Cross Country

Brian Herberger

Cross Country
by Brian Herberger
...

ISBN-10: 1-946229-97-0
ISBN-13: 978-1-946229-97-7

Birch Cove Books
Washington, DC

Distributed by Bublish, Inc.

Cover illustration by Michael Gelen, Inkwell Studios
Design by Jeffrey Herberger

Publisher's Cataloging-In-Publication Data
(Prepared by The Donohue Group, Inc.)

Names: Herberger, Brian.
Title: Cross country / Brian Herberger.
Description: Washington, DC : Birch Cove Books, [2018] | [Place of distribution
not identified] : Bublish, Inc., [2018] | Interest age level: 012-018. | Summary:
"Having her father away in Vietnam wasn't easy for Bets, but she soon discovers
having him back home comes with its own set of problems. When a letter from
her friend Emmie arrives along with a ticket to the Woodstock Music Festival,
Bets has a tough decision to make. Should she stick it out back home or leave
her problems behind for a cross-country adventure?"--Provided by publisher.
Identifiers: ISBN 9781946229977 | ISBN 1946229970 | ISBN 9781946229984
(ebook)
Subjects: LCSH: Vietnam War, 1961-1975--Veterans--Juvenile fiction. | Wood-
stock Festival--Juvenile fiction. | Automobile travel--United States--History-
-20th century--Juvenile fiction. | Nineteen sixty-nine, A.D.--Juvenile fiction.
| Bildungsromans. | CYAC: Vietnam War, 1961-1975--Veterans--Fiction. |
Woodstock Festival--Fiction. | Automobile travel--United States--History--
20th century--Fiction. | Nineteen sixty-nine, A.D.--Fiction. | Coming of age--
Fiction. | LCGFT: Historical fiction.
Classification: LCC PZ7.1.H47 Cr 2018 (print) | LCC PZ7.1.H47 (ebook) | DDC
[Fic]--dc23

To my father, who taught me everything,
and to my son, who showed me
how much I still have to learn.

We are stardust
We are golden
And we've got to get ourselves
Back to the garden
~ Joni Mitchell

"...the man next to you is your brother,
and you'd...better treat each other that way."
~ Chip Monck - Woodstock Stage Announcer

Ticket

The day the ticket arrived, I checked the mailbox when I got home from school just like I did every afternoon. I brought the mail in every day, because I knew my parents wouldn't. My father was usually away, working on base, or if he did happen to be home when I got there, I knew he wouldn't be in any condition to step out the front door and walk to the mailbox at the end of the driveway. My mother was either busy in the house getting things ready for dinner, or she was at a neighbor's, at a bridge game or luncheon that lasted longer than planned.

I rolled up on my bike, letting my feet drag on the gravel at the edge of the road to slow me to a stop. I opened the mailbox door, pulled out the contents, and tossed the mail into my bike basket without even looking at it. It wasn't until I'd leaned my bike against the side of the house and let myself in that I even flipped through the letters.

Just like getting the mail had become part of my routine, I was used to letting myself into the house. Other kids came home to empty houses, I'm sure. Some had parents who both worked, just a few that I knew about had parents who were divorced. I was a sophomore in high school and certainly responsible enough to take care of myself until my mother or father got home. It wasn't a big deal.

In fact, there was part of me that let out a breath of relief when I came up to the door and found it locked. That meant my father wasn't home yet. My father was my absolute favorite person to be with, but when he was home early, things were different.

There wasn't usually any mail for me, but I flipped through it each day anyway. An envelope addressed to my mother from my aunt, a bill or two, something official-looking for my father, and then, surprisingly, an envelope with my name on it. I tossed the rest of the mail on the kitchen table and held up the envelope addressed to Elizabeth Wells.

Here's the thing about my name. I can count on one hand the people who call me Elizabeth: teachers and my mother. There was a time when I thought my mother did it to aggravate me. Now, I know she just does it because that's the name she gave me, and she's sticking with it. Friends call me Bethy, and that's fine. But my father calls me Bets, and that's what I call myself. Emmie Hatcher knows all this, and after a year of friendship she'd shorten my name, sometimes, except when she addressed a letter to me. Then she always used Elizabeth, like the postman wouldn't know who to deliver it to unless it had my full name on the envelope.

Emmie Hatcher. I don't really call her by her full name either, but for a while that's how I thought of her. Back then, it was just a name on the inside cover of a journal I'd ended up with. Emmie Hatcher. After I met her and returned her journal, I thought of her as just Emmie I guess, but I'd only ever seen her once. Well, twice. The first time she was unconscious and covered in blood, but that's another story. I hadn't seen Emmie in almost a year. We had written, sometimes a lot, sometimes a little. Even during the times when we weren't writing, I knew I'd eventually get a letter from Emmie. And I always did.

I slipped a finger under the envelope flap and tore down its edge. Something fell out. My hand was already pulling out the folded letter, but I stopped with it halfway out and picked up the small slip of paper on the table instead. Something about its shape and size and the feel of the paper told me it was a ticket, even though I'd never really seen a ticket before. I'd never been anywhere that required one.

It was divided into four sections. The first had a red diagonal slash across the words, with FRIDAY standing out in capital letters. Next to it SATURDAY was decorated with a red star. The third section - SUNDAY - had a red moon, and the fourth section proclaimed in the same capital letters, THREE DAY TICKET. Three days of what?

Across the top of each section were the words "Woodstock Music and Arts Festival", and below that was a date. August 15, 1969, was on the Friday section with a price

9

of $6.00. Eighteen dollars total. Eighteen dollars was a lot of money. It would take me weeks of working my part-time job at Johnson's Grocery to earn as much, and that was if I didn't spend half of it on ice cream or pizza at Sonny's. Why was Emmie mailing me a ticket that cost almost a month's worth of work?

I pulled out her letter. Folded within the paper was a page torn from a magazine. The side I saw first was covered with an advertisement, a full page photo of a man on a horse smoking a cigarette. I didn't really understand what the horse had to do with cigarettes, but I didn't think that was what Emmie was sending me, and I flipped the page over.

The first thing my eyes noticed was the simple but colorful image—a dove, perched on the neck of a guitar. "3 Days of Peace and Music" stood out above the dove. My eyes scanned the rest of the page. There were dates again. August 15, 16, and 17, and a list of performers. Joe Cocker, Arlo Guthrie, Richie Havens. These were names I knew even though I didn't have any of their records. I'd heard their songs on the radio. I kept reading; It was a long list. Janis Joplin! I played her records all the time. The same with The Grateful Dead, Joan Baez, Jefferson Airplane, and Jimi Hendrix. The more names I recognized, the more I wanted to know what it was all about.

The rest of the advertisement went on to explain the festival. There would be performances by some of the most popular singers and bands, the festival would take place over three days, and it would all be happening on a farm a couple hours outside of New York City.

New York? I lived in California, in a small town outside of San Francisco. New York was just about as far away as I could imagine.

I recognized Emmie's handwriting scrawled across the top of the ad.

You have GOT to go to this with me!

I finally got to Emmie's letter, realizing I'd really gone about things backwards, taking things in the order they fell out of the envelope and trying to piece together what it all meant, when Emmie's letter would likely explain it all. I spread it flat on the table and scanned its lines. The explanation was not one I could have pieced together in my wildest dreams.

Emmie and two friends made plans to spend the summer traveling east, driving cross country. They'd be sleeping in their van, stopping along the way to pick up odd jobs and earn a little money, seeing the country from one coast to the other, and eventually ending up in the small New York town that was hosting the Woodstock Music and Arts Festival. One friend had backed out, and that left an extra ticket and room in the van. The ticket was for me, and Emmie was inviting me to join her on this cross-country adventure.

The thought of traveling across the country, with a friend and without my parents, and eventually ending up at a three-day concert that included some of my absolute favorite singers and bands was still sinking in when the door opened and my mother walked into the kitchen.

"Hello, Sweetheart. How was your day?"

My mother and I had not always had the best relationship. "Hello Sweetheart" was a big step up from where we were a couple years ago.

How was my day? Well, it was a school day like any other. I'd been lucky most school years and ended up with some pretty good teachers. This year... well, I was learning at least. But there was never anything happening at school that was worth reporting at home. In fact, Emmie's letter and the Woodstock ticket were not only the most exciting thing that had happened to me all day, they were easily at the top of the year's list. So I don't really know why I folded them in half and slipped them into my back pocket before I turned to my mother and said in a bored voice, "It was okay."

1969

I sat in history class, the teacher's voice in the background talking about dates and places. Freshman year I had the best history teacher ever. In fact, he was such a good teacher, he got himself kicked out of the school. Mr. Flynn made history come alive. Well, at one point a little bit too alive. He somehow tricked us into getting interested in what he had to teach, and once we were there with him, curious and involved, the bell would ring and he would send us off to our next class full of questions and chatting with classmates about our opinions and ideas.

Ms. Simms was not Mr. Flynn. If whoever was in charge of the universe was striving for balance, they could put Mr. Flynn on one side and Ms. Simms on the other. They were exact opposites. Ms. Simms taught history-book history. In her class, history wasn't something to have opinions about. It wasn't something to debate or consider. It definitely wasn't alive. In Ms. Simms' class, history was dead and buried. It happened long long ago, and the textbook gave the facts. Who did what, where they did it, which countries were involved. Tenth grade was world history. I'm not sure whose world it was, but the way Ms. Simms taught, it definitely didn't feel like ours.

I was probably supposed to be taking notes. It was hard to tell in Ms. Simms' class. She'd told us at the beginning of the year that we'd be expected to take notes and that she would collect notebooks regularly and grade them. Five or ten hands shot up immediately, and the first boy she called on asked, "How will we know what to take notes on?"

"You'll just know," Ms. Simms answered. "Take notes on whatever is important." By that standard, there should be a classroom full of empty notebooks. The few words I'd written on the page in front of me had gradually been fringed by a puffy white cloud. I added another below it and one off to the side, and then doodled an airplane high above them, heading toward the upper right corner of the page.

When I was sure Ms. Simms wasn't going to see me, I slowly reached under my chair, slipped my three-ring binder off the top of the stack of books that was under there, and set it on my desk. The binder was covered in a blue cloth that looked like faded denim, and just like my jeans, I'd drawn flowers and peace signs all over it. I'd cut a file folder in half and taped it to the inside front cover of the binder to form a pocket for keeping homework and an extra pen or pencil. That morning I carefully took the ticket and magazine page, folded them inside Emmie's letter, and slipped them into the pocket.

After Ms. Simms paused to ask a question about what she'd just read, answered it herself when she didn't get any volunteers, and then continued reading the next section in the textbook, I carefully pulled the letter out of the pocket and unfolded it enough to let the ticket slide free. I tried to imagine a concert that lasted three days and reread the words in each section of the ticket.

FRIDAY   SATURDAY   SUNDAY
August 15, 1969 | August 16, 1969 | August 17, 1969

As far as being a high school kid goes, I had it pretty good. Homework, a few chores at home, and a part time job that gave me just enough hours to keep money in my pocket for whatever I wanted in town. But even with the few responsibilities I had, I couldn't remember ever having three days to simply do nothing but enjoy music. I'd never been away from my parents for three days, and Emmie's idea for driving across the country would practically take months not days.

That guilty thought forced me to fold up the letter and hide everything back in my binder. But it was only minutes before the clouds and airplane at the top of my page were joined by a dove perched proudly on the neck of a guitar. Like the one in the magazine advertisement, I drew a hand with fingers placed on the guitar strings and then imagined who the hand might belong to and what song they could be playing. The bell to end the period rang, jarring me from my daydream, and saving me from Ms. Simms' version of history.

☮ ☮ ☮

"They'll never let you go."

"She's sixteen."

"They'll never let her go."

I was walking between school and the library with two friends, Cassie and Susan. I'd met them both, along with Cassie's younger sister Anne, when I'd first moved to Forestville. Cassie was a year older than me. She was a junior and the pessimist in the current conversation. Susan was in tenth grade with me, and we'd been lucky enough to end up with a couple classes together last year. This year was no different, and we should have been heading to Susan's to work together on a science project that was due in a couple weeks. Instead, we were going to the library. Cassie was tagging along in order to rain on our parade and provide me with all the reasons I shouldn't even consider spending an entire summer driving across the country to a three-day music festival.

El Molino High School had several buildings spread out on a small campus. Most students had classes in different buildings during the day and class changes meant hundreds of students streaming down sidewalks and across grassy areas, trying to connect with friends before the bell for the next class rang. But things cleared out quickly at the end of the day. So, other than a few boys tossing a Frisbee around and a couple clusters of kids chatting, we had the place to ourselves.

It was mid-May and kids were ready for summer even though the end of school was still a month away. Juniors and seniors had final exams or projects in most classes, but a nearly empty library made it seem like they'd already happened and everyone had passed with flying colors. The mild weather could be blamed for some kids lack of interest in school, but in 1969, there was enough happening that exams and final projects just didn't seem important.

Martin Luther King Jr. had been killed the year before, and the peaceful movement he'd started in order to work toward racial equality had grown angry and was turning into something that was anything but peaceful. One group that seemed to have taken advantage of the empty space left by King called themselves the Black Panthers. Some newspaper articles made them seem like a political party, and one of their members even tried to run for president, but other articles described the members as militant and violent.

On TV the previous summer, we'd watched athletes from around the world compete in the summer Olympics in Mexico. We saw two African-American athletes receive their gold and bronze medals, and then as "The Star-Spangled Banner" played, they raised their fists in a salute that had become a symbol of the Black Power movement.

Forestville was a small town, and other than the anti-war demonstration I'd unleashed on our main street a year earlier, news didn't really happen in our little town. We just read about it in the paper or turned on the TV to watch it happening in other places. But still, it was getting harder to know who to trust, and people who used to greet strangers with a smile and a handshake were crossing to the other side of the street to avoid people who they'd decided were not like them.

The war in Vietnam had gotten progressively worse. Our country continued to send young men to Vietnam, just boys really, and more and more we saw them return in flag draped coffins. To try to destroy an enemy that was able to kill our soldiers and then simply fade into the surrounding villages and jungles, our planes carpet bombed, dropped fiery napalm, and sprayed chemicals to kill vegetation, making it harder to hide. All the while, people back home tried to figure out how farmers and villagers in some far away country could be our enemies. There were peaceful protests, but often those protests turned violent as people realized that taking over a building or starting things on fire got them more attention than waving a two-fingered peace sign in the air.

Not that a high school kid spends too much time thinking about politics, but the presidential election of 1968 had gotten everyone's attention. A young Senator from New York, Robert Kennedy, seemed likely to win the Democratic nomination and continue on to win the election, bringing his energy and new ideas with him. He was talking about equality, social justice, and some were saying, a peaceful end to the war. But that ended in June of 1968, when he was assassinated. Richard Nixon went on to become president and many of the changes we were hoping for never happened. The war just seemed to get worse.

And with the war, came the draft. Draft was a word that had snuck its way into our vocabulary over the last few years. It wasn't like we'd learned it in English class or looked it up in a dictionary. One day it was just in our mouths, like it had always been there. Draft.

What it meant was that boys were getting called up to fight in the war. My father was in the army already. He'd made a career out of it. He spent most of his time on a base working on engines, keeping planes flying and trucks moving. When he went to Vietnam, I worried about him, missed him, wished every day that he could come home. Even though he wasn't out doing the fighting, he was still in danger while he was over there, but the difference was that he'd signed up for the job. He had made that decision for himself.

The draft was different. The draft was plucking boys up like an unlucky lottery ticket. They might have had plans to be a doctor, or a scientist, or a teacher, or a father, and then, just like that, they were a soldier. They weren't taking high school age boys, but the juniors and seniors at El Molino were certainly thinking about what they were headed for, because at age 18 you had to register, and then when your number came up, you went. And lots of the kids at school had older brothers. Some had already gone, and some hadn't come back.

The one bright spot in all this bad news had our attention focused over two-hundred thousand miles away. While people argued about politics, struggled for equality, and tried to find an end to war, three men would soon leave behind Earth and all its problems entirely. Neil Armstrong, Buzz Aldrin, and Michael Collins were preparing to travel to the Moon. We'd sent astronauts into space before, but this time would be different. This time, they'd actually be landing on the Moon and walking on its surface.

That's the world we were living in in 1969. We went to our classes, we talked with friends, and made plans for the weekend. But all the while, it seemed like there were clouds hanging over us. Emmie's letter, the prospect of a cross-country trip, and a three-day concert helped push them away for a little while.

I'd come to the library for a map, and I'd dragged Cassie and Susan with me as I told them about the ticket and Woodstock. We found Cassie's sister Anne at a table with a stack of books in front of her, and she looked a little surprised to see all three of us.

"What's up?" she said, looking from one face to the next.

"Bets is preparing to have her parents tell her no, by planning out a route for a trip she'll never be allowed to take," Cassie jumped in.

"Honestly Cassie," Susan said with a sigh. "Like I said before, she's sixteen. She can decide to go if she wants to. What are her parents going to do? Lock her in her room?"

"Lock her out of the house when she tries to come back is more like it."

An angry hush from the librarian coupled with a hard stare cut the conversation short and gave Cassie the last word.

We wandered around the library looking for an atlas or some other book with a map in it. I was scanning a shelf full of books on each of the states, when a wave from Susan got my attention. I wound my way around a bookshelf and saw what she'd found. In a corner of the library, a rack of pull down maps was mounted on the wall. We pulled down two world maps and a map of Europe before we realized the bottom edge of each map was labeled. Susan flipped through, found the U.S. map, and pulled it down with a flourish just as Cassie and Anne walked up behind us.

Maybe it was because it was so much bigger than the tiny maps in our history textbook, but standing in the corner of the library looking up at the wall map, the enormity of our country began to sink in. Cassie decided to illustrate that fact by putting her finger on the map near San Francisco and then moving it eastward, making painfully slow progress while sputtering car sounds came out of her mouth. She'd barely made it to the edge of California when Susan stepped up beside her and pushed her off to the side. Our laughter drew another stern look from the librarian.

I stepped forward, close enough to the map that it filled my vision. There were no roads on the map, but my eyes traced an imaginary route through the states: California, Nevada, Utah, Kansas, Nebraska, Iowa, Illinois,

Indiana, Ohio, Pennsylvania, New York. Or a string of other states if we took a route farther north or south.

There was so much country, so much space. It didn't seem possible that all those places, all those states and cities and towns were like my own. When I thought about all the news that weighed us down each day, all the issues that lingered in our minds, it seemed like they couldn't possibly be spread out across the entire country. There must be places where life just went on day to day and people didn't worry about the war or the draft, where people walked down the same sidewalk no matter what color their skin was. If there weren't places like that, then surely our country could use a few kids driving across it in a van, spreading peace and love and happiness.

I was scared. I couldn't imagine being away from my parents, couldn't imagine being on the opposite side of the country from both of them. I couldn't imagine being gone for an entire summer. But I decided at that moment, looking at the map of our country, that I absolutely wanted to go, that I would find parts of our country where there was just a little bit more happiness, or if I didn't, I would make them happier by being there.

I moved my face in close to the New York part of the map. The town of Woodstock was too tiny to be labeled, and I didn't even really know where in New York State it was. But I let a patch of green in the middle of the state fill my eyes and I imagined three days of peace and love and music.

Broken

My father's car was in the driveway when I got home. He always pulled it carefully into the garage, but instead it was parked off to one side of the driveway at an angle, one wheel resting on the grass. I took my feet off the pedals and let them drag in the gravel at the edge of the road. I caught myself wishing that I had deliveries to make at Johnson's, but pushed the thought away. I wasn't ready to admit to myself that I didn't want to be home with my own father.

When we moved to Forestville, my father was getting ready to leave for Vietnam, so my parents picked a town with my mother and me in mind and didn't consider my father's drive to and from Oakland Army Base near San Francisco. He'd only been with us for just over a month before he left, so he put up with the long drive and saw us each night. But now that he was back home, driving back and forth wore on him, and it was three hours out of his day that he could be working.

So he came up with a schedule where he stayed on base during the week. Then he could drive home and spend the weekend with us. My mother and I missed him while he was away, but we could see it made things easier and less stressful for him, so we decided it was for the best. Besides when he was in Vietnam, we didn't see him at all for an entire year, and most of the time we didn't know for sure if he was okay or not. At least now, we saw him each week, and the most dangerous thing he encountered was the traffic leaving San Francisco on a Friday afternoon.

But sometimes he didn't follow that schedule. Sometimes he would come home unexpectedly. Rather than working all week, he would arrive home after three days or after just two. He usually arrived in the evening after putting in a full day on the base, but sometimes he would show up mid-day, like he'd only been on base a few hours. One day he'd left home early in the morning heading for Oakland, and showed up back at home before I left for school, like he'd turned around halfway there. And when he came home a day or two early or showed up at an odd time, he was different.

Different. That was the only way to describe it. My father was the person who always understood me. He knew when I needed to talk or when I just needed a hug. He knew when I was in a silly mood, and he was willing to just be stupid and laugh with me. He knew when I felt serious, and he was ready to sit and listen to whatever I had to say. My father was still all of those things—sometimes, but since coming back from the war, more and more he seemed like a different person.

One afternoon, I came home from school to find him in our living room, pacing the floor. When I first came into the house and heard his voice, I thought my mother was home with him and that he was talking to her. I took in a surprised breath when I realized he was alone, talking to himself, or maybe talking to others who were only with him in a memory.

Nothing he said made any sense. Shouted names of people I didn't know, orders to men who weren't there, and panicked whispers about an enemy that was hiding in the tall grass and ready to sneak into camp at night. My skin shivered when I heard the urgency in his voice, and I looked over my shoulder, as if an invisible enemy was right there in our living room with us.

I stood there helplessly watching, not knowing what to do. I was afraid to call out or step in front of him or do anything to pull him out of the memory he was in, and at the same time, I wasn't able to bear another second. I knew only a little bit about my father's time in Vietnam, but standing in our living room with him that afternoon was like looking through a window at the year he was away from us. I didn't like what I saw.

Other times, my father would be home early and he would seem just fine. Normal. Well, maybe to other kids he would seem normal. To me, he seemed like a TV father, from one of the shows where the parents were always perfect, always happy and calm, even when the kids did something horrible like buying bubble gum with all the money they'd earned delivering newspapers.

The TV shows might have been entertaining, but seeing my father act that way was nothing but frightening, like his smile was painted on and the cheerful things he said were rehearsed lines. But I could sense what was hiding behind the smile, and it felt like if I didn't play my part, if I didn't smile back and respond cheerfully, that the TV comedy we were playing in would turn tragic in a breath.

So when I rolled into the driveway on my bike that afternoon and saw my father's car in the driveway, I didn't really know what to expect. I slid off my bike, pushed it around the corner of the house, and leaned it against the wall. Seeing it there reminded me of the day my father gave it to me, the day he left for Vietnam. It came with a basket on the handlebars and the job he'd lined up for me at Johnson's store. He'd taken care of everything. The bike was absolute freedom, and I couldn't keep myself from smiling whenever I rode it.

But it didn't look right leaning against the house. When my father gave it to me, it had a kickstand. That had been almost two years ago. The spring that held the kickstand broke a couple months after my father came back home. It ended up dragging on the ground when I rode the bike and wouldn't stay in place to hold the bike up when it leaned over. My father removed it from the bike, took a look at what was broken, and told me he would fix it that weekend. I'd been leaning my bike against the wall ever since.

I don't know how long I was standing there thinking and running my hand along the curve of the bike's banana seat, but I realized I was stalling for time. I looked down at my feet, scuffed a stone across the ground, then roughly grabbed my backpack out of the bike basket and headed for the front door. It was unavoidable.

The house was quiet when I opened the door. My eyes darted around the kitchen, then through the doorway into the living room and down the hallway. I slid the strap of my backpack off my shoulder, pulled a chair out from the kitchen table, and set the backpack on it.

"Daddy?"

Quiet. I walked slowly around the kitchen table and pulled a glass and a plate out of the cupboard. I carefully set them down on the counter so they wouldn't make a sound, and did the same when I pulled a knife out of the drawer and set it on the plate. The small clinks they did make sounded noisy in the silent house, and I bit my lip, wishing I'd been more careful. I opened cupboard doors and brought out bread and peanut butter and then tiptoed to the refrigerator for jelly. I let the cupboard door close softly, keeping the tips of my fingers behind it until the door touched the cupboard without a sound.

I remembered an afternoon not long after my father had returned from Vietnam. After being without him for a year, I was still excited to see him each day when I came home from school, and I burst through the door shouting, "I'm home!" I had a split second to see the quiet conversation my parents were having before the screen door slapped closed behind me and interrupted everything. My father cried out in a panicked voice I'd never heard him use before. His arms instinctively went to his face as if he was protecting himself, and he crouched to the floor, using the kitchen table as protection from the imagined dangers that surrounded him. Since then, I'd gotten very good at being quiet.

"Daddy?" I called again, a little louder this time. I made myself a peanut butter and jelly sandwich, and then as an afterthought I pulled another plate and glass of out the cupboard. I made a second sandwich and poured two glasses of milk. I picked up the plates and carried them toward the living room. I could see the top of his head sticking up just above the back of the couch, and I walked around it and set the plates down on the coffee table.

"Daddy, I made you a sandwich," I said in the same quiet voice I'd used when I was in the other room. It didn't matter. My father was slouched down on the couch staring straight ahead like he was watching TV. Except that the TV wasn't on, and his eyes were focused on the blank wall above it.

I sat down slowly in the chair next to the couch and watched my father. I guess I was waiting for him to react, waiting for him to see me or hear me. But I knew he wouldn't. Just like me calling his name when I came into the house. I did it because it was the normal thing to do. Kids were probably getting home all over town saying things like "Hi, Mom. I'm home!" or "Dad? Hi, I'm home." I did it hoping that he'd call back and say hello or ask me how my day was, but I knew all the while that he wouldn't.

On the days when my father came home early from the base, we'd sometimes find him on the couch staring at the wall or laying on my parents' bed staring at the ceiling. If my mother and I were home when he arrived, he would simply walk past us like we weren't there. I wondered what would happen if I stepped in front of him instead of just letting him walk by, but I never tried it. I didn't really want to find out. The staring and the silence was weird and awkward and a little bit scary, but there was other stuff that was worse.

My father wasn't always like this. Most of the time he seemed the same as before he went to Vietnam. He and I could always tell what the other was thinking. We both talked with our hands and our faces as much as we did with our voices, and maybe that made it seem like we could read each other's minds, because we could say so much to each other without saying a word. My father always knew what I needed, whether it was a Coke or a trip to Sonny's for pizza, his arm around me or a bike before leaving for Vietnam. And all of that was still true, except when it wasn't.

I should have just gone back to the kitchen to start my homework or walked away to quietly listen to music in my room for a few hours. I knew that eventually, once my mother was back home and there was enough going on in the house, my father would be back to normal. Like slowly waking up from a sleep, he'd blink his eyes a few times, stand up and walk around the room, and then he'd start talking to us like nothing had happened. He'd ask us about our day or chat about something he saw on the news, and then everything was back to normal—sort of. When you've seen your father staring blankly at the wall, totally oblivious to anyone else in the house, it's hard to ever really feel like things are normal.

But I didn't go back into the kitchen or into my bedroom. I didn't just wait for whatever was wrong to pass. I reached out and I touched his arm. Simple. Like waking someone from a nap or getting a friend's attention in school while the teacher's back was turned.

My father reacted like my fingers were on fire and he'd just been burned. His body flinched back and he took in a sudden gasp of breath. His hands sprang up in front of his face, not covering it like he was hiding, but hovering between the two of us, like he was protecting himself and at the same time, ready to strike out at whoever was in front of him.

The worst part was his eyes. They were looking at me and at the same time flicking around the room. I could tell that he recognized me and knew where he was, but I also felt like I could see a touch of the other things those eyes had seen when they were staring at the wall. Whatever it was had crawled up my spine and left me tingling.

I instinctively took a step back. "It's okay," I whispered. "It's okay." Another step back, first raising my own hands. I don't know why. To show that they were empty, that I wasn't going to hurt him? Or was I protecting myself? As I moved farther away, my father seemed to relax. His eyes still looked at me, but it was more like they were looking through me. His arms settled back down to his sides and he turned back to stare at the wall again.

I took what felt like my first breath in hours. I was taking slow steps toward the kitchen, still whispering comforting words. "It's okay. It will be alright. It's okay." I don't know if they were for my father or for me.

I saw him lean forward and reach for the sandwich I'd made him. He settled back into the couch and lifted the sandwich to his mouth to take a bite. That was good. I didn't like the surprise reaction I'd gotten, but touching my father's arm had at least gotten him out of his daydream. Or was it a nightmare? Could someone have those in the middle of the day? I watched and waited. He took another bite.

"Daddy?" There was a silence long enough that I was ready to call his name again.

"Hey, Bets." I closed my eyes and let out a long breath. His voice was distant, like he was half asleep, part greeting and part question. But it was his voice and it was the best thing I'd heard all day.

"Hi, Daddy. You're home early." I paused, wishing I could pull the words back and trying to figure out what I could cover them with. "You were napping. Feeling better?" A mumble was the only response, but the sandwich was at his mouth again and he was chewing another bite. I couldn't expect much more than a one-sided conversation, at least not at first.

"Here, I poured you some milk. It'll be perfect with the sandwich." It's amazing how in the scariest of situations, something like a glass of milk and a peanut butter and jelly sandwich can be so comforting. I grabbed the glasses off the counter and turned back toward my father. I could see him through the large doorway that joined the kitchen with the living room. So when I walked past the kitchen table, I was watching him enjoy his sandwich instead of looking where I was going.

Sandals had become more and more popular at school over the last year, and I wore them most days. But the thing about sandals is that they don't really do anything to protect your feet. So when you're wearing them, you should really look where you're going.

The little toe on my right foot hit the leg of a chair, and the pain was immediate. It tore up from my toe, through my foot, and into my leg. I screamed. I let go of the glass of milk in one hand, and I clenched my throbbing foot before I heard the glass hit the floor. The sound must have scared me enough that I let go of the other glass and brought my hand up to try to hold back a second scream that had already escaped my mouth. In the silence that had filled the room a second before, the breaking glass seemed like a bomb going off.

At first I didn't realize that the screaming I was hearing was no longer mine. My father was standing, his arms waving, an unrecognizable sound coming from his mouth. I had never heard my father yell before. I can remember a few times when I knew he was angry, when I could see it in his eyes and on his face. It was never anger directed at me. Something in the news had bothered him more than usual or an injustice he'd seen in town or on the base. There were times when I'd disappointed my father, and I could sense that too, without him needing to say anything. But he always turned that around and managed to help me learn a lesson while praising something else I'd done that made him proud. But I had never seen him so angry before, and never felt that anger directed at me.

Mixed in with the screaming and yelling were words, but I couldn't tell what he was saying. He'd look in one direction then twist his neck around in another, sometimes bringing his hands up in the same defensive way he'd done when I touched his arm.

Without warning he bent down and picked up his plate from the coffee table. In a flash it was flying across the room toward me. Without time to think, my body reacted instinctively and my legs bent, my back sliding down the door of the refrigerator as the plate shattered just above my head and showered me with glinting white slivers. My hands had gone up to cover my face and my eyes were squinted closed.

Then above the screams coming from my father, I heard my mother's voice. With a single spoken sentence that somehow started with a shout and ended with a comforting whisper, my mother ended the chaos in our living room like she was turning down the volume on a record player.

I opened my eyes to see her standing between us, holding up her outstretched hands like a traffic cop toward my father, who still held the second plate in his hands. Her eyes flicked in my direction and sized me up. I could read her face as she assessed my condition—still breathing, not bloody.

My mother turned and took five or six steady steps toward my father. In the time that it took her to reach him, the second plate slid from his hand. It broke on the coffee table, but he didn't seem to notice. His head hung down and his hands covered his face. My mother wrapped her arms around him, and his body heaved with sobs. It was impossible to imagine that this was my father.

Without moving away from him or lifting her head from my father, my mother made eye contact with me. She gave me a long look. There was no judgment or accusation in her expression. She'd already made sure I was physically fine. Now she was looking deeper. I used to think that my father and I were the only ones who could read each other's faces and body language as easily as we could listen to each other's voices. But now I wondered.

My mother seemed okay with what she saw and her eyes flicked toward the still open front door and then back at me. I got it. I'd seen enough. Go someplace else for a while. Things were in my mother's hands now. I looked back at my mother before stepping out the door. Her expression said everything. "I love you. It will be okay. I love you. He'll be okay. I love you. We'll be okay." Then she buried her face in my father's hair and I stepped outside.

Outside with the afternoon sun on my face, what had happened with my father seemed impossible. I breathed in the sun-filled air, knowing I would never be able to wash away the memory, but wanting for the moment to dull the ache. I went around the corner to grab my bike without even thinking about it. It was the only thing I could do.

I'd already thrown my right leg over the seat and was straddling the bike before I felt the stab in my left foot. I cried out in surprise. It hurt. A lot! I hopped off my bike on the right side to avoid standing on my left foot, and once I did, my bike tumbled away from me. I crouched onto my hands and knees and then sat on the ground.

I could see the blood even before I flicked the sandal off my foot. So much, I must have left a trail of it on my way out of the house. I winced and closed my eyes at the sight of it. My head spun a little so I opened my eyes and forced myself to focus on the ground in front of me. Once I felt better, I looked back at my foot. Even though it was covered in red, I could see the piece of glass sticking out of it.

I held my breath. There was another stab of pain as soon as I touched it, but I kept my hand from jumping away. I knew it was going to get worse. I let out a slow breath and then closed my eyes and pulled. The pain exploded red behind my eyelids, but the glass was out. It seemed like forever ago that I'd stubbed my toe. The ache in my right foot was nothing now compared to the stabbing pain in my left.

Opening my eyes and seeing the glass in my hand gave me another spell of dizziness, but it faded. The glass was thick, not a shard or a sliver. It looked like it had come from the bottom of one of the glasses and I could even see the curved edge where the thin side of the glass turned into the thicker base.

I knew I should probably go back into the house to clean and bandage my foot. Who knows, judging from the amount of blood and the pain, there might be a trip to the emergency room and a couple of stitches in my future. But instead, I carefully put my sandal back on and struggled to my feet. I managed to stand, and I figured once I was on my bike I could keep weight off the foot.

I pulled my bike upright and once again swung my leg over the seat and straddled the frame. I realized I was still holding the piece of glass. I don't know why I didn't just toss it away. I wanted to. I wanted to throw it away from me as hard as I could, like I wanted to get rid of the memory of everything that had just happened. But I didn't. Instead I dropped it into the basket on the front of my bike and somehow managed to slide onto the seat and pedal down the driveway.

Phone Call

I drifted through school. I arrived in the morning, I went to some classes, and then I walked out of school to my bike. What happened in the classes, what we read, what the teacher told us to do for homework, none of that remained by the end of the day.

Parents ask kids what they did in school or what they learned. Most of the time, kids will answer "nothing," even though they did a whole bunch of stuff and probably learned a lot more than they realize. Kids just say "nothing" because it's the easiest way to end the conversation, so they can get outside to do whatever it is they wish they had been doing all day while they were in school.

If I was asked by my mother or father what I did in school, which I wasn't, I honestly could have answered, "nothing." Sure, there were things happening in school, but I didn't do them. Things were being taught, but I didn't learn them. Not that day, or the day before, or the day before that.

When I came home after everything that had happened with my father, our house looked like it always did. My mother had already cleaned up the broken glass and shattered plate. She'd mopped up the milk, and even put a fresh bag in the trash can. It was like all evidence had been swept away, like it never happened.

My mother was good at acting like nothing was wrong. I'd spent most of the time that my father was in Vietnam wondering how she could be so emotionless, how she could go about her routine and not break down crying. Because that's what I wanted to do every day he was gone. I'd come to realize that her emotions were there, but just hidden. It was a defense she'd built up through years of my father being away. It wasn't a defect like I'd thought. It was her strength. She did it for herself, and she did it for me, because it was better to go through each day with a strong smile, even when you felt like curling up in a corner with your knees pulled up to your chin, crying until there were no tears left.

So she was doing it again. She could have hugged me, could have told me it would be okay, could have let me cry into her shoulder. But she didn't. She made the house look perfect and cleared away anything that would have hinted at the earlier chaos. A year ago, it would have annoyed me, would have left me angry and confused. Now, I at least knew it was just her way of making things easier, but it didn't change the fact that I just wanted to cry and needed a hug from my mother.

She saw it on my face and knew. "Not now, Elizabeth, your father's sleeping." That was better. Talking about it and dealing with it later was better than pretending absolutely nothing was wrong. We made enough eye contact to understand where we both stood. She understood I was upset, knew I had every reason to be, and knew I needed to talk about it.

But that was three days ago. The day after the plate throwing, I didn't see my father before school and assumed he was sleeping off the events of the day before. When I came home from school, both of my parents were in the kitchen, clearly in the middle of a conversation that stopped as soon as I came in the door.

"Hey, Bets. What did you do in school today?" my father asked in a voice that was a little too upbeat.

"Nothing," I said with a shrug.

"We were thinking of going to Sonny's tonight. How does that sound?" my mother jumped in, realizing the exchange between me and my father was going nowhere without her help. The memory of an interrupted conversation on our first day in California surfaced. Back then, we were dealing with our move to a new town, a new school, and my father's leaving for Vietnam. The issues were different; the pretending was the same.

"That sounds nice," I said with a smile.

Sonny's was the best pizza place in Forestville. It was also the only place. There wasn't really a dining area, just a space in the front of the building where someone had put a few tables. Empty pizza boxes were stacked in one corner waiting to be filled, and a counter with a cash register was the only thing keeping the kitchen from taking over the whole place.

But the pizza was good enough and the families that couldn't find an empty table at Sonny's in the evening just grabbed a pizza to go and found a park bench on Front Street. That's where we ended up, and I was glad for it. A bench meant we were all sitting in a row, looking out toward the town square rather than sitting across from each other and avoiding each other's eyes.

Normally, I would have expected a heart-to-heart with my father. Whenever something was bothering me or when he had something important to talk to me about, he'd find some reason for us to step out of the house and then we'd sit somewhere and talk. Normally. But when your father's staring at the walls when you come home and then starts screaming and throwing stuff at you, normal has gone out the window. If my father couldn't handle me touching his arm or dropping a glass, he wasn't going to be pulling me aside to have a conversation that would make everything okay. We ate pizza, we watched the world go by, and we let another day end.

And then, I was back at school. The Woodstock ticket was still tucked into my binder. I don't know why I kept bringing it with me. I'd struggled all year to keep my school stuff organized, and more than once I'd lost an important assignment. The possibility of losing the ticket at school terrified me, but I was even more nervous about leaving it somewhere in my room for my mother to find.

I'd had a scare one night while I was doing my homework. My binder was open on the kitchen table, and I had papers spread from one side of the table to the other as I worked my way through each subject. I'd gotten up to go to the bathroom, and when I walked back to the table, I could see Emmie's letter and the Woodstock ticket sticking out of the binder pocket in plain sight. I looked at my mother, washing dishes with her back turned to me. Then I looked back at the ticket and wondered if I'd left it sticking out that far. Had I been that careless? Had she pulled it out and then slipped it back quickly when she heard me returning, or was I just getting paranoid. I'd only been gone a minute, but the thought of my mother discovering the ticket and letter made me break out in a sweat, and I suddenly found it hard to breathe. So I kept bringing it to school with me, and I made sure it was pushed down into the binder pocket and out of sight..

I needed to talk with Emmie. She'd be expecting an answer about Woodstock, but I didn't think I could just decide on my own. I hadn't said anything to my parents yet. I wasn't ready to do that, but I felt like talking with Emmie would help me decide, would help me figure out what I wanted to do and how I should tell my parents. Plus, I just needed to talk to someone who would understand about my dad.

Susan, Cassie, and Anne were my good friends, but I had a connection with Emmie that I didn't have with them. I'd ended up with Emmie's diary when we both got tangled up in an anti-war demonstration that had grown out of control. I'd discovered that her father had been killed in Vietnam, when all I wanted in the world was for my father to come back. So I could talk to Susan and the others, but what I really needed was to talk with Emmie. And I needed to hear a voice, not write a letter.

I'd never used a pay phone before. There was one on the street in front of the library and another closer to the Town Hall, but I never really had a reason to use either. The only people I would have called were my parents, and if I needed them I'd just ride my bike home.

The day before was a grocery delivery day, and while I was putting orders in boxes, I asked Mr. Johnson for change. He normally paid me in ones and fives which was fine for Sonny's and the ice cream place, but I knew I needed change for the pay phone. He started giving me four quarters for a dollar, but I asked for dimes instead. He gave me a curious look, but opened the cash register again and let ten dimes clink onto the counter.

I'd squeezed myself into the phone booth and closed the door behind me before realizing I had no idea what number to call. Could the operator help me if I just asked for Emmie Hatcher in San Francisco?

Emmie lived in a group house. I'd seen a few of the people she shared the house with when I visited. If there was a phone in the house, any one of them could have put it in their name. Was Emmie her full name or short for something else? I didn't even know. In spite of the odds stacked against me, I pulled the phone book out from the shelf beneath the phone and flipped toward the H section.

Forestville was a small town. Nearby Santa Rosa was bigger, but still not big enough to deserve its own phonebook. So I was in luck that the title across the cover of the thick book read, "San Francisco and Surrounding Area." Forestville was a surrounding area I guess, but the important part was that the book included San Francisco. If it had just been for Forestville, it wouldn't have been much more than a few sheets of folded paper.

I found names beginning with "Ha" and scanned the tops of the pages until I got closer. I finally found a row with "Hatcher" in it and let my eyes follow my finger down the list of first names.

Donald
Edward
Kenny
Leonard
Lorraine
Richard

No Emmie. I got a sinking feeling that I'd be making the decision on my own, mailing Emmie rather than hearing her voice. Then my eyes popped back to the list of names—all men except Lorraine. In 1969, most married couples didn't decide whose name would be listed in the phonebook, the phone company just put in the husband's name. Unless there was no husband.

I picked up the receiver and held it to my ear while I dug a dime out of my pocket. I slid it into the slot, holding it for a second longer than I needed to. Letting it drop into the phone felt like a decision made, and I was rewarded with the hum of a dial tone. I propped the phone receiver against my ear with my shoulder, traced a finger along Lorraine Hatcher's number in the phonebook, and dialed.

A voice somewhere in the phone line, louder than I was expecting, surprised me. "There is a long distance charge for this call. Please deposit an additional twenty cents." I reached back into my pocket and dug out a few more dimes. I put two more in the slot and let the others drop back into my pocket.

There was a long pause where I could hear nothing but silence and partially imagined clicks as phone line connected to phone line between Forestville and San Francisco. Finally, the phone blurted out a ring. I held my breath and waited. Ring. I waited. Ring. Ring. Ring. I didn't know if the money I'd put into the phone would be enough to let it ring until someone picked up. I hoped so.

"Hello?" a voice said. There was concern in the voice, like the ringing phone, wherever it was ringing, was out of place. I hesitated long enough that the voice said another hello, with more concern.

"Hi... ummm, I'm sorry. Hello, Mrs. Hatcher. I'm..." Who was I? Emmie's friend? Not really. I was just someone who happened to scoop her off the floor after the police had started knocking people around at the protest. Did that make Emmie my friend? Because right now I really needed one.

"Hello," I started again. "Mrs. Hatcher, I'm Bets... um, Elizabeth Wells. I'm a friend of... uh, do you have a daughter named Emmie?" I realized the assumption I'd made in the phone book could be totally wrong.

"Yes... yes, Emmie is my daughter." I breathed a sigh of relief and tried to figure out what to say next. I started again with an introduction, a little more sure of myself this time.

"Hello. I'm Elizabeth Wells. I'm a friend of Emmie's, and..."

"Are you the girl from City Hall? The one who helped Emmie when she got hurt?"

"Um, yes. Yes." It made sense, I guess, that Emmie's mother would know about what happened to her at the City Hall protest. Although I wondered if Emmie had done the editing when she told her mom what had happened, or if her mother was editing for my sake. "When she got hurt" certainly didn't tell the whole story.

Emmie and I had both been at an anti-war demonstration in front of City Hall in San Francisco. Well, Emmie had been at the demonstration. I was there for a field trip gone terribly wrong. When the protesters stormed the building and the police arrived to break things up, Emmie got slammed into a wall that I happened to be standing next to. Even Emmie's mom saying I'd helped her was a distortion of the truth. Stopping her from hitting the wall would have helped her. I held her head while she bled all over the place. Although I suppose me holding my sweater against the wound and slowing down the blood helped a little.

"And you're the girl who organized the protest in that little town up north, right?" I smiled, remembering. I'd somehow gotten most of my school to cover the front of their shirts with tomato juice, ketchup, red paint, whatever we could find to mimic my bloody shirt from San Francisco. We lined both sides of Front Street and had most of the town out there with us by the time we were done.

"Yes, ma'am. That was me." I couldn't hide the smile or the pride in my voice, and I was suddenly feeling much more comfortable about the conversation.

"Well, it's good to meet you... Bets. Is that right?"

"Yes, ma'am. Bets. Um... that's what my father calls me."

"What can I do for you, Bets?" The hesitant voice I'd heard when she first picked up the phone was gone. I no longer felt like I was talking to a stranger, getting ready to make some odd request.

"I was hoping you'd have a number where I could reach Emmie. All I have is her address, but I'd really like to get in touch with her today, instead of sending a letter."

"Sure, Bets. Just a minute. Let me check." I heard the clunk of the phone being set down and then what was probably her footsteps. I waited, listening to the silence in someone else's house.

Then the loud voice interrupted the silence. "Please deposit another ten cents."

"What?"

"Deposit another dime please or this call will be disconnected." The operator again. Emmie's mom had sounded like she was in San Francisco. The operator sounded like she was inside the phone right next to my ear.

"No, wait! Just a second." I dug in my pocket. "Don't disconnect us!" I fished another dime out and pushed it into the slot. The operator disappeared and left me to continue listening to the silence. I put my hand back in my pocket to inventory my remaining dimes and hoped Emmie's mom would return soon. I still had another call to make.

Then she was back. I had to put the phone down while I dug in my backpack for a pen and something to write on, desperately hoping the operator didn't return and ask for another dime while the phone wasn't to my ear. Then I picked it back up and scribbled the number down as Emmie's mom read it through the phone. I thanked her and was saying goodbye when I thought of something else.

"Ma'am?"

"Yes?"

"I...um, I'm sorry. I'm sorry about your husband." I didn't know if this was the right thing to say, or the right time to say it, or if it was right to even say anything. But I felt like I should. I guess I'd want someone to say something to me if I were in her place. But there was a long silence on the other end of the phone and what sounded like a long sigh. I crossed my fingers that the operator wouldn't pick that second to cut back in, and my fingers nervously played with the remaining dimes in my pocket, ready to snatch one out and deposit it in the phone.

"Thank you," a weak voice said on the other end of the phone line. The first voice I'd heard—the one that sounded concerned and nervous about the phone ringing—was back again.

"I'm sorry ma'am. I... I didn't know if... I just wanted to... Sorry. I'm sorry. I... I don't know what else to say."

Another silent pause. "Sorry is all there is to say." There was almost a laugh in her voice, but it had a helplessness to it that left me feeling uneasy and empty. "You have a nice chat with Emmie, Bets. Tell her I say hello." Then there was a click and she was gone.

Talking

I didn't call Emmie right away. After getting off the phone with her mother, I felt empty and weighed down by the way things had ended. I wanted to talk to Emmie about my father and about the trip to Woodstock. I wanted her to help me figure out what to do about both. But talking on the phone was more work than I could manage at the moment.

I decided to walk around town and look for friends I could talk to in person. I hadn't made plans to meet Cassie, Susan, or Anne, but I figured at least one of them would be hanging around somewhere in town. Forestville wasn't a big place. It had one main street that was nothing but a highway number a half mile outside of town in either direction. Other than the school on Front Street, there was a town hall, Johnson's store, a few other shops and businesses mixed in with some older houses that were there before the town spread into the surrounding area, and two places to get food. Well, I suppose there were more than two, but as far as a high school kid was concerned there were only two that mattered: Sonny's and a place that sold ice cream, burgers, and fries. I walked down Front street and figured if I didn't see one of the girls at the ice cream place, I'd find one of them at Sonny's.

I walked, and I thought. Emmie's father had died over a year ago. To most sixteen-year-olds, a year can seem like a pretty long time. I thought about Emmie's mom, and her reaction to just the mention of her husband. If the pain and hurt she was feeling from his death had faded at all over the last year, it hadn't faded much. Or maybe it had, and what I'd sensed on the phone was just a fraction of what she was feeling a year ago. Either way, the thought terrified me.

My father had been away from me for a year. It didn't get any easier the longer he was gone, but I got used to him not being home. I got used to not talking with him, and I got used to not seeing him. But getting used to something doesn't make it any easier. I thought about how I would have felt if he hadn't come back. And then with a sinking feeling that made me suddenly dizzy, I thought about what it would be like if the way my father had been acting became something I'd simply have to get used to, if plate throwing and staring at the walls became a normal part of living with him, as the memory of how things used to be faded away.

I was relieved when I saw Cassie, Susan, and Anne all outside the ice cream place, because I don't think I could have made it all the way to Sonny's alone with my thoughts. They all held ice cream cones and were busy chatting when I walked up. Cassie had our favorite, marshmallow fudge.

We'd discovered we all liked that flavor the day we first met, but all four of us would scan the list of flavors anyway and occasionally try something different. Susan held a cone with two heaping scoops of strawberry, and Anne had chocolate. I don't think I'd ever seen Cassie with anything but marshmallow fudge though.

Ice cream choices aside, all three friends knew something was wrong the second they saw me. Cassie elbowed Anne, and she turned and ducked back into the ice cream place. By the time we were seated at a picnic table in the grassy area next to the building, she reemerged with a second marshmallow fudge and handed it to me. Whether or not I needed a heart-to-heart at the moment, one thing was for sure, I definitely needed ice cream.

We sat, ate ice cream, and didn't talk much except for comments about people walking by across the street and giggled conversation about boys at school. But I knew as I reached the pointy end of my cone that I'd eventually have to talk.

Susan finished her cone first and asked, "What's going on, Bethy?" Her tone was friendly and pleasant, but her eyes didn't leave me, both watching for any reaction I might have and letting me know that avoiding the conversation was not an option. Cassie and Anne tossed the tips of their cones into their mouths at the same time and joined in.

This is what I wanted, what I needed. As uncomfortable as it was, as much as I wanted to avoid talking about my father, I really just needed to sit with friends and talk. I hadn't really told anyone, hadn't even really talked with my mother about it. Not about what happened or about anything that lead up to it. I told Cassie, Susan, and Anne everything, starting with the first time my father was home early. I shared how it had been happening since he'd come home from Vietnam, and how it seemed to be happening more and more often. And then I told them about the other day, about coming home from school and finding him already home, about my father's frightened reaction when I touched his arm, and about him throwing the plate.

All three girls sat and listened, not commenting. No big reactions or surprise, just nods and comforting smiles. Again, exactly what I needed. I finished talking, and there was a moment where we all just looked at the ground or scanned the other side of Front Street for something interesting. Cassie was the first to say something.

"Jeez, Bethy. Give someone else a chance to have issues once in awhile." She laughed a little when she said it, but I still looked at her, surprised and trying to figure out if I should be upset. "Seriously," she continued, no longer able to hide her joking smile. "First you're moping around town for a year, depressed about your father being gone. Now he's back and you found some other thing to be upset about."

"Cassie, don't be a jerk!" Anne elbowed her sister with a shocked look on her face, but she understood the joke and laughed while she did it. When Susan finally gave up on holding in her giggles, I joined in and laughed until I got tears in my eyes. We took a minute to settle down, but when someone at another table gave us a disapproving look, we started laughing uncontrollably all over again. When we finally caught our breath, Cassie was the first to talk.

"I mean it though, Bethy. Lots of people have issues with their fathers." Then she added, "and their mothers."

"Jimmy McNeil's dad is yelling constantly. That poor kid can't do anything right," Susan said. "I hear it all the time, and he lives three houses away from ours."

"Carol Peters' dad is always heading into Santa Rosa. Spending all his time in bars, my mom's friends say."

"Jackie Anderson's mom kicked her dad out of the house for a month. No idea why, but she must have had a reason."

"Andy Spencer's parents never stop arguing." Cassie pointed a finger at me. "Probably your fault, Bethy. Andy told me his dad's a big Nixon supporter, but his mom turned against the war after the protest you organized last year. They haven't gotten along ever since." Cassie and Anne wrapped up the list of problem parents with a playful show, mimicking a bickering mother and father, and we all broke down laughing again.

It didn't take away my worries about my father and what was wrong with him, but being with the three girls did take away the lonely feeling I'd had since talking with Emmie's mother, and as unexpected as Cassie's take on my situation was, it did put everything in a different light. Emmie had lost her father. Mine might be acting strangely, he might have gotten unfairly angry and more than a little bit scary, but I still had him.

☮ ☮ ☮

Anne convinced Susan to walk with her to the library. She said she had to work on homework, but we all knew it was about Jimmy McNeil. He had practice for El Molino's spring musical, and the library was right next to the theater.

Cassie's house was in the same direction as mine, so we left Anne and Susan and decided to walk together. "Have you figured out Woodstock yet?" We'd walked a block in silence, and her voice brought me out of my thoughts. I only shrugged. I hadn't figured anything out. I guess I'd been focused on other things.

"I don't know." I let those three words linger while I decided what else I could say. "I want to go. I really want to go!" I stopped, realizing how much I sounded like a kid pleading with a parent for a trip to the zoo. When she didn't say anything in reply, I glanced over at Cassie. I was a little surprised at how much she'd grown up over the last year. She was just a year ahead of me in school, but she looked like she could have been in college. She wore a long flowing dress that almost covered the worn leather of her sandals. How did they get so worn? Mine still smelled like the store they came from. Cassie's long hair was pulled back by a braided headband. Lots of kids at school had learned how to make them, but Cassie's didn't look fresh and new and handmade by kids. Like her sandals, it looked like it had a story behind it. The beaded necklace and the braids around her wrists were the same. Maybe the difference was that all the stuff I was wearing had been bought for me by my parents, and Cassie's comfort with her own wardrobe made it look like it was all hers, maybe even something her parents wouldn't approve of.

"What are you going to do when your parents say no?" Again, her question pulled me back from my own thoughts.

"When they say no?"

"Bethy, come on. We had this conversation the other day. You want to go. You really want to go, and your parents are going to say no. They're really, really going to say no. So, I'm just asking. What are you going to do?"

I honestly hadn't thought about it. Until Cassie asked, in my mind, my parents saying I couldn't go to Woodstock meant that I wouldn't be going to Woodstock. I hadn't occurred to me that I had other options. Without an answer, I looked back at Cassie. Her raised eyebrow asked the question again.

"I don't know," was my only answer.

Disruptive Behavior

Ms. Simms was talking at us about World War II. Talking was really the best word for what she was doing. It would have been nice to say we were learning about World War II. Even saying that Ms. Simms was teaching us about the war would have been an improvement. But what was happening in room 231 didn't resemble teaching, and we definitely weren't learning.

The details were fuzzy. I wasn't really paying attention, so I can't say for sure. She told us about the Japanese attack on Pearl Harbor. She told us about all the countries Germany invaded in Europe and about the Holocaust. That much my ears had caught even through my brain was in San Francisco, or Woodstock, or flying through the sky, or absolutely anywhere but Ms. Simms' classroom.

I raised my hand.

No one ever raised their hand in Ms. Simms' classroom. If she wanted to ask us questions, she just called on someone. It didn't really matter who, because whether their answer was right or wrong, Ms. Simms would continue talking and just give us the answer she wanted anyway.

So when I stuck my hand high in the air, she didn't even see it at first. Kids near me noticed and looked up at my hand and then at my face to see if they could figure out what the heck I was thinking. A couple kids snickered, and there was a murmur from the back of the room. In my two years of high school, I'd gotten a reputation for stirring things up. Whether it was punching a boy with a strong right hook, disrupting a pep rally, or organizing an anti-war demonstration, kids knew that if I was doing anything at school other than taking notes or studying, something worth seeing was going to happen.

Clearly, Ms. Simms had the same thought. When she saw my hand, she did her best to ignore it, sticking her nose in her book or looking anywhere in the room but in my direction. When I got tired, I switched arms, holding my other hand high in the air until that arm got tired too, and then I switched back. I'm sure Ms. Simms could have ignored me the rest of the period, but when the giggles and talking from my classmates interrupted her reading, she gave in.

"Yes, Elizabeth?" she said in a breath, a stabbing finger holding her place in the textbook.

"People had some very good reasons for fighting in World War II," I said simply. Everyone had quieted in anticipation, but no one quite knew how to respond to what I ended up saying. Ms. Simms seemed especially unnerved.

She'd been expecting a confrontation, and while what I'd said was technically an opinion, it certainly supported everything she'd been reading.

"Yes." She hesitated, not quite sure I was done. "Yes, that's right, Elizabeth." She inhaled, ready to continue reading, but I spoke again before she got out her next word.

"We don't have any good reasons for fighting in Vietnam." My words hung there. Ms. Simms' mouth froze open, like the word she was about to read had gotten wedged inside. My classmates stifled giggles again. They were getting what they'd expected from me and were sure to have a story to tell at lunch.

"What did you say Elizabeth?"

"You heard me. We don't have a good reason for sending soldiers to Vietnam. People are getting killed for no reason. It's a bad war. We need to stop fighting and bring our soldiers home." Those few sentences had more opinion in them than everything else that had ever been said in Ms. Simms' classroom combined.

"Elizabeth, today we're talking about World War II."

"No, we're not," I jumped on top of her words. "You're talking about it. We're just sitting here. But that's my point. Why bother talking about a war that happened decades ago? Vietnam's happening now. Let's talk about that. The textbook doesn't say anything about Vietnam, but it's all over the newspapers. Let's read them. Let's talk about something we care about. How many people here know someone in the war? Or someone who was killed in the war?" I was spouting sentences like rocks thrown at windows. I wasn't waiting for answers to my questions, but I saw more than a few hands go up.

"And let's not just talk about Vietnam. Let's do something! We can write letters, letters to the people in charge, letters to the newspaper. Why waste our time reading a textbook full of old stuff, when we can be doing something about what's happening right now!" At some point I stood up, and I was shouting without realizing it.

Kids cheered and clapped. Some stood on their chairs or crumpled the day's notes and tossed them across the room. I could see from the expressions on some faces that they felt the same way I did. Others just seemed like they were glad for a break from the classroom routine.

Ms. Simms didn't say anything. She walked to the far side of her desk and scribbled something on a small pad of paper. She tore off the top sheet and held it out for me. I knew what it was, gathered my things, and grabbed it from her on my way out the door. I looked at it once I was out in the hallway.

From Rm 231 to Office - Disruptive behavior.

She'd underlined the word disruptive and signed her name at the bottom. As horrible a teacher as Ms. Simms was, she knew how to handle a classroom full of high school kids. A less experienced teacher would have engaged in the argument with me, would have tried to convince me and all the kids shouting and clapping that I was wrong. It would have been a losing battle and the teacher would have ended up defending her own opinions while the class spiraled quickly out of control. By sending me to the office, Ms. Simms eliminated the instigator and sent the message to everyone else that they could easily be next.

I looked down at her note again. Disruptive Behavior. I guess that was a bad thing, but it really depended on what you were disrupting. If people disrupted a bank robbery, or a fight, or a war, that would be a good thing. I decided, as I turned a corner and walked past the cafeteria, that disrupting history class was indeed a good thing.

I knew how the main office worked. I'd been there before, a couple of times. I'd sit in an uncomfortable chair outside Mr. Higgins' office while his secretary sat at the desk and tried to look busy. I'd eventually have to stand in front of his desk and explain why I did what I did to someone who'd already decided I shouldn't have done it. I wasn't sure if disruptive behavior in a classroom was reason enough to call my mother and have her come to school. Either way, the afternoon was sure to involve a lot of sitting and waiting, and more than my fair share of listening to adults tell me how to behave.

I looked at the note again, then crumpled it up and tossed in a trash can. I could see the office just down the hallway, but instead of continuing, I turned and went straight out the front door.

Choices

Walking around Forestville when I should have been in school gave me a weird, out-of-place feeling. The light wasn't right. The sun was high in the sky, and it would be hours before it cast long afternoon shadows. The town wasn't entirely empty, but with kids in school and most people at work, I was sharing the sidewalks with just a few people, an older couple and a mother pushing her baby in a stroller. No one seemed interested enough to ask a high school kid why she wasn't in school.

The change left from my call to Emmie's mother was in a small dish on top of my dresser at home. I certainly wasn't going to go home to get it and risk running into my mother, or worse, my father. I also couldn't go into Johnson's without raising suspicion. I could have gotten change at Sonny's, and grabbed a slice of pizza while I was there, or walked down to the ice cream place. But both places were used to the rush of kids after school let out, and I figured someone would wonder why I was showing up hours early.

I settled on the post office, but before the bell above the door stopped ringing, I'd already started to doubt my choice. There was a line of four or five people waiting to step up to the counter. Any one of the them could be a friend of my mother, someone who would recognize me and wonder why I wasn't in school. I stood with my face to the floor, watching my feet as I shuffled forward.

When I finally got to the head of the line, I realized I didn't have anything to mail. I guess I could have just asked for change, but I felt like I should have some other reason for being there. I thought fast, as the person ahead of me finished and I stepped up to the counter.

"Stamps please." The man behind the counter didn't say anything at first. Instead he eyed me up and down. I braced myself for his question and my brain raced for an excuse.

"How many?"

"How many? Oh, uhh.. How much do they cost?" We'd gotten lots of letters from my father while he was in Vietnam, and my mother and I sent just as many. But I guess I'd never paid attention to the stamps, and I wondered if stamps for sending letters to another country were different. But I didn't even need stamps. I just needed change.

"First class stamps are six cents." If the man had been suspicious when I first stepped up to the counter, he must have decided I was okay. Rather than looking at me, he seemed to be sizing up the line behind me, and I felt pressure to get my change and get out.

"Uhh, I'll take ten." It seemed like a good amount—not too much money, but enough to make it worth the time it took to dig in the cash register and make change. But as soon as I said it, I remember the operator interrupting my call with Emmie's mother. Was forty cents going to give me enough time for the conversation I needed to have?

"Sorry. Umm, I'll actually take... uh." I quickly did the math. "Seventeen." I put two dollars on the counter, and the man rolled his eyes.

"You don't have a couple pennies or a nickel?" I shrugged silently and shook my head. The man took my two dollars and started counting out my change in quarters. When I stopped him and asked for dimes instead, he rolled his eyes again with a loud sigh, glancing toward the people behind me. He methodically counted nine dimes, one nickel, and three pennies, and slid them across the counter to me along with the seventeen stamps. I thanked him, sliding them off the edge of the counter into my cupped hand and exiting the post office, again keeping my head down in case anyone my parents knew was waiting in line.

Although it was farther, I walked to the phone booth in front of the Town Hall instead of using the one near the library. The library was right next to school, and I felt like the shorter walk was not worth the risk of someone from school seeing me.

I dug Emmie's phone number out of my purse, put a dime into the slot, and dialed. I deposited two more when the operator's voice came through the phone, and then set the remaining dimes on the shelf under the phone. The ring sounded like it was far away in San Francisco. I waited, listening to the empty space between rings and holding my breath hoping Emmie was home. I had no idea what her schedule was like or when she went to classes. I also caught myself hoping that she'd be the one to answer. I'd seen a few of her roommates when I visited, and they seemed a bit out of it, like they'd need to think for a while before they even remembered that they had a roommate named Emmie.

A click on the other end of the line stopped the ringing, and then there was a thunk loud enough to make me pull the phone away from my ear. I heard a distant voice mixed in with more thunks and clunks. Someone was having trouble holding on to the phone.

"Yeah?" a man's voice finally said.

"Hi," I said hesitantly. "Is Emmie there?" There was a long silence on the other end as I held my breath.

"Yeah," the voice said again, then I heard the phone receiver set down loudly. I waited. I just barely heard other voices, not a shout for Emmie, but a conversation in another room maybe. At one point, footsteps got louder as they approached the phone then faded again. More conversation and laughter. The operator cut in and asked for another ten cents. I put it in the phone and eyed my stack of dimes, wondering if it would last.

"Hello?" I'd listened to the sounds of Emmie's house long enough that her voice on the phone surprised me.

"Emmie? Hi, it's me. Um, it's Elizabeth Wells. Uh, I mean, it's Bets."

"Hey! Cool! I was wondering when I was going to hear from you." Hearing her voice felt good. Hearing the excitement in her voice felt wonderful. I felt an overwhelming need to talk with Emmie, and knowing that she was glad to hear from me made that a little bit easier.

"Are you coming with us? Woodstock? Please say you're coming!"

"I... yeah, I want to. I just don't know. I... do you have time to talk? For a little bit?"

"Yeah, that's cool." There was a smile in Emmie's voice, and I could picture her settling into a comfy chair or folding herself crossed-legged on the floor, like we were in the same room enjoying each other's company. Making myself comfortable in the phone booth was not an option.

I filled her in on everything. It was hard to pinpoint the sinking feeling I'd been holding inside, but talking to Emmie helped. I started with a run down of classes and teachers and could practically hear Emmie's eyes rolling when I told her about Ms. Simms. I talked about the things I was seeing on the news. Maybe some people wouldn't understand how racial unrest, assassinations, and politics would matter to a kid in tiny, middle of nowhere Forestville, but Emmie got it. I talked and fed dimes into the phone.

I knew everything I shared with Emmie added to how I was feeling, and I also knew it was all building toward my father. That was not a conversation I could just jump into. So I got everything else out in the open, and then I was ready to tell Emmie about the rest. There was mostly silence on the other end of the phone, just the sounds of someone listening. That was what I needed and Emmie knew it. Eventually, I got it all out. I wiped away tears, and Emmie let the silence stay a little longer.

"You've got a lot going on, Elizabeth." I caught myself opening my mouth to correct her and then was glad we were only talking on the phone and not in person. I hadn't talked to Emmie in a while, so she could be forgiven for using my full name, but if she wanted me to drive across the country with her, we were going to need to fix that.

"You've got a lot going on," she repeated. "It seems like sometimes when things are weighing you down, it's best to get away from them. And sometimes getting some distance helps you sort everything out. Other times the only way to get through difficult times is to stick with it, right where you are, and sort it all out while you're surrounded by it." Emmie had a way of speaking that made me feel like I was listening to her thoughts, like she was figuring things out while talking, and then what she'd said was just out there waiting for me to pick it up, or not. It was the opposite of someone telling me what to do. It was a million times better.

"Funny how things work out sometimes," Emmie continued after a while. "You've got a choice to make. Take a trip or not. Sort things out by getting out of town, or sort them out by staying put. If you didn't have a choice, you'd feel stuck. But having a choice becomes a whole new conflict." Again, the feeling that Emmie was just thinking out loud, and I was lucky enough to be there listening.

"This is all your choice to make, Elizabeth. I really want you to come with us, but you have to decide on your own. We're heading out in two weeks, and we'll make Forestville one of our stops. Take some time to figure things out, and then come with us or not."

We talked for a few more minutes. I told her about Forestville and some places they could park for the night. She thought a spot along the river on the edge of town would be their best bet. We both decided stopping by my house would not be a good idea. I had two weeks to decide whether I was joining her. If I wanted to go, I would meet Emmie by the river on the night she was in town. Finding her would be easy. Deciding whether to join her or not would be the tricky part.

We said goodbye and I hung up the phone. Talking to Emmie made me feel better about the things that were bothering me. It didn't make those problems go away, but knowing that someone else knew about them and understood made it a little easier.

Still in the phone booth, I looked around at the world outside. The sun was lower in the sky and other kids milled around town. I'd lost track of time and had no idea how long I'd been talking with Emmie. There was one dime left on the shelf below the phone. I pushed back the folding door of the phone booth and stepped out into the cool afternoon air. I left the dime on the shelf. Someone might need to make a call.

History

I was used to riding my bike around town. I worked at Johnson's store part-time after school delivering groceries. The bike my father had given me before he left for Vietnam made the job easier, and even though I'd already put hundreds of miles on it, riding it was still exciting for me and biking all over Forestville never felt like work.

Still, the ride out to Miss E.'s farm made me realize I was out of shape. It was definitely outside of town, far enough that roads with names and houses with numbers were few and far between. People who had lived in Forestville all their lives didn't use the road names anyway. "Out where the Petersons live" or "two driveways past old Volkers' place" was all you'd get for directions from some folks.

A year ago, I'd ridden out to Miss E.'s farm once a week to deliver her groceries. Well, I'd started out just delivering, but before long, the trips out of town became more like visits than deliveries. I knew all the customers I delivered to. I knew a little bit of their stories. Heck, I knew what they ate and what brand of toilet paper they used. But Miss E. was special.

I hadn't been out to the farm in almost a year, but I knew the way without thinking, so I could let my mind wander. I had two weeks to decide about Woodstock and the cross-country trip with Emmie. Cassie was right. My parents would never say yes to the trip. So it wasn't just a decision to go or not go. It was a decision to leave without my parents knowing, without their permission.

I'd heard about kids who ran away from home. The evening news shared information about them occasionally, hoping someone had seen them. I could never figure it out. What would make someone want to leave home? I'd always been perfectly happy at home, and couldn't imagine leaving. Until now.

I kept thinking about the concert and all the music that would be happening there, but my excitement couldn't drown out the darker feeling that lingered just below that. If I went away with Emmie, I wouldn't just be running off to a music festival. I'd be running away from my father and the tension that had sunk into our home. But I wasn't really running away, right? I was just going away, like a vacation, and I'd be back, right?

The question trailed behind me as I crested the hill in the dirt road and saw Miss E.'s farm nestled in the low flat ground below. I spun my pedals backwards, braking hard enough to cause the back wheel of my bike to skid along the gravelly surface. I slid my feet slid off the pedals as a cloud of dust drifted off in the direction I'd been going.

I hadn't really thought things through when I decided to head out to Miss E.'s farm, but now that I was looking down the hill at the farm, I wasn't sure I should go any farther. It wasn't like I'd be trespassing. I guess technically Miss E. still owned it, but she hadn't been there in almost a year and I was pretty sure she wouldn't ever be back. There was no one around to know if I rode my bike up her driveway and walked right into her house. And who would care if I did? No one in town knew much about Miss E. while she lived here, they certainly wouldn't bother themselves with her business now that she was gone.

But it still didn't feel right. My parents had taken me to the beach when I was five or six. I'm not really sure if I remember being there or if I just remember the story my parents tell. We walked along the beach and came to a spot where some other kids had built a whole village of sand castles. They'd left, and the tide had already claimed some of the castles closest to the water, but I wouldn't let my parents walk through them and insisted on walking up near the dunes and sea grass to avoid stepping on the castles. Someone had built them, had taken the time to carefully construct them. Even though the builders were gone, no, especially because they were gone, I'd decided it was important to leave the castles just as they had left them.

Miss E.'s farm was like that. My last memory of Miss E. was of her landing at the airport in Oakton and then flying away again. I hadn't really thought about what came before that: leaving the house where she'd spent the last thirty years, climbing into her plane, and flying away. Did she take anything with her? Maybe all the photos that hung on her wall? Her red pickup still sat in the driveway, and the doors of the barn that had held her plane for so long hung wide open. Why bother closing them. It would have been absurd to open them, start up an airplane and roll it out of the barn, only to hop out to close the barn doors and hop back in. Absurd. Yet, the barn door hung open as a reminder to me that the woman who'd opened them was never coming back.

I threw a leg over my bike and planted two feet on the ground. I leaned the bike over until it rested on the gravel surface of the road, and then I sat next to it, pulling my legs in so my chin rested on my knees. In all the times I rode my bike out to Miss E.'s farm, I don't think I ever saw a car driving the dirt road that led to her farm. I felt pretty safe sitting down in the middle of it. And knowing some of the cars that drove around Forestville, if one did come down the road I'd have time to stand up and walk to the side before it slowly passed me by.

I had no idea what to do next. I realized I'd crossed a line. Walking out of school seemed exciting and the only right thing to do at the time, but it didn't lead to any good options for me. There wasn't really a way to avoid what I'd done at school. It was going to catch up with me the next day. And if someone from school hadn't already called my parents, they would soon. I'd totally trapped myself, but it somehow still felt like the right thing to do.

There were bigger issues to deal with. The problems at school and the confrontation with Ms. Simms seemed insignificant compared to what was going on with my father and the decision I had to make.

The decision.

My talk with Emmie had framed that decision in an entirely different way. It made the question of whether or not to go to the concert feel like a kid's birthday wish. Sure I wanted to go to Woodstock. What high school kid wouldn't? It wasn't a decision to go or not go. And the concert wasn't the problem. As much as I wanted to go, I wouldn't just leave without my parents' permission. There was more.

Hopping into Emmie's van and following one road after another as we wandered our way across the country was inviting. But it wasn't just about where I'd be going. It was about what I'd be leaving. I spent a year alone with my mother while my father was in Vietnam. It took me almost a year to figure my mother out—the silence at dinner, her upbeat attitude when all I wanted to do was cry, barely acknowledging that my father was gone. It drove me crazy and made me feel entirely alone, but I finally saw things from her perspective and started to understand why she was the way she was.

The problem with my father was different. I had absolutely no idea what to do. Maybe what made it so difficult was the contrast. My father and I had always been close. We enjoyed each other's company no matter what we were doing. We always knew what the other was thinking and always knew what to do or say around each other. That was before the war. My father came back a different person. Some days it felt like my father was still in Vietnam and someone else was living in my home. In spite of my best efforts, it was still difficult and awkward—sometimes scary—to be around him. After almost a year of watching things gradually get worse, simply getting away from the whole mess felt like the best option, maybe the only option.

I looked down at the farmhouse at the bottom of the hill. On a day that seemed forever ago, Miss E. sat with me at her kitchen table and told me her story. She'd run away, sort of. And I knew that a big part of the unhappiness in her story was that she hadn't run toward something she wanted, she'd run away from something she didn't want. But the day she told that story felt long ago, and the story she told, longer still. None of it helped or seemed to fit with what I was feeling. All I wanted was to get away. I didn't know what else to do. It didn't matter whether I was running to something or from something. Getting away was enough, which was an exciting and horrible feeling all at once. It offered some relief, but at the same time, I'd never wanted to be anywhere but home.

I couldn't hold it in any longer. I tucked my face into the dark space created by my arms wrapped around my knees, and I cried. It was the kind of cry that shakes your whole body. I cried as hard as I ever had, and when the sobs finally slowed down and I started to think I was done, it all started again, worse than before.

I don't know how long I would have gone on like that if the sound of car tires on the gravel road hadn't invaded my space. I lifted my face from between my knees and looked up, ready to jump out of the way, but what I saw was worse than a car accident. My mother's car rolled to a stop in front of me.

I wanted to tuck my head back between my knees and start crying all over again, but instead I quickly wiped the tears from my eyes and ran my fingers through my hair to straighten it. By the time my mother had climbed out of the car and closed the door behind her, I was sitting comfortably, staring down at the farm at the bottom of the hill like I hadn't even noticed her approach.

She sat down next to me without saying anything. A year ago, I'd gotten used to the silence between us, had hated it and at the same time had gotten comfortable with the day to day routine of it. Now it immediately felt like something was wrong, like my mother's silence meant she was angry at me or that my silence meant I was hiding something.

We must have looked like a pair, sitting in the middle of the road at the top of the hill. My mother sat close enough to me that our elbows brushed, and she pulled her knees up to her chest and wrapped her arms around them, mirroring my pose. I turned to look at her, thinking eye contact would force the conversation to start so we could get it over with. But I only saw the side of her face. She gazed out at the farm in front of us, and after a few seconds waiting for her to acknowledge me, I turned back to do the same.

I lost myself in memories of the farm and the woman who'd lived there. My eyes moved slowly from barn, to house, to pickup truck, and my thoughts wandered with them. I'd only come out to the farm once each week to deliver groceries, but my visits to Miss E. had gotten me through a difficult year. I replayed conversations and remembered feelings for long enough that I'd nearly forgotten that I was sitting next to my mother, until she spoke.

"Hard to lose someone you care about." She fell back into silence and let her words hang in front of us awhile. I didn't know what I was expecting her to say. I figured she was angry about me leaving school and would lecture me about that. The idea that she'd discovered Emmie's letter and the ticket flittered through my mind, bringing with it a brief panic, but if that was what she'd driven out to talk to me about, she would have done it as soon as she got out of the car.

So I'd written off both of those possibilities, but it hadn't occurred to me that she'd break the silence by comforting me about Miss E.'s disappearance. I didn't understand how she could ignore all that had happened in the last weeks, in the last few months, and instead think I was upset over something that happened almost a year ago. I opened my mouth to argue, but her words cut mine off before they could get anywhere.

"You haven't lost your father, Bets." I turned to look at her, surprised that she'd used my nickname, and just as quickly realized I'd misunderstood what she'd first said.

"Those buildings down there are empty. But our home's not. Your father came home from the war, which is more than a lot of kids can say. You can talk to your friend Emmie about what losing a father is really like." I felt the blood rush out of my face and tried to hide it. Did she somehow know I'd talked to Emmie on the phone? Maybe she had seen Emmie's letter. Emmie and I had sent letters back and forth over the last year, but it had been months and months since I'd mentioned her to my mother. I would have thought she would have forgotten her name at least, if she remembered Emmie at all. My mother bringing her up out of the blue made me wonder if she knew. And at the same time I wondered if I was just feeling guilty and becoming paranoid.

"We may not like what your father's going through right now, but having him at home the way he is, well, that's a whole lot better than not having him come home at all. I'm not defending what he did the other day. That was wrong, and I'll do what I can to make sure you're not put in a situation like that again, Bets." Again, my nickname, my father's name for me. It felt wrong coming out of my mother's mouth, and at the same time it felt wonderful.

"You have a decision to make." I held my breath. She knew about Woodstock for sure.

"And you won't find any answers by running away to a farm." A farm? Woodstock was being held on a farm. She absolutely knew. My mind frantically composed my explanation and my defense, but I caught myself before the words escaped my mouth. I'd run away from school to Miss

E.'s farm. I swallowed what I was going to say and again felt my face go white at the close call.

"How you're going to manage things with your father and the way he is right now is your decision. You can avoid him, you can be angry at him, or maybe you'll do what you can to help him through it. But don't make things worse by creating more problems for yourself. And problems for me." She pushed herself onto her feet and stood. She looked tired.

"Mr. Higgins called. I told him you'd gotten sick and were at home with me. When I passed through town and didn't see you, I figured you'd be out here." My mouth hung open in disbelief that my mother had lied to the principal in order to cover up what I'd done. "Figure it out, Bets, but don't take too long. Your father needs you, and so do I."

Then she turned and walked back to the car. She gave me a small wave as she backed up slightly and swung the car around. Then she turned the wheels in the other direction, rolled forward, and completed the turn, disappearing down the road and leaving a lingering trail of road dust behind her.

I wasn't upset that she didn't offer me a ride. A car ride with my mother was the last thing I wanted at the moment, and she knew it. I'd come out to Miss E.'s farm to think, and I needed more time to myself to do that. Rather than offering a solution to the choices I was wrestling with, my mother had heaped another decision on top and left me sitting in the middle of the road more confused than ever.

Saying Goodbye

The next two weeks were excruciating. What I wanted to do changed day to day, hour to hour. There were times when I absolutely knew that what I wanted was to go with Emmie to Woodstock, but that was clouded by thoughts of what I *should* do, what common sense told me to do, or worst of all, what my mother or father would want me to do.

The day my father left for Vietnam, he gave me a bike and arranged a job for me, but what he'd really given me was freedom. I remembered that feeling, as I struggled with the decision I had to make, and I imagined asking that father, the one from before the war, what to do. He'd lean back on his heels like he needed to be a little farther away from me in order to size me up. He'd cross his arms on his chest, tilt his head to the side a little like he was really thinking about his answer, then he'd raise his eyebrows and smile. But he'd say nothing. He'd look at me like that and make me wonder what his answer was going to be, but I knew that his silence meant he was waiting for me to decide.

My father expected me to make decisions. That didn't mean he'd let me do whatever I wanted to do, but he wouldn't make the decision for me. He'd let me scuff my feet in the dust and look at my toes while he smiled and waited. And when I finally made my choice and told him, if he agreed, he'd laugh and ruffle my hair and the nod and compliment me. Or his raised eyebrows would drop into a furrow and he'd bring a hand up to rub the stubble on a chin that had been clean-shaven that morning. "Why would you do that, Bets?" he would say. That would be my chance to convince him I was right. He'd listen, and sometimes he'd nod and agree with me. Or he'd keep rubbing his chin until I'd finished my argument, and then he'd give me his thoughts and help me see why my choice might not be the best one.

But the point was, he expected me to decide. He wouldn't let me do anything really stupid or anything that he really felt was wrong, but he wouldn't just tell me I couldn't do it. He'd let me decide and make me defend my choice. Sometimes while I was trying to convince him, I'd decide for myself that what I wanted wasn't any good for me. I knew a lot of kids who just got told by their parents what they could or couldn't do, so I appreciated the way my father treated difficult choices.

But that was my father before the war. I couldn't guess how my after-the-war father would react. He might get angry. Would he throw something again? He might just sigh and walk away from me so he could go back to staring at the walls. But I'd learned enough from my father before he left for Vietnam to figure out that what was most important was that I could make decisions for myself.

So I kept deciding, again and again. I'd think about everything on the ride to school and decide not to go. Then after parking my bike and walking toward my first class, I'd overhear a classmate talking about a singer I liked. One time I heard a group actually talking about Woodstock and how much they'd like to go. Whatever I heard was enough to change my mind, and that was it. I was determined to go, until my ride home when I'd start to think about my parents and how they'd react when they discovered I was gone. The sinking feeling inside me would change my mind back.

One night when we were out for dinner at Sonny's, I almost told them. It was a day where I'd changed my mind again and again and finally landed on the idea that I wanted to go, truly should go because of the once in a lifetime experience it offered, but couldn't go without telling my parents. I listened to their part of the conversation and nodded at the right parts, but my mind was wording and rewording what I was going to say.

I sat there waiting for the right moment to bring up what was on my mind. I waited for something that would let me turn the conversation toward Woodstock or music or travel. When the opportunity didn't come, I fidgeted in my chair, determined to just jump in, but I didn't. My mother started talking about some older kids in town who had wandered off to San Francisco. Their parents had called the police thinking they'd been kidnapped or something, and they were finally found and brought back to Forestville. My mother's telling of the story didn't touch on why they left home or why they went to San Francisco, but instead dwelled on the embarrassment their mothers must have felt having their kids come home in a police car. Heading to Woodstock with Emmie was a difficult topic to bring up after that.

Figuring things out with friends wasn't much easier. It was close enough to summer vacation that everyone was talking about what they were doing after school ended. I'd listen attentively while others talked about their plans, leaving an awkward silence when they finished talking and looked at me expectantly. When anyone actually asked me what my plans where, I'd shrug and make a face. "Working at Johnson's I guess. Just like last summer." I was bursting to tell them about Woodstock and about traveling across the country with Emmie. But how could I? If someone I told went on to tell their parents, and their parents told mine, the debate I'd been having with myself for weeks would have been for nothing. As soon as my parents found out, I'd be stuck at home all summer hoping to catch a few seconds of Woodstock mentioned on the evening news.

I'd only told Cassie and Anne and Susan. They knew I was struggling with what to do, and mostly they knew enough not to ask. They'd gone through a couple days of me changing my mind every time I turned around. They'd finally gotten tired of listening to my reasons for staying or going, but there were more silences in the conversation when we walked together after school, like they were waiting for me to say something. I didn't, mostly because I was still figuring it all out, so we didn't talk about Woodstock until an afternoon when Anne and Susan stayed after school and I was alone with Cassie.

"Be careful, ok?" was all she said. There was only the sound of our sandals on the sidewalk while I figured out what that meant. I finally just looked at her with a question on my face. "Just be careful," she said in a frustrated voice. "Forestville is middle-of-nowhere-ville. There's lots going on in the world, and none of it makes it to our town." I mumbled something about San Francisco to remind her of the riot I'd managed to survive, but she only shook her head. "Yeah, Bethy, I know about San Fran. You don't need to remind me."

Again, I was struck by how much older she seemed. I could see it in the way she dressed, the way she moved, and the way she talked to me. My uncle was fifteen years older than my mother, and he had a daughter who was almost closer in age to my mother than she was to me. We were cousins, but she felt more like she was part of my parents' generation, and I felt like a little girl when I was with her. Lately, hanging out with Cassie felt a little bit like that, and the feeling made me want to go to Woodstock all the more, just to prove that I wasn't a little girl, that I was as grown up as Cassie, or Emmie, or my cousin.

There was more silence as we walked, and when I couldn't stand it anymore I stopped. Cassie took a few more steps before she realized I was no longer beside her and turned around. I stuck my hands on my hips and planted my feet, ready to argue, ready to be angry at her for treating me like a kid. Instead, all I managed was little more than a whisper.

"I'll be careful." There was a tremor in my voice, and I was terrified at the certainty of it, but I knew at that instant that I would go with Emmie, that I couldn't possibly do otherwise. Cassie was right. There was a lot going on in the world. If I couldn't make any of it better, I at least had to see it, had to be a part of it.

"Yeah, I know you will." Cassie was next to me in what seemed like one long gliding step, and her arms were around me. We didn't have to say anything else, and we just stood there holding each other until it felt right to stop. Cassie moved her hands behind her neck and untied the braided necklace that had become a permanent part of her wardrobe. Then it was around my neck and Cassie was reaching behind me to tie it. "Give it back to me at the end of summer," she said with a smile, and then added, "and you better have some stories to tell." Then she walked away. She turned around briefly to wave as she crossed the street, and then she was gone.

Stepping Out

Planning to sneak out of my house, and actually sneaking out were two different things. Once I actually had to do it, I found myself wishing I'd decided on a different way to meet up with Emmie. I could have just left from school or told my parents I was going for a ride on my bike after dinner. Instead I was kicking myself for waiting until night and trying to get out of my dark and sleeping house without my parents hearing.

But I knew why I'd waited. Part of me wanted a few more hours of the routine—coming home, chatting with my mother, eating dinner with my parents, sitting with them while they watched the evening news. I also felt a seriousness to what I was doing. I was leaving home to drive across the country. That wasn't a journey that started with a detour on the way home from school or a fib about an after-dinner bike ride. I was getting into something for real, and if I was going to do it, I'd better be ready to sneak out of my parents' house in the dark of night. If I couldn't manage that, I would be better off staying in bed.

I'd started watching the evening news with my mother while my father was in Vietnam. It rarely gave us any information we wanted to hear, but it was a backdrop for my mother and I sitting together and wishing that my father was home. The routine continued after he came back, but depending on what the news was, my father would often get up and leave halfway through. If there was a local news story, or something about the President or a vote in Congress, he'd stay there between my mother and me, but when news of the war came on, he'd stand up and drift into my parents' bedroom without even saying goodnight. My mother would follow a minute later.

Of course, the night I needed to sneak out of my house was a slow news day for Vietnam, and my parents stayed on the couch with me listening to the weather and the news anchors bantering until the very end. They even stayed up for Johnny Carson's monologue on the Tonight Show before my father patted my knee and said, "Well Bets, time for bed." He got up as my mother stretched and nodded agreement. My father turned off the TV as he walked by and then disappeared down the hallway.

I was left on the couch alone, wanting desperately to tell them everything. I wanted to tell them about Emmie, and Woodstock, and the cross-country trip that I was about to begin. Most of all, I wanted to tell them how I was feeling.

How I was feeling about school, and everything that was happening in our country, and with my father.

That was the hardest part, because that evening he had been fine. He had been himself. There was no hint of the changes I'd seen since he'd come home. I was leaving with Emmie to get away from everything that was happening at home, but on that night, things at home seemed to be fine, and I didn't want to go anywhere.

My mother bent to kiss my forehead. She looked me in the eyes and smiled, her eyes darting quickly toward my father. I remembered her talking to me weeks ago on the hill above Miss E.'s farm, and I tried to smile back. She told me to get to bed and then followed my father.

I stayed on the couch with my thoughts, waiting for the noises that came with getting ready for bed to end. I caught myself staring at the blank wall above the television and had a sudden memory of my father doing the same. Maybe it wasn't such a bad thing after all. I was just letting my mind drift, sorting things out. My father certainly had much more to think about and sort out than I did. Maybe it was okay that he acted the way he did. Then, I thought of the plate crashing into the wall above my head.

I stood up and went to my room. I'd already packed clothes into a canvas bag and hidden it in my closet. I pulled out the bag and set it carefully by my bedroom door. I felt like every movement made a sound that was loud enough for my parents to hear. I slowly opened my desk drawer and pulled out Emmie's note and the Woodstock ticket. I felt a flush, imagining what it would have been like to leave it behind and drive all the way across the country only to discover that my ticket into the festival was back on the west coast. I unzipped my bag and stuffed the ticket in between some clothes where it would be safe. My fingertips brushed something flat and smooth as I pulled my hand out. Maybe a belt buckle or the bottom of a sandal. I'd already forgotten half of what I'd put in the bag and was starting to think I'd packed too much.

Then I held Emmie's letter in my hand and wondered what to do with it. I had already tried to write a note to my parents. My first attempt was full of all the things that were bothering me. It was balled up and tossed into a trash can at school. With the second note, I just tried to tell my parents what I was doing so they'd know where I was and wouldn't worry. It came out sounding like a note I'd scrawl after school if I was going over to a friend's to work on homework, like driving across the country was something I did all the time.

Instead, I unfolded Emmie's letter to me, pressed it flat, and left it on my desk. It would be enough to let my parents know where I went. I took a few steps away from my desk before the sinking feeling of guilt hit me. I imagined what it would have been like if my father had left for Vietnam without saying goodbye. I turned back to my desk and scrawled a quick note at the bottom of Emmie's letter. My handwriting was different enough that my parents would know it was mine.

I have to do this. I love you. Bets

My bag felt a little heavier than I expected when I lifted it from the floor. I half-shrugged and slung it over my shoulders, balancing with its weight while trying to push the rush of feelings aside. My eyes made a quick survey of my empty room as I pulled the door closed. My parents would wake up to a lazy Saturday morning and let me sleep in. It would be nine or ten o'clock before they knocked on my door and eventually opened it. I had no idea where I'd be by then. Still in town? Still in California? Or already far away?

I closed the door as softly as I could, but its sound still seemed to fill the quiet house. My feet were on autopilot, moving through the dark living room and into the kitchen. I brushed a hip on the edge of the kitchen table. If I'd been an inch closer, I probably would have hit it hard enough to scrape the legs across the floor, or I would have yelped in pain, or both. As it was, I held my breath and thanked my good luck for a near miss.

The door outside from the kitchen was easy to get through. We never kept it locked. With as much turmoil as there was in the country, we still felt safe in our little town, safe on our quiet street. The door swung easily on hinges that my father oiled as part of the routine he had for taking care of everything around our house. But as easy as it was to get out the door, it was that moment when I felt the most tension. I was so close to the outside, so close to being away.

I could almost feel my parents' eyes on me, and my muscles tensed waiting for a hand to grab my shoulder. What if I got caught at that instant, with one foot out the door and one still inside? And then I was out, and the door was closed behind me.

My bike was leaning against the side of the house as always. I tossed my bag into the basket in front where I'd put so many deliveries from Johnson's. I rolled it partway down the driveway, and then with one quick motion stepped onto a pedal with one foot while throwing the other leg over the seat. One rotation of the pedals, and I was down the driveway and out into the street.

It felt strange to be biking at night. Even on shorter days in the winter months, I was always home from deliveries before dark. The moon was almost full and high in the sky, so I could see where I was going, but at the same time I felt invisible as I glided along the dark and silent streets.

I rode right into the middle of town on Front Street and then turned down a side street to ride past the high school and out toward the narrow river that ran along the north edge of town. The dark windows of shops and houses stared at me as I rode by. The empty town might have felt eerie if I were walking through it, but sailing through on my bike, I felt like I owned it, like everyone had gone someplace else and left me in charge. I let out a nervous giggle that turned into a full laugh. I didn't care if anyone heard me. The freedom I'd always felt on my bike was amplified by the cool night air in my face, and I laughed again as my bike carried me out of town.

The road to the park where Emmie was going to meet me was another story. Once outside of town, the road narrowed and the trees closed in. Brush and tangles lined the edges of the road, and anything could have been behind them in the shadows. The few houses I passed were set back off the road, partially blocked by trees and bushes. They looked like someone had pulled a curtain aside to peer out from the shadows. I pedaled hard to get beyond one house, only to find myself on a darker stretch of road and in front of an even darker house.

My heart raced and I pulled in panicked breaths as I pushed the pedals harder to go even faster. And then decisively, I pedaled backwards instead, locking the rear wheel and skidding to a stop.

I was on the very first part of a journey that would take me across the country. I wasn't sure what the trip would be like, but I was certain that I'd never get anywhere if I couldn't ride past a few dark houses without getting the heebie jeebies.

I swung my leg over my bike and let it fall to the side. Standing in the middle of the road, I crossed my arms on my chest and glared at the house in front of me. I was certain that in the daylight it would have been a welcoming home. There was likely a friendly family that lived there, probably even someone I knew.

I stomped my foot and then walked forward. Reaching down without slowing my pace, I grabbed a handful of wildflowers growing beside the road and charged up to the darkened house. As I walked up to the front door, I remembered the first time I nervously approached Miss E.'s house, and then how comfortable I felt once I'd been invited inside and met the woman who lived there. I skipped a step on my way up to the front porch and then took another two or three quick steps to the door. Without hesitation, I pulled the screen door open far enough to fit the stems of the flowers inside and then shut it on them so they were held there, waiting for the owner to discover them in in the morning.

With the flowers there, the house immediately changed its tone. I noticed the rockers on the porch with what looked like comfortable cushions. I pictured the people who lived there enjoying their morning coffee with the flowers in a vase next to them. I walked back out to my bike and saw that the bushes that had been partially hiding the house were ringed with flowers, grey and black in the dark, but surely a bright yellow and red by day.

I was ready for what was coming next. I stood my bike up and hopped on. I pedaled another minute or two, and then around the next turn, the trees pulled back from the road to reveal the riverside park where Emmie said she would meet me. Moonlight reflected in dancing patches on the river, and parked next to the river's edge was the boxy shape of a Volkswagen camper.

I'd seen a bunch of Volkswagens on the two trips I took down to San Francisco last year. With their funny shape, they were easy to spot, looking more like mini versions of city buses and nothing like the rest of the cars on the road. The Andersons, who lived a few miles outside of town, actually owned one, and for months after they bought it, they attracted attention and questions wherever they drove it. So I'd seen Volkswagen buses before and lots more of the smaller, rounder VW bugs, but I'd never seen a Volkswagen camper.

The roof was popped up at an angle, canvas sides creating a wedge that made the VW look like it was half car and half tent. The large, square sliding door on the side was open wide, lantern light and music drifting out into the night. It looked warm and comfortable inside, a contrast to the dark ride I'd just taken out of town.

I heard Emmie's voice and then her laughter. For the first time in weeks, everything felt right. The decision I'd been wrestling with no longer felt so serious, no longer felt like an all or nothing choice. The funny looking bus nestled by the river in front of me was going to take me to Woodstock. Its round headlights looked like smiling eyes, and its curved bumper added to the cheerful expression. And more important, I knew the person inside. I knew her, and knew all the ways that she was like me. That night, while I stood in the middle of the road looking down at the little bus that would be my home for the next month, I was certain that Emmie Hatcher was the person I felt closest to, the person who I wanted to be with most of all.

Cool and Creepy

I walked my bike off the road and down the hill toward the Volkswagen. As I got closer, there was a squeal of surprise. Emmie's shape sprang from the open door of the bus. For a brief second she was silhouetted against the square of flickering lantern light, then she was beside me. She threw her arms around me, and I let my bike fall to the side so I could do the same to her.

"You came! I'm so happy! So cool that you decided to come!" I smiled at Emmie's favorite expression. Everything was cool with Emmie. And then as if she was affirming her own assessment, she added, "Yeah, cool."

Emmie was just as I remembered her. Her long blond hair had grown since I last saw her and was now brushing her waist. Mostly it hung in loose waves, but here and there a thin braid swung, weighed down by tiny beads that had been worked into the strands. She wore a long flowing dress that was covered in an intricate pattern of flowers. A memory shoved its way into my consciousness, and I could see the dress Emmie had been wearing in San Francisco. That dress had been covered in blood, her hair too. I pushed the memory away as quickly as it had come.

"Yeah, I'm excited!" I said, matching Emmie's enthusiasm, and then I added sounding less certain, "I always wanted to... it was just... well, it was a hard decision... for other reasons." Emmie nodded her understanding. My father and I always understood what the other was thinking without saying much at all. I figured it was just because we'd spent so much time together and I'd grown up learning to talk with his gestures and facial expressions. But with Emmie, it was different. I'd barely spent any time with her, I only knew her for a year and saw her only twice, and yet I felt the same connection. The best explanation I could come up with was that we were just so much alike that we thought the same things.

"So you just left? Without telling your parents?" I nodded. Emmie's eyes searched me. Even in the dark, they caught some of the light that spilled from the camper and shown their hazy blue. It wasn't uncomfortable having Emmie look at me like that. It wasn't like the suspicious glares of some adults in town after I'd organized the protest. Emmie was just looking me over, making sure everything was okay. It was comforting, mostly because I knew she could see that everything wasn't okay. Everything wasn't okay, and it felt good to let someone in on that secret.

"Things have a way of working themselves out, Elizabeth." This time she saw my eyes roll, even in the dark.

"Sorry," she continued. "Bets. Things have a way of working themselves out, Bets. Being out in the open, following a road, being someplace new. It lets you see things in a different way, and the stuff that's bothering you starts to look more like something you can find your way through." I didn't know Emmie when she'd gotten the news that her father had been killed in Vietnam, but I knew she was speaking from experience. Her arms were around me again. "It'll be good, Bets. You'll see. It'll be cool."

My face was mostly buried in Emmie's hair, but I could see the light change, and I lifted my head. The shadow moved toward us with the lantern held low to the ground. Its bouncing light flashed up, blinding me, and then swung down again leaving me squinting into darkness. I couldn't make out any details. The shadow seemed to shift from side to side as it walked.

"Hey, girly girl," said a gritty voice, and the shadow lifted the lantern so I could see his face. I squinted again at the sudden light and tried to focus on the shape in front of me. Dark waves of oily hair tumbled to his shoulders and framed a face with angular features. A sharp nose stuck out above a thin mustache, and a half grown beard dirtied his cheeks and gathered into a wedge of hair on a pointy chin. His eyes were as dark as his hair, but the lantern light glinted off of them and made me feel like he was looking right through me.

The man looked me up and down in a way that made me want to pull my arms in across my chest and look down toward scuffling feet. He looked at me with the same contempt I'd often seen on the disapproving faces of adults in town, but along with it came the uncomfortable feeling I'd get when the boys at school stared too long.

"Hey, Bets. This is Seth." Emmie's cheerful voice didn't match the person she gestured toward. Emmie's letter to me said she was heading to Woodstock with a friend. I'd either forgotten that or had decided it wasn't important. Or I guess maybe I'd assumed Emmie's friend would be another girl—a girl like Emmie, and like me.

"Nice to meet you, girly girl." Seth stuck his hand out toward me in a sudden movement that seemed to throw him off balance for a second. He shifted his feet to stay upright, and the movement rippled through him, reminding me of a snake.

I tried to convince myself that Seth was like the darkened houses I'd passed on my ride out to the river and Emmie's campsite. Intimidating in a way that caught you off guard, but as harmless as any of the houses I rode by every day. But I couldn't brush off the eerie feeling. Instead, the longer Seth stood in front of me, the more I thought that the dark house was frightening after all. The bushes weren't hiding flower beds, they were tangled with poison ivy. The comfortable rocking chairs had been smashed and shoved off the edge of the porch in a heap, their cushions gathering mold. A dead animal smell hung in the front yard, and I shuddered to think what I'd find if I stepped through the front door.

But I gathered my courage as best I could and planted my feet the same way I'd done in the middle of the street in front of the dark house. "My name is Elizabeth," I said in as firm a voice as I could muster. Seth's immediate response was a cackle that filled the dark around us. The hand he'd extended to shake mine went to his chest as he clutched himself in uncontrolled laughter. He sauntered off, his feet following a curved and staggering path as the lantern swung beside him.

Emmie looked at me embarrassed. "Seth's okay when you get to know him, really." She could see the doubt on my face and added, "He's okay when he's not... well, he's okay most of the time." Emmie's standard "cool" was conspicuously absent from her assessment of Seth, and I couldn't help feeling like she was trying to convince herself along with me.

"He's one of my roommates," she continued. "Well, sort of a new one actually. He came to the house about six months ago. He's dating one of my friends." Then she paused like she was figuring out how to say what came next. "Or was dating, I guess. She dumped him, and then decided not to go to Woodstock with us. Which is where the extra ticket came from." None of what Emmie was saying took away the sinking feeling I'd gotten from meeting Seth.

"He calls me girly girl. I am anything but girly," I said with a huff. What he called me was the least of all the things that bothered me about Seth, but the nickname he'd immediately adopted for me was the easiest to articulate. It didn't matter. Emmie saw the concern on my face.

"Look, Bets. He's annoying and weird, but he's not dangerous. He's... just... creepy." Yes, he was creepy, but not just creepy. Creepy. I wanted to agree with Emmie, to nod and go along with everything she'd said. Emmie was friendly and optimistic, upbeat and cheerful, and I wanted to be like her and think like her. But I'd known Seth for less than five minutes, and I already didn't want to be around him. I didn't want Emmie to be around him either, but I needed to trust Emmie. I'd just snuck out of my parents' house and was getting ready to cross the entire country, and I desperately needed to trust someone. Emmie was it.

I rolled my eyes and crossed my arms on my chest in a gesture that told Emmie I thought she was crazy and completely stupid to be going anywhere with Seth, but the smirk on my face gave me away, and she could tell how happy I was to see her and that I'd go absolutely anywhere with her.

"So where do we sleep in this thing?" I asked, pulling my bike back onto its tires and rolling it along next to me as I walked with Emmie toward the camper. It hadn't occurred to me until after I said it that Emmie and Seth might have already figured out sleeping arrangements of their own that didn't include me.

Emmie must have seen what I was thinking and made a face. "Seth can sleep in the great outdoors. The girls get the camper." She smiled and added, "If it rains we might let him sleep inside on the luggage." We both giggled and then laughed. "We get to sleep up in the pop-top," Emmie said, gesturing toward the slanted roof of the camper. The roof had been lifted in front to reveal screen and canvas sides. It didn't look like much from the outside, but there must have been enough room to lie down up there.

I leaned my bike against the back of the VW. It instantly reminded me of all the times I'd leaned it against my parent's house, but I pushed the memory away. The glow from inside the camper made it look warm and inviting, and I wanted nothing more than to crawl in and fall asleep. In spite of the struggle I'd had making a decision, in spite of creepy Seth and the uncertainty I still felt, I was excited about what was to come, not just where we were going, but how we were getting there and everything that we would see and do on the way. As I pulled my bag from the bike basket and climbed into the VW, I knew one thing for sure. It wasn't what I was used to, but the VW would be the closest thing to a home that I'd have for a while.

East

101 S, 116 E, 12 E, 80 E

Rolling down the highway in the VW was nothing like riding in my parents' car. When I was in their car, I felt contained and surrounded. The roof was hovering just over my head and small windows restricted my view of the world moving by outside. I usually ended up in back, separated from my parents by the bench seat that divided the car in half. My father absolutely always made me wear my seat belt.

Riding in the VW was different. I couldn't even find the seat belts in the back of the camper. There were separate seats up front with space between them, so we could move from front to back seat as easily as moving from a chair to the couch in the living room. Some of the Volkswagens I saw driving around had two rows of back seats, but since Seth's was a camper, there was only one bench seat in back with open space in the center and cabinets along the side opposite the large sliding door. There was even a sink and a little stove.

And the view! That's what made riding in the VW spectacular. The top half seemed like it was made entirely of windows. I could turn around completely and see the world surrounding us, and because we sat higher up than in a car, I felt like I had a bird's eye view. The huge curved windshield up front made me feel like I was at a drive-in watching a movie that was nothing but moving highway.

Seth was doing most of the driving, and Emmie usually sat up front, but we traded places occasionally. I liked sitting up front and seeing everything that we were speeding toward. But I didn't like sitting next to Seth.

He was mostly harmless when he was driving because he could only glance over at me while trying to keep his eyes on the road. When we stopped for gas or food or to stretch our legs, he could set his eyes on me with that piercing stare he had. Something about Seth made me feel like at any moment he could jump at me or lash out, but knowing that he had to keep at least one hand on the steering wheel and a foot on the gas pedal offered some comfort. When he was driving he seemed to drift into his own world anyway, and for a while I could forget that he was there with us and just talk to Emmie like we were hanging out in her room.

But the first morning was different.

Emmie and I had climbed up into the space created by the pop-top, leaving Seth to the darkness outside. He didn't even seem to notice when we slipped into the camper to go to bed. After spending a minute or two looking around the cozy little space and telling Emmie one more time how excited I was to be with her, I fell asleep without even realizing that I was doing it.

I woke up to dappled sunlight in my eyes. Like waking up in a hotel while traveling or finding myself at a friend's house after a sleepover, it took me a few seconds to wake up fully and remember where I was. I had a feeling of disbelief and at the same time, excitement. I found the little hatch between the sleeping space and the lower part of the VW, slid my legs over the edge, and lowered myself to the floor.

I guess I could hear it while I was still up top, but I wasn't aware of the yelling until I came down and stepped out of the open sliding door. What I saw didn't really make sense. Emmie was standing next to my bike with one hand on the seat, holding it upright. She stood there silent and still while Seth raged in front of her. He yelled, and stomped, and threw his arms around in motions large enough to jerk his body side to side.

Although I could hear him easily, what he was saying didn't really register in my brain until I walked toward them and woke up enough to take everything in. He was yelling at Emmie about my bike. She continued to stand in front of him without talking or moving. She seemed like someone standing in the path of an oncoming tornado. No, Seth was more like a wild animal, yet Emmie stood tall in front of him, her eyes meeting his. Then she held up a hand, and surprisingly, Seth quieted.

"The bike's coming with us," she said, her eyes still leveled on Seth. "You can put it up top or I will. You can yell at me until you lose your voice, or you can walk into the river for all I care. But the bike's coming with us." Seth looked like he had a fish hook caught in his throat, but there was still fire in his eyes and a snarl on his face. He yelled one last time, something incomprehensible, and stomped off to the other side of the camper.

Emmie and I stood where we were for a minute more, letting Seth's rage drift away from us like dust settling to the ground. Finally, she broke the silence. "I figured you'd want to take your bike. I mean… we're heading out today, and we can't just leave it here." I hadn't really thought about it when I decided to ride my bike to meet up with Emmie, but once she'd said it, I realized she was right. I couldn't just leave my bike beside the river for someone to find and take.

There was a small rack on top of the VW behind the section of roof that popped up to create the sleeping space. There was enough room inside for Emmie and Seth's things along with my bag and still room left to sit and move around comfortably, so they hadn't bothered to put anything up on the rack.

I sized up the bike and the distance up to the rack. If Emmie and I worked together, I figured we could probably get it up there without too much of a struggle. She stepped up onto the rear tire and quickly grabbed the edge of the rack for balance. Emmie reached her other hand down, ready for me to lift the bike up to her. I raised the front and then grabbed the back part of the frame. In one motion, I lifted the bike up and raised the back tire to shoulder level, high enough that Emmie could easily grab the handle bars.

Without warning, something fell from the basket and hit me on the forehead. My hands instinctively shot up, maybe to protect my face but probably out of shock from the sudden pain between my eyes. I no longer held the bike, and Emmie was left holding it in one hand while she struggled to stay standing on the tire. She lost the battle, but she had enough time to swing my bike off to the side before she fell, so it didn't land on me and she didn't land on it. The bike hit the ground with a crash, and Emmie managed to land on her feet, stumbling a little but close enough to me that I could put my hands out to help steady her.

A quick look at Emmie assured me that she was okay, and then my eyes immediately went to the ground, looking for whatever had hit me. I saw it after just a few seconds of searching. A curved chunky piece of glass stood out against the gravelly ground, its edges catching the morning sun. It was from the glass I broke in our kitchen, the day I came home from school to find my father staring at the walls, the day he was angry enough to throw a plate across the room at me.

The day seemed like it was years ago, but the memory still hurt like it was yesterday. Anger at what had happened that day filled me, and in one motion I knelt down, picked up the glass, stood again, and raised it over my head, ready to throw it away from me as hard as I could.

"Wait!" Emmie called before the glass left my hand. "What is it?" I knew Emmie's question wasn't just curiosity about the object that had fallen on me. She could see that what bothered me went beyond aggravation at getting hit on the forehead. I paused and looked at her, my arm still raised over my head. Then I managed the few steps needed to make my way over to the VW's open sliding door and slumped into a sitting position on the edge of the floor with my legs hanging out the door and my feet on the ground. I dropped the glass and hung my head, staring at it between my sandaled feet and remembering the day I'd stepped on it and cut my foot without even knowing it.

Emmie settled down next to me, and I filled her in. I'd told her most of the story when we'd talked on the phone, but I guess I'd left out the part where I cut my foot, mostly because I'd forgotten about it, forgotten about the cut and tossing the piece of glass in my bike basket.

Emmie just nodded, bent down, and picked it up. I thought she was going to give it back to me for some reason and I couldn't imagine why, but instead her hand disappeared into her bag and when it came out the glass was gone. Emmie wore her bag like a piece of clothing. It wasn't something she carried, it wasn't an accessory. It was just part of her, always hanging from her shoulder, always against her hip. I'd forget it was there until she pulled something out of it or put something in. Somehow Emmie managed to find whatever she needed without looking, without rummaging around like most girls did, digging for lipstick or gum or a pen in their purse. Emmie just slipped a hand in and pulled it out holding whatever she needed.

I looked at her expectantly, wondering why she'd decided the piece of broken glass was worth keeping, especially considering where it had come from. It wasn't a memory I wanted to hold onto . I also wondered how long it would be before Emmie reached into her bag for something and cut herself on the glass. Emmie just shrugged.

"There's a weight to it, Bets. I can feel it in you. There's a weight to the day, to what happened." Then she patted her bag and said it again, like she wanted to make sure I understood. "There's a weight to it." There was a long pause, like Emmie was sifting her thoughts. "That weight doesn't go away just by throwing away the memory. Trying to do that just makes it heavier."

And that was it. She didn't need to explain herself. I knew what she meant. After all, I rode a bus home from San Francisco wearing a bloody t-shirt and jeans because I understood that the event they were attached to had an importance I had to sort through, a significance that couldn't be washed away by a simple change of clothes. So I got what Emmie was telling me, even though I still wanted to grab the piece of glass and throw it as far away from me as I could.

Endless

80 E, 50 E, 722 E

Emmie and Seth were in no hurry. Our first day of driving put us only a few hours away from Forestville. The sun was high in the sky on the second day before the camper pulled out of the field we'd parked in the night before and rolled onto a narrow two-lane highway.

The only map I'd seen was stuffed into the small compartment in the passenger-side door. I pulled it out while sitting up there, but I hadn't seen Emmie or Seth use it yet. I looked at it a few times, trying to figure out where we were or how far we'd already traveled, but I didn't bother trying to give directions. We were sticking to the smaller roads, but while some occasionally bent north or south we were mostly heading east.

We didn't really need to hurry, which was another opposite to driving with my parents. Whenever I'd traveled with them, the goal seemed to be to get as far as possible in a single day, waking up early, stopping as little as possible, and driving until dark. Even trips around town had a predetermined timeline that had my mother hissing about being late if a slower than average driver pulled out in front of her or a traffic signal seemed to stay red longer than expected. My father was a little more relaxed, but I didn't really ride in the car with him anymore.

We had over a month to make it to New York and the Woodstock festival. The VW wouldn't break any speed records, but we still could have made it across the entire country in four or five days if we really wanted. Instead, Emmie and Seth found something interesting in every little town we passed through, or rather Emmie did. Seth didn't grumble about the stops and didn't seem rushed at all, but more often than not it was Emmie who would point to something while we rolled through a town, urging Seth to a parking spot beside the road. There were even stops while in an open expanse of nothing, Emmie hopping out her door to observe an animal disappearing over a hill, the sun on trees, or a passing cloud.

I was sitting up front when we had to stop for the convoy. Emmie was humming quietly in back. Thankfully, Seth was ignoring me. The dry ground was flat in all directions, and the road was level and straight. Through the big front window of the VW, I could see for miles, and I saw the dust from the trucks long before I actually saw their dark shapes.

Seth let the VW roll to a stop as we approached the intersection, and both our heads turned to watch their approach. The first truck thundered past filling the air with sound and dust. If Seth hadn't been paying attention or if he'd ignored the stop sign, the truck would have rolled right through us. The roar of the first truck barely faded, as the second truck and then the third stormed through.

I sat, turning my head from left to right and tracking each truck as it passed. At first I waited for the end, sitting patiently in my seat and watching for the last one. It didn't come. Just the sound of the next passing truck, and the next. The rumble of each blended together by the time I'd lost count. It stopped being the sound of individual trucks and simply turned into a rhythm: the engine, the tires on pavement, the rush of air, and then the next one.

They were army trucks, all painted the same drab green, big monstrous things with tires that looked as tall as me. The soldiers inside seemed just like their trucks, all the same, all drab green. Two sat up front, the sun's glare on the windshield making them faceless. More sat in back under the camouflage canvas canopy.

Without really thinking about it, I opened my door and stepped out onto the road. The sound of the trucks was louder outside, almost overwhelming. And along with the sound came the push of air as each one gusted past, bringing with it the smell of fuel and hot rubber and green paint.

Without me even noticing her approach, Emmie was standing beside me. She put an arm around me, and we just watched. It would have been impossible to talk, and I don't know what we would have said if we could. I was having a hard time thinking about the sheer number of trucks and soldiers. I'd lost count after the first minute of watching, somewhere in the thirties. How long had I been watching, standing there next to Emmie? How many trucks filled with soldiers heading to war?

Emmie and I had been in protests against the war. It was exciting to be a part of one, looking around at all the people gathered with the goal of stopping the war, soaking in the collective determination. But it wasn't really that difficult to stand and shout and shake a sign, easier still if there was already a crowd of people that you could just join.

And there were lots of reasons to feel good about it. You could see people's reactions as they walked or drove past. Did they look confused? Did they disagree? Had they stopped to think? And all the attention turned into a story in the newspaper or on TV, or maybe it just landed you in the principal's office. But you'd gotten people's attention and changed some minds. Heck, the first protest Emmie was part of—the one I became a part of without really meaning to—practically shut down City Hall in San Francisco.

But had anything really changed after all of that? The papers wrote about it, and we felt like we'd made a difference, but the trucks rolling down the highway in front of us told a different story. All the soldiers rushing past us were on their way somewhere. We were still at war.

Seth had stepped out of the VW too. He was standing dangerously close to the passing trucks, making offensive gestures and yelling stupidly into the wind. Just another demonstration of uselessness. He wasn't changing anything. Did they even see him? I guess so. A bottle came hurling out from the back of one of the trucks, spinning in an arc and smashing at Seth's feet. He only stabbed his fingers in the air more aggressively and kept yelling.

I realized Emmie had raised her arm as well. She held a peace sign high, the two fingers of her left hand making the familiar V shape. Was it any less useless than Seth's gestures? Probably not, but I couldn't stop myself from joining her. There was hope in it, even if the trucks roaring past made me feel hopeless.

I thrust my right hand into the air, my two fingers reaching, like hope was up there somewhere just above my finger tips. My left hand brushed Emmie's hip, and her hand slipped off my shoulder to clasp mine. The wind of the passing trucks blew hair into my face, most of it mine and some of it probably Emmie's, but I couldn't brush it away without lowering my hand or letting go of Emmie's, and I wouldn't do either.

Some of the trucks blew a loud horn, the sound mixing with the push of air they created and making it feel even more invasive. It was just a horn, but somehow it felt aggressive, one long blast that hurt my ears long after the truck had disappeared down the road. Others I could tell were more friendly, like the sound a friend's car would make if they saw you on the sidewalk while they drove through town. A quick *beep beep* to say that they saw us. I thought I saw a few trucks, just a few, drive by with an arm stuck out the window, fingers in a V. Some others made another gesture. I figured those were aimed at Seth.

Then, like the trucks were never there in the first place, the last one passed, disappearing over the small rise in the road ahead, pulling the wind away with it. We were left alone in a silence that felt empty and overwhelming at the same time.

We didn't do anything at first, just stood there. But just when it felt like too much time had passed and one of us should say something, Emmie sighed, let go of my hand, and then sat down, cross-legged right there in the middle of the road. I didn't know what else to do, and I didn't want to walk away, so I sat down next to her. I crossed my legs like Emmie, and when she rested her hands lightly on her knees, I did the same. I guess if anyone drove by at that moment, they would have laughed at the two hippie girls meditating on the pavement where some nameless road met US-50.

"OK, let's go." Seth came lumbering back toward us. I hadn't seen him go, but he must have decided his shouts and gestures weren't enough and had gone chasing after the convoy to get a few more insults in before the trucks left him in the dust. "Com'on, let's go," he repeated with a growl.

Emmie said nothing, just turned her head slowly to face him, opened her eyes long enough for Seth to see the icy blue of her glare, and then turned her head back to center. Seth let out a sputtering sound that was part laugh and part growl and then disappeared behind us, mimicking a meditation mantra. "Ohmmmmmmmm, oohommmmmmmm." Then he cackled and let out another Ooohmmmmmmmmmmm that faded as a he walked away. I half wondered if I'd hear the engine of the VW start up behind us. But it didn't, and I slipped back into the silence.

I didn't really know what I was supposed to do. Were we meditating? If we were, why were we doing it? And was I doing it right? Those thoughts bounced around in my head until I started to get uncomfortable sitting on the pavement. I cracked open an eye and looked sideways, trying to see what Emmie was doing without turning my head. I couldn't.

Eventually my mind wandered from the hard road I was sitting on, I stopped peeking at what Emmie was doing, and I let my thoughts settle back on the trucks. They were overwhelming when they were driving past, unbearable. But thinking about them once they were gone was easier. They were just trucks. Just trucks full of soldiers. Soldiers heading off to fight a war we shouldn't be fighting.

I let my mind hop from one thought to another, and then when I realized what was happening I became aware of my body again, straightened my posture in an attempt to refocus. The trucks. Should I be thinking about them or trying not to think about them? I thought about them.

They were all the same. All those trucks, and all the soldiers inside them looked the same. Nameless. Faceless. Uniform. Not my father. That thought surprised me. I'd been so caught up in seeing Emmie, dealing with Seth and his creepiness, being in the VW, and finally going somewhere after weeks spent deciding. I felt a pang of guilt for spending so little time thinking about my parents in the last few days.

My father. My father wasn't like all those soldiers in all those trucks. There was no one like him and no one like Emmie's father. I hadn't met him and she hadn't really told me much about him other than about how he died and how she'd found out. But I was sure that Emmie felt about him the same way I felt about my father. He was an individual, he was someone with his own story and his own dreams.

Then I thought about the soldiers I'd seen flashing peace signs as they drove by. Most of the soldiers seemed like they were just staring straight ahead, not even seeing us, some of them were angry and shouting, but some, I guess, were a little more like us than I'd expected. Maybe some of them were sitting in those trucks right now hoping for an end to the war so they didn't have to go and fight, not because they were afraid to, but because they'd decided that it was wrong. That was an oddly comforting thought, and I let my mind dwell on it.

I eventually let my mind shift to that final image of the trucks rolling away down the road and over the horizon. That was comforting too. Just like the noise and the dust and the wind faded with the real trucks, I let the troubling feelings I'd had drift away with the memory of the trucks.

Then, for a minute or two, there was nothing. No trucks, no fathers, just the sound of my breathing. I gradually became aware of my eyes being closed, and so I opened them. And I was back on the road, sitting cross-legged next to Emmie. It wasn't that I'd forgotten where I was or who I was with. I just felt like I hadn't thought about it in a long, long time, and then gradually, I was thinking about it again.

Out of the corner of my eye, I saw Emmie turn toward me, so I slowly turned my head toward her and smiled.

"Cool, huh?"

"Yeah, cool," I replied, and the joke wasn't lost on Emmie. She laughed, and then we laughed together. We stood up and walked back toward the VW.

I somehow felt better. It wasn't that I'd pushed the memory of the trucks away, instead it felt like I'd put it in the right place. Put it in the right place and figured out what it meant, figured out how to use it instead of letting it fester inside me.

We drove through a town later that day, and Seth pulled the VW off the road after the houses on the outskirts of town thinned to fields and forest. I hadn't traveled in the camper long enough for it to feel like a routine yet, but emerging from the VW and starting to convert it from vehicle to sleeping space already had a comforting feeling, and it helped the events of the day mellow into memory.

While Seth started a fire, I asked Emmie to help me pull my bike off the top of the VW. I didn't even consider asking Seth. Together Emmie and I were able to slide it off the roof with much less difficulty than we'd had putting it up there, and then Emmie drifted away to start making dinner. I thanked her for her help and tossed a few things into the bike basket.

Riding my bike never got old. No matter how many times I rode it, there was still a hint of the same excitement and thrill I'd felt the day I rode it for the first time. It felt odd riding away from the VW. After just a few days of driving, I was already far from home, but the memory of sneaking away from my parents in the middle of the night was still fresh. The VW was the closest thing I had to a home, and I wasn't riding into familiar Forestville where I knew all the streets and was likely to see a friend or two.

It was easy enough to trace our path back toward town. The road we'd followed had only crossed one of two others, and they were so much smaller, one of them not much more than a gravel driveway. So there was no question about which way to go at intersections. The town was small, but there were still some people milling around, chatting outside of stores, or getting into cars to make their way home for the evening.

I missed the post office on my first pass through town, but I stopped and asked a woman who was loading some groceries into the trunk of a car. She looked at me for a moment before answering, like she was trying to figure out how a kid she'd never seen before had ended up in her town on a bike, and then she gestured back toward a building I'd passed by but hadn't noticed. It was too big for a post office in such a small town, but when I biked back toward it I realized why I'd missed it at first. It was town hall, library, and post office all rolled into one. All three were closed already, but all I needed was a mail slot.

I let my bike roll to a stop and reached into the basket that hung from my handlebars. I pulled out a postcard and then rummaged deeper for the booklet of stamps I'd bought as an excuse for getting change from the Forestville post office. The front of the postcard showed a desert landscape not unlike what we'd driven through over the last few days, but I hadn't really paid much attention to the picture. The writing on the back was what mattered. I'd already filled out the address and written my message. I licked a stamp and placed it carefully in the corner of the postcard, then I pulled open the small door of the mailslot and dropped it in.

Powerless

50 E, 15 N, 50 E, 70 E

After breakfast the next morning, Emmie and I lifted my bike back on top of the VW. Seth always seemed to disappear each morning just long enough for breakfast to get cleaned up and things packed back in the camper. If it wasn't intentional, it was a well-timed coincidence.

He was still gone when Emmie walked off toward the "bathroom," which was usually just a cluster of bushes on days when our camping spot was a field by the side of the road, and that was most days. I turned around to give her some privacy and leaned into the VW's big sliding door to put the dishes from breakfast into the little cupboards. There wasn't a whole lot of room, but if things were stored neatly, everything would fit. I opened the cupboard where we were keeping food to see what was left and figure out how soon we'd need to stop in a town. From the look of the empty shelves, we'd be stopping in a town soon for more than food.

As free as I felt out on the road and traveling across the country, the money we'd started off with would only get us so far. I wasn't sure how much gas the VW used up each day, but what was left of the food made me think we should probably stop in the next few towns we passed through to see what jobs were out there. I was just closing the door of the cupboard when Seth's laugh made me jump, and I slammed it instead.

"Hey, girly girl."

I stood up quickly and turned around to find Seth right behind me. He was close, too close. I stepped back only to bump into the little step that stuck out just below the VW's sliding door. It pressed into the back of my knees uncomfortably, but Seth leaned toward me and I instinctively leaned backward.

"You stealing food, girly girl?" The laugh in his voice made it seem like he was kidding, but the sharp look in his eyes made me nervous and defensive. My eyes flicked over Seth's shoulder to the bushes, but I didn't see Emmie.

"No, I... I was just..." I stammered, but Seth just laughed.

"No sweat, girly girl. I know we're running low on stuff. Got to pick a place to stop soon, huh?" I managed a nod, but Seth's face was so close to mine all I wanted to do was turn away. His hair hung in oily black strips across his face, and his breath was a mixture of cigarette smoke and whatever he'd been drinking the night before. Clearly when Seth wandered off every day after breakfast, he wasn't brushing his teeth. He laughed again and a fresh cloud of his breath enveloped me.

"You having fun, girly girl?" I wanted to tell him to stop calling me that. Hearing it made me grit my teeth. I wanted to push him away from me and shout my name, but what name would I want him to use. Elizabeth? Bethy? Bets? I didn't want Seth calling me any of those names. What I wanted most was for Seth not to talk to me at all. But that wasn't happening.

"You know, I wasn't happy about you joining us at first. I was looking forward to spending the whole summer with Emmie, just the two of us. I didn't even know she invited you until we were on the road and she told me we had to head up to that little town you live in. All of the sudden I'm sleeping on the ground instead of in a bed, and I'm driving around with a bike strapped to the top of my VW." He laughed again, but there was anger in his eyes. "What do you think about that, girly girl?"

Seth moved closer, his nose nearly touching mine, so close that his eyes were all I could see. I shifted my weight and tried to lean back farther, but I was already off balance, the back of my legs pressed painfully into the edge of the step. My feet skidded on the gravelly ground, and I felt like they'd slip out from under me if I leaned back any farther.

"But I'm glad you're here now, girly girl." Seth's eyes drilled into me. He was impossibly close. "Emmie's okay, but she's a heavy, you know? Always crying about her daddy or doing that crazy meditation stuff. Not you though, huh? You're fun to have around, girly girl."

I couldn't take it anymore. My muscles tensed and my fingernails bit into the palms of my hands. I was ready to hit him or push him away or shout at him. Then my feet slipped out from under me, and I fell backward through the open door and landed hard on the VW's floor.

I can't really be sure what Seth would have done if I let him. He might have just laughed and walked away. Maybe he would have just stood there, waiting for me to get back up so he could continue to intimidate and mock me. Maybe worse. I didn't wait to find out; I reacted.

I guess some of the stuff that had happened to me in the last year played a part in what I did. There was the boy who I knocked to the ground with one punch because he'd been harassing my friend for months. There was the protest, and Emmie, and the police. I'd discovered that bad things happened to people because they were in the wrong place at the wrong time. Mostly, I think my reaction was because of what I'd learned about the importance of standing up for what I believed in—including myself.

Whatever the reason, I felt trapped in the VW with no way out but the door that Seth was blocking, and I'd had enough. It was easy really. My feet flew up in the air when I fell backwards. My hands were gripping the edge of the door and my feet hovered in front of Seth's chest.

Putting every muscle into it, I straightened my legs and gave Seth a shove backwards as hard as I could. As my feet connected with his chest, I saw the surprise on his face before he toppled over.

I scrambled out of the VW and onto my feet, and then I stood over Seth while he struggled to suck air back into his lungs. He had a panicked look on his face, and I knew exactly how he was feeling. I'd fallen while climbing a tree when I was seven. We were in a park, having a picnic with some of my parents' friends and their families. Hitting the ground was enough to knock the wind out of me, and I lay there, feeling paralyzed, helplessly gasping for air, wanting to cry out for help—or simply cry—and unable even to breathe.

It felt like forever until my father came to me, kneeling down beside me and looking me in the eyes. I still couldn't breathe, and the feeling was made even worse knowing that there was nothing my father could do about it. He could only talk to me and try to comfort me, but I was so focused on my empty lungs that I only saw his mouth move and heard no words. It was all over in just a second or two, but it felt like much longer.

Seth got no comfort from me as he struggled on the ground trying to pull in air. I stood above him, my feet firmly planted and my hands clenched into fists, my arms drawn up to my chest, ready to strike out. I could see the panic in his eyes as mine simply drilled into him, remembering the feeling of having his face far too close to mine.

He finally sucked in air with a gasp and let it out in a rasping cough, then rolled onto his side in a feeble attempt to get up. Seth took another minute to catch his breath and then pushed himself shakily to his knees.

There was hate in his eyes when he was finally able to raise his head to meet my gaze. He wiped the back of his hand across his mouth and coughed again, as he struggled to his feet.

I might have been inspired by all that had happened to me in the last year, but there was no teacher around to break up this fight, no policemen or paramedics to rush in when things got out of hand. Having Seth talk to me the way he did and stand intimidatingly close was intolerable. I knew my reaction after I'd fallen was the right one, but I also realized that I'd pushed things from bad to worse. Seth dragged himself back to his feet and took a tentative step toward me. He was still taking in short rasping breaths, but his eyes were focused and intent on me.

"Everything okay?" It was Emmie. I don't know where she'd been so long. Maybe it wasn't even that much time and it just felt like forever, but I was overwhelmingly re-lieved to have her back. I didn't know how much she'd seen. Had she seen Seth when he was standing so close? Had she seen me pushing him backwards or standing over him while he gasped for breath?

Her eyes leveled on mine, and I could tell that Em-mie understood things were definitely not okay. But I also had a feeling that pushing Seth any further would only be asking for trouble. He'd been humiliated, tossed on his back by a girl a foot shorter than he was. He was unpleasant with me on a good day, and I was pretty sure that his anger was a breath away from turning into rage.

"Yeah," I said. "Everything's cool. Seth was just helping me clean up from breakfast." I looked at Emmie until I knew she understood. I wasn't about to cover for Seth or to hide what had just happened, but I also thought it was smarter to wait, talk to her when Seth wandered off after dinner that evening or whisper to her that night once he'd fallen asleep. I'd also make sure I didn't end up alone with Seth again, and I was pretty sure Emmie was thinking the same thing.

By the time Emmie and I climbed into the VW, Seth was already in the driver's seat and had the engine started. Emmie stepped in the sliding door with me rather than through the front passenger door, and I thought for a second that she was going to sit in back with me. It struck me as a subtle snub—letting Seth drive while we relaxed in back, or perhaps a way of making it clear which side she was on. She made eye contact with me and held it, confirming that we were thinking the same thing as far as Seth was concerned. But after she closed the door, she slipped up the small aisle between the front seats. And I understood that too. Subtle or not, snubbing Seth at that moment wouldn't have been wise.

Before she even sat down, Emmie turned the radio on. We listed to the radio about half the time we were on the road, the other half we mixed conversation with aimless gazing out the windows at the world around us. Sometimes we didn't have a choice, there simply weren't that many radio stations to pick up in some of the places we were driving through.

But I knew Emmie turning the radio on that morning was intentional. Any conversation we could have had wouldn't have gone well. Seth was still on edge. I could see his eyes in the rear-view mirror and there was unmistakable anger in them. So engaging Seth in conversation wasn't going to happen, and listening to Emmie and I chat would likely fuel his anger. So finding some music to fill the tense space was a good idea.

Emmie turned the dial and skimmed through static, looking for a station that had something on worth listening to. She paused on a news report where a garbled voice described the preparations that were being made for the Apollo launch, but she turned the dial again when the voice starting discussing troop movements and exit strategies, then stopped briefly on a country-sounding song with a strained and tired voice. Emmie finally discovered a station that was playing a mix of rock and folk, the sort of music we were driving thousands of miles to hear. She nearly skipped over it, hearing only the DJ's voice at first, but he must have sounded groovy enough to catch Emmie's attention and she turned the dial back just in time to catch a Joni Mitchell song. Joni wouldn't be at Woodstock we'd heard. She'd been asked, but was appearing on a TV show that weekend instead. But she was absolutely worth listening to, and I let her voice fill my mind while I watched the scenery roll by.

One song faded to another as the miles and hours passed. I might have slept a little bit. If I had, I didn't miss any conversation. The VW was silent other than the wind blowing in through the windows, the hum of the tires on the road, and the music on the radio. We seemed to go on all day like that until Seth slowed and pulled to the edge of the road and into a gas station.

It looked like no one had stopped there in years. Maybe it was just from the VW pulling off the road, but dust hung suspended in the air and seemed to have settled on everything: the gas pumps, the sign advertising cheap gas and Coca-Cola, the station owner. They'd all been motionless, waiting for us to arrive.

The owner sat tipped back on a rocking chair in front of the small building next to the gas pumps. I guess it was a store, although other than Coke and gas it wasn't obvious that it sold anything. The rocking chair sat motionless as well.

The gas station owner's dark skin glistened in the heat of the day. A fan or a patch of shade certainly would have offered some relief, but instead he sat in full sun, sweating in spite of his stillness. I had a pretty sheltered life in Forestville I guess. Not everyone in town agreed with my activist approach to current events, but for the most part, they were all just like me: white, middle class, average Americans, if there was such a thing.

I was ashamed to realize that I couldn't really remember the last time I'd seen a black person, until the gas station. Not in Forestville. The riot in San Francisco? There were hundreds of people there. They certainly weren't all white. In another state, in one of the places

I'd lived before? I didn't know, or didn't remember. I was embarrassed by the narrowness of my world and wanted to hop out and start up a conversation just so I could... so I could do what exactly? Say that I hadn't led an entirely sheltered existence surrounded by people just like me? That felt even worse, like I'd be meeting the man's race instead of a person. Instead I sat and struggled with my feelings.

Seth shut the engine off and hopped out. The radio cut off with the engine and the silence emphasized the stillness outside the van. Seth circled around the back of the VW to the opposite corner where I could hear him unscrew the gas cap. He fumbled with the nozzle and then leaned back against the pump as the tank filled.

The gas station owner slowly rocked forward in his chair and then gradually pushed himself up to a standing position. He was old. What was left of his close cropped hair had turned grey and his body never fully straightened after getting out of the chair. I watched him shuffle around the back of the VW and join Seth at the pump. I wasn't sure if the station was full service or self serve, but Seth hadn't waited for the old man to work his way over to the pump. He'd already started the pump and was slumped against it with arms crossed and a smirk on his face, watching the station owner.

I decided I couldn't let the man's encounter with us end up being as unpleasant as Seth. I grabbed the handle of the sliding door and pulled it open, eliciting a shout of surprise from Seth as the door slid backwards and bumped the nozzle sticking out of the gas tank.

After hours of sitting in the VW with nothing but the radio, it felt good to hop out the door and plant my feet on the ground. I had an overwhelming desire to break the silence that had invaded the VW, and the gas station owner had become my savior.

"Hi. I'm Bets," I said taking a step toward the man and putting my hand out.

"Well little lady, pleased to meet you," the man said in a slow drawn out voice that matched his walk. "My name's…" His introduction was interrupted by Seth.

"Get back in the car, girly girl," he hissed. My eyes narrowed and my hands balled into fists. Seth saw it, and I watched the expression on his face change as he remembered the events of that morning. But then there was something else. There was anger, then frustration, then resolve. "Get back in the car," he said again with a determination in his voice that caused me to take a step back. If he was afraid I'd knock him on his back again, he'd shoved that fear down deep inside where I couldn't see it.

"Well now, no need for that," the gas station owner said in his tired, dusty voice. "This here young lady's smile is the brightest thing I've seen since before I can remember." The man had the kind of voice that made you want to smile, so I did. I couldn't help it.

"Pleased to meet you. Bets. I'm…" but his introduction was interrupted again.

"Back in the car. Now. And close the door," Seth growled. At that moment, the VW's gas tank was filled and the pump snapped off, making me jump in surprise.

The old man's eyes met mine and then flicked toward the open sliding door. He got it. After spending only a minute standing next to Seth, he somehow understood that it was better to do what he said.

"Thanks," I said, and then added, "I'm sorry." I liked the connection I felt with the old man. There was more to him than what I saw when we first pulled up to the gas station, and I couldn't just walk away from it. I stuck out my hand.

The man grasped it immediately. His hand was firm and he gave mine a quick shake that traveled up my arm. Our eyes met, and he nodded in a way that made me feel like I was doing something right even if I didn't know what. Then he let go, and I turned away from him and climbed back into the VW, sliding the door closed after me and catching a glimpse of Seth just as his expression turned from threatening to sly and his gaze shifted from me to the gas station owner.

"Everything okay?" Emmie's voice drifted back from the front seat.

"Yeah, I guess so." I paused. "No, not really. Something's weird." I didn't know what it was, but something wasn't right. I twisted in my seat and watched Seth pat the old man on the back. I heard him say something about getting his wallet out of his seat, and then I watched Seth walk around the back of the VW, leaving the old man standing expectantly at the pump.

Seth's face glided along each of the of the VW's long windows, the longest one across the back, the small vent window in the rounded back corner, then the two on the side, before he got to the driver's side door. Like frames in a strip of movie film, he changed a little bit in each window. That sly smiling expression was still on his face when he left the old man. But with each window the smile disappeared a little bit, and the eyes—which were never really smiling in the first place—grew more intense.

And as he passed each window, part of an idea clicked into place in my brain. Seth filling the VW up with gas. Next window. Seth mentioning that morning that we were almost out of food. Next window. Seth getting his wallet. Next window. And then I figured it out.

"No!" I shouted to Seth and the old man at the same time, twisting my head back and forth so I only caught a glimpse of each in the turning blur between them. "No!" I shouted again, still trying to figure out what to do first: somehow stop Seth, or tell the old man what was happening. But, helplessly, I did nothing.

Instead of standing outside the door and leaning in to find his wallet, Seth grabbed the handle above the door and hopped up into the seat. He'd left the key in the ignition, and his hand was on it before his left foot left the ground. If I'd had time to think, maybe I could have grabbed them before he climbed into the VW, but I didn't, and it was too late. He turned the key and the VW's engine sputtered to life in the funny sort of way that it always did, sounding both eager and reluctant at the same time, like it was ready to roll down the road but wasn't quite sure it could.

I saw the old man's expression through the back window, saw his mouth open in a silent yell that was drowned out by the revving engine. My heart sinking, I watched his shaking fists as we pulled away, spitting gravel and churning up dust.

"Seth, what are you doing?" Emmie yelled, but the only response was a joyful cackle. Seth's attention wasn't in the van. His eyes jumped to the rear-view mirror and then out the front window. The VW's tires bounced from the gravelly parking lot to the road just as Seth cut the wheel to the right and caused the van to skid into a turn.

We were facing back where'd we come from. I could see the old man through the windshield. His hands were still shaking and waving above his head, and his face was confused and disappointed. Seth jammed his foot on the gas pedal again, propelling us forward, and I thought for one panicked second that he was going to run over the man.

Instead he leaned out the window. Had Seth actually rolled the window down during all that mayhem, or had it always been down? I didn't know. It didn't matter. Seth was leaning so far out the window I thought he was going to fall out. Part of me wanted to push him out. His right hand was still on the steering wheel, and he must have been standing up on the gas pedal. His other arm was out the window shaking a clenched fist.

"Wooo hooo. Black power!" he shouted and laughed. "Black power!" he shouted again. The old man got it. I could see it on his face. The raised fist, Seth's shouted words. Not only was Seth stealing his gas, he was insulting him. He was insulting him, simply because of the color of his skin.

I knew the word racism. I'd read newspaper articles about the different groups that were working toward equality. The papers mostly reported the riots that had happened in some cities, but the opinion pieces and the letters to the editor said more than any of the articles ever did. Pulling away from the gas station, I realized I was witnessing racism for the first time. Seth stealing gas was a crime, but his turning around for a drive-by to taunt and mock the gas station owner was worse. It wasn't about not having money for gas. He was treating someone differently because of the color of their skin, as if his color made him less. I was left with a sinking feeling that I only partially understood. It was unsettling, and I didn't want to think about it, but I knew I had to.

The VW bounced back onto the road a second time, and Seth cut the wheel again sharply, tires now screeching on pavement. The van made a tight turn that threw me to one side, and then we were pointed down the highway again, driving by the gas station one more time before leaving it behind for good.

"Seth, what the... What was that?" Emmie yelled. The VW, after having been filled with nothing but fading, staticky radio stations for miles, was now overflowing with voices. Emmie shouted. Seth yelled back. I think my voice was somewhere in the whole mess too.

"What are you doing?" Emmie pressed Seth again for an explanation.

"We're out of cash, Em," Seth shrugged, his voice now calm, like stealing gas was the most ordinary thing in the world. "And we're almost out of food. We could choose between running out gas in the middle of nowhere or having boiled water for dinner," he said with a laugh in his voice. "Me? I want to get to where we're going and I want to eat tonight. So, we drive away without paying for some gas. Chill out, Em."

"No. Absolutely not, Seth!" Emmie was the calmest person I knew, even when talking about difficult topics like her father being killed or what I was going through with my father or the war. It wasn't that she didn't get emotional. She did. But she took the time to sift through her emotions in a thoughtful, measured way before she reacted, and most of the time her reaction took the form of a slow deliberate voice rather than an action. Not today. I could see the anger on her face, anger at what Seth had done and anger at the way he'd done it. I thought again about his raised fist and shouts of "Black Power" as we pulled away.

"Turn around, Seth." She was shouting, and the sound of Emmie's normally peaceful voice raised to that volume surprised my ears. "Immediately! Go back and give that man his money!" She leaned across the narrow aisle that separated the two front seats and reached out to grab his arm.

Seth's reaction was immediate. His right arm shot up, and he shoved her back into her seat with enough force that her head banged against the side window. "Back off, Em!" he yelled and turned his head to glare with eyes full of fire. The camper veered half off the road, two tires bumping along the dirt and gravel shoulder before Seth jerked the wheel back and got us pointed in the right direction again. The whole time his foot must have been firmly planted on the gas pedal. We never slowed, the brake pedal an unused accessory.

I don't know what sort of reaction Emmie was expecting from Seth, but the shock of getting pushed back into her seat was enough to keep her there. Or maybe it was fear that we'd end up driving off the road if she came at Seth again. I could only sit in the back seat, mouth gaping open helplessly. I just watched Emmie, trying to figure out what she would do next, how she would handle the situation we were in.

"Yeah, okay. It's cool, Seth. Yeah, cool," she said. I don't think Seth noticed the slight tremor in her voice; his attention was thankfully back on the road. But I did, and that was the worst part of everything that had happened. Emmie had pretty much been unconscious when I met her, eyes flickering closed and head bleeding into my lap. But in spite of that introduction, I always thought of her as unfailingly strong, probably the strongest person I knew, except maybe my parents, I guess.

So it hurt to see her just sit back and act like everything was okay. Seth had just stolen—I didn't even know how much. I had no idea how much a tank of gas cost. But I'd seen the gas station, seen the man who owned it, seen the empty stretch of highway that it was hunkered down next to. I knew that however much money the gas cost, it was likely the only money the man was going to see that day.

My gaping mouth snapped closed. I needed to say something. Emmie, still turned in her seat to face Seth, must have caught the determined look on my face. Her head shook, barely noticeable, more like a shiver from a sudden chill than a headshake, but I got the message that Seth wasn't meant to see. *Drop it.*

Sunset

We stopped in a town long enough for Seth to pull over at a small corner grocery store. "Come-on, Em. Help me get some food, huh?" he said as he climbed out his door. The miles of road we'd covered after leaving the gas station had lifted the tension a little and Emmie managed an eye roll and an aggravated head shake as she followed Seth, but she didn't mention the theft or confront him.

I sat in the VW and waited, thinking about what had happened earlier that day and trying to figure out what to do next. Could I just leave? I was hundreds of miles from home. There were whole states between me and my parents. What would I do? Just call them on the phone and ask them to come pick me up? I only had minutes, seconds, before Seth and Emmie came out of the store. Time enough to grab my stuff and run down the street—run into another store, or a restaurant, or someone's home. Time enough to run away, but not time enough to think it through.

Was this the best I could do? I ran away from home because I couldn't deal with my father. I was kidding myself that it was about going to Woodstock. I couldn't deal with my father, and instead of talking to him or to my mother or trying to sort it out on my own, I ran away. So after a week of camping out and listening to unfamiliar radio stations as we passed through states, things on the road got a little tough. Seth was a jerk. I knew that from the start, but I came anyway, and now I was willing to run away again because I didn't like the way things were going.

And then there was the war. Had I made my stand? Fought my fight? I survived San Francisco and came away with a bloody t-shirt and a deeper understanding of current events. I organized my little protest and ended up in a couple newspapers. Was I done? The war certainly wasn't. People were fighting against the war, against racism, against poverty. What if they all had the same fickle determination as me? Was I really done? Was I really going to run away from running away? I didn't have time to figure out the answer.

Seth and Emmie emerged from the grocery store and hopped back into the front seats. Doors closed, the engine started, and we were back on the road, my thoughts and questions drifting away.

Seth turned down a side street, then took a few turns that seemed random, but we eventually ended up back where we started. Another pass down the main street—I caught a glimpse of a street sign, it actually was called Main

Street—and Seth determined that the town had potential. We would see if we could pick up a few jobs and earn enough money to get us further down the road.

A few miles outside of town, Seth found a spot between the road and a cornfield that was wide enough to park the VW. He hopped out as soon as he shut off the engine then circled around the front of the camper to the sliding side door. I jumped in surprise when he flung it open. "I'll make dinner tonight, Em," he said, grabbing the bag he'd brought out of the store. "Why don't you two go take a walk?" There was a smile on his face, and his voice sounded sincere, but none of it fit with all that had happened earlier in the day. Emmie seemed confused by the change as well, but dismissed it with a roll of her eyes then looked at me and tilted her head to the side in a follow me gesture. We both stepped out of the VW and left Seth behind.

We walked up the road a little bit until Emmie saw a small hill that poked above the tops of the corn. We dove between the stalks, immediately losing site of the hill, leaving the road behind, nearly losing each other. Emmie reached a hand out behind her without saying anything and I instinctively took it. She led the way, and after a few minutes of walking she somehow found the little hill.

It seemed out of place in the field, like an island in a sea of corn, but I guess if I knew a little more about farming it would have made sense. It was easy enough to drive a tractor back and forth and plow a flat field, but the hill was just steep enough to keep a tractor off its sides. And as we climbed it, I realized it was more rock than dirt. It wasn't going to be plowed, only an occasional wisp of field grass would grow on it. The farmer probably cursed the land he couldn't plant, but we were happy for its smooth flat crest.

There were a million things I wanted to ask Emmie. We hadn't had a chance to talk after my run-in with Seth that morning, and then the gas station incident happened. I didn't know where to start so I stumbled and stuttered, trying to begin the conversation in three places at once.

"Emmie, this morning... Seth... he was... did you see... and the gas station..."

"Shhhhhhh..." The sound drifted out of her and faded so slowly I couldn't tell where the sound stopped and the silence began. I'd barely sat down, still trying to figure out what words to say, but Emmie already sat cross-legged, her eyes closed and her hands resting lightly on her knees. I'd immediately seen our walk as a chance to talk about the day's events without Seth intruding on the conversation, but Emmie clearly had other ideas.

I settled next to her and mimicked her position. Even though I'd meditated before, after we'd watched the army trucks drive by, it still felt funny, like I was just pretending. But I did my best to erase that thought and everything else from my head. It was tempting to replay everything that had happened, to try to make sense of it, but I pushed those thoughts away too. The second my mind wandered, they tried to sneak back in, but I pushed them away again.

Then, when it seemed like my head was completely empty, I felt it. Sunlight, warm on my face. I wanted to open my eyes to see it, but then realized I didn't have to. Feeling it was better. The sun had been there all along, it wasn't like it had suddenly come out from behind clouds. I was just too busy thinking about other things to notice.

So I sat there, still, free of thought, letting the sun dance on the contours of my face. For a minute, or two, or more, there was nothing else. No recollection of the day, no consciousness of the hill I sat on or the clothes against my skin. Just my face in the sunlight, growing warmer. I could see its glow, even beneath my eyelids. Then I felt it fading, for real, not in my mind. The sun was setting.

I still sat with my eyes closed, feeling the last rays. And then I opened my eyes and let the world back in. Emmie was there beside me again. Her eyes remained closed for another minute or two, then opened.

"Better?" she said straightening her legs and standing up.

"Yeah," I said and then again, "yeah," because somehow it really was better.

We retraced our steps through the cornfield and found our way back to the VW. Seth had somehow managed to make something edible. The better part of it had come out of a can, but at least some of the meal involved chopping food and cooking on the camper's stove. While some of the ill feelings I'd been able to get rid of on the hill crept back just by being around Seth, having a belly full of food after a long day was comforting no matter what.

Seth popped up the second our plates were empty and took them from us. "You two might as well go to bed. Get a good night's sleep. I'll clean up." Emmie and I looked at each other with raised eyebrows, but we both shrugged, stood up, and happily left our dirty plates behind. Seth gave us a smile that was a little too sweet as we turned toward the VW. I could already hear the clinking of dishes being gathered, and I looked over my shoulder before stepping up through the sliding door. The smile was gone. It had been replaced by the fire-filled eyes I'd seen earlier that day. Our eyes met for an instant, and then the smile was back. In spite of the warm summer night, I shivered a little as I climbed into the VW and closed the door.

Seth had already popped the top on the camper, but we took a few minutes to straighten up the small area below before climbing through the hatch into the sleeping area above. We already had routines that helped turn the vehicle we traveled in all day into the space we slept in at night.

The small sleeping space in the top of the VW felt comforting and close, and I was more than tired. It was tempting to just drift off to sleep and leave the day behind, but I couldn't. I needed to talk about it.

"Emmie?" I whispered with a question in my voice even though I knew she was still awake.

"Yeah."

I didn't talk at first, not really knowing what to say or how to start. "Seth." That was all I could think to say. "Seth. He's..."

"I know," Emmie interrupted then paused and let the silence creep back in.. "I know. He's..."

"Horrible. He's horrible," I finished for her. There was an uncomfortable silence, but I didn't think I needed to say anything else. It was Emmie's turn.

"I know. He's... well, he's okay... some of the time."

"No Emmie, he's not." I couldn't help but jump in on top of her words, still trying to whisper but finding it hard not to shout. "This morning, and the gas station, and him pushing you. He's horrible." My words hung in the small space. "He's horrible," I said again because there was no better way to say it. "Why are you even on this trip with him?"

Emmie let out a long sigh and then a start-stop series of half spoken words. "He... I don't know. It's just... we made these plans, and then... I don't know... my friend dumped him, but... he's okay, sometimes..." I didn't stop her, and when she ran out of things to say, I let the silence fill the small space around us. I gave her time to think, and then she started up again.

"Look, Bets... Seth's a creep. I know. He's bad news. But he's harmless. I mean, he gets angry and all, but let's give it a couple more days, okay? Let's see what it's like in town and how he is in a day or two. I think... I think being

144

together in this close space day after day... I mean, we're going to get on each other's nerves, right? I think it will be okay being in town for a few days."

She was making excuses, and I could tell she was trying to convince herself as much as me. What I couldn't figure out is why. Emmie was a strong person. She'd figured things out after her father died and after she'd been hurt at the protest. I sort of wondered why she didn't just punch Seth in the teeth and get rid of him. But I could tell that for some reason she wanted everything to be okay. Was it just the ride to Woodstock? Was there something between her and Seth that I just didn't get? Or was there more to Emmie than I knew? Whatever it was, for Emmie's sake I was willing to give it a few more days.

I nodded. "Yeah, okay."

"Let's get some sleep, huh?"

I nodded and settled into my pillow, turning my head so my face was up against the screened side of the pop-up. But I wasn't done thinking about Seth. Whatever Emmie's reason was for sticking with him, I didn't get it, but I was willing to stick with Emmie. I'd keep my distance from Seth and keep an eye on him. Maybe spending a few days in town with other people would make it okay. Maybe he wasn't all that bad, like Emmie said.

But one thought kept me awake long after the rhythm of Emmie's breathing told me she was sleeping. She didn't want me to notice, had tried to hide it by flitting around the camper picking things up and putting them in their place. But I saw it anyway. Emmie had locked all the VW's doors before going to bed.

Parachute

Riding my bike into town the next day felt like I was going back in time. It hadn't even been two weeks since I'd ridden my bike on dark streets into Forestville and then out the other side. But it felt like forever. Remembering school and Johnson's store and eating pizza at Sonny's all felt like another life. Then I remembered my parents, but I pushed that thought away. I wasn't ready to think about them.

Seth had suggested heading into town separately. Our plan was to pick up jobs for a week, and he said our chances would be better if the people in town didn't see a bunch of hippies all pile out of a dusty VW. That seemed odd at first, partially because he'd grouped me in with the hippies. A year ago, the only hippies I knew were on the pages of Mr. Johnson's newspaper, and I just thought of myself as a regular kid. But I guess if I was going to be part of anti-war demonstrations and ride a Volkswagen bus across the country to a music festival, I better get used to the label.

The other unsettling thing about what he had said was that the people in town might reject us. For what? I couldn't wrap my head around people getting angry at other people because they wanted a war to end. Did that mean that there were really people who wanted the opposite, wanted the war to just keep going and going? I'd heard Mr. Johnson grumbling about hippies, but they were other people, not me. He wouldn't just stick me in a group and reject me. None of the other people in Forestville had, although some looked at me funny. But everyone in Forestville knew me, knew my friends, knew my parents. No one in this new town did. Would they judge me by the way I looked, stick a label on me, put me in a group, and decide I wasn't welcome?

I didn't want to leave Emmie with Seth at first. They said they were going to find a better spot to park the VW. There was a river that ran by the edge of town, and Seth figured they could find a shady place there, close to town but not so close that people would get upset about hippies camping in their backyard. Thinking about Emmie being alone with Seth gave me an unsettled feeling in my stomach. I starting thinking of all the bad things that could happen, but then I reminded myself that he'd been perfectly polite that morning. When we climbed down from the camper top, Seth was already awake, cutting up fruit for breakfast with a pot of coffee warming on the stove. He seemed upbeat, not irritable and impatient the way he'd been for most of the trip. And he laid out his plan for a new camping spot and going into town separately, then asked us what we thought rather than just telling us what to do and walking away with a smirk.

I still thought it could all be an act, just Seth knowing that he'd gone too far the day before and realizing he'd need to do something fast to convince me and Emmie that things were okay. But when Emmie met my eyes, she gave me a nod and said simply, "It's cool." I didn't argue. She was older, she'd seen and done more, she'd known Seth for longer. I trusted her, mostly I think because at the moment I needed to trust someone.

So I rode my bike into town. We were in the mountains. Well, surrounded by them at least. There wasn't much traffic on the highway that led to town. It was still early, but I'm not sure there was ever much traffic, so I felt comfortable twisting my head side to side and taking in the view. I'd come through the mountains with my parents on our way to California, but it wasn't like this. How could riding along in a car closed in by windows and a roof compare to being on a bike, surrounded by scenery. Maybe flying would have been better, but I didn't have an airplane, I had a bike.

I crested a hill and saw the town below me. I slowed to a stop and put my feet down, straddling my bike and the yellow centerline of the road. Maybe Highway 6 got more traffic later in the day or in a different season, but that morning it was all mine. I'd stopped next to a road sign and craned my neck to read it.

PARACHUTE, COLORADO

Population 436

Parachute? It seemed like an odd name for a town. There were words that meant something, and then words that were just names of people or places. Parachute was both, I guess. At the moment, something to control a fall, something to catch me when I was in trouble was exactly what I needed. I pushed down a pedal, hopped up on my bike seat, and coasted down the hill into Parachute.

If the bike ride into town reminded me of Forestville, all resemblance faded once I rolled into town. Northern California did everything in moderation: cooler temperatures but not too cold, mountains that were really just big hills, and enough rain that people had lawns and trees and shade.

Parachute seemed the opposite. It was still morning and I remembered being chilly in bed the night before, but I could already tell it was going to be a warm day. There were a few lawns where people had clearly made some effort, but the most common plants were clumps of scraggly grass and low twisted bushes hoping to one day become trees. And the mountains! Riding along the highway, the mountains just felt like scenery, but Parachute was nestled in a low bowl with mountains all around it, and once I'd ridden down the hill into town, I felt surrounded. I stepped off my bike and walked in a circle, looking at the peaks above me. How did people get out? Maybe they didn't. Maybe they didn't want to.

I rolled through town, only occasionally pushing down a pedal and moving just fast enough to keep my balance. There were mostly houses. I kept thinking I'd get to the next intersection and there would be a corner store or a restaurant. Finally, the view changed slightly. There were sidewalks along the sides of the road and there were more intersections, a few of them with something on the corner that looked like a business.

I eventually saw what seemed to be a grocery store and steered my bike to the side of the road. I figured if I had to find a job in an unfamiliar town, it might as well be a job I already knew. I leaned my bike up against the front of the store and pushed the door open, making a bell jingle.

I immediately felt the closeness of the store, but it wasn't a cramped feeling. The aisles were narrow and the building itself was less than half the size of Johnson's, but the space felt just right. If anything, the small size made the store feel more inviting, almost comforting.

"Help you find something?" a voice said from someplace I couldn't see. I peeked down aisles and around corners, looking for some sort of checkout counter and the store owner. "You look a little bit lost, Missy," the voice said again. The sentences were short and to the point, but not unpleasant., if only I could see their owner.

I finally found him.

A low counter stood near the door, hiding behind cans of coffee and bags of flour. Still, I didn't think anyone was there until I stepped up closer and saw the man sitting in a chair behind it. I wondered how he kept tabs on his store from a spot behind the counter like that, but somehow he did. He'd seen enough of me to know I was clearly out of place before I could even figure out where he was.

"I...ummm, no, not lost," I stammered. "I..." If I wasn't lost, what was I? I didn't know. Was I in there to buy something? Was I just scouting things out for Emmie and Seth, trying to figure out if this town was worth staying in? Or, was I actually looking for a job?

"What'd ya' need, Missy?" There wasn't anger or impatience in his voice, just a straightforwardness, and a desire to get to the point. But calling me Missy? It was almost as bad as Seth calling me girly girl. The man was old, his grey hair combed back neatly from his forehead, a scruff of beard on his face. I couldn't tell if it was intentional; it wasn't long enough for me to be sure. But his eyes hinted that the gruff questions and offensive nickname could be more act than actual.

"My name's Elizabeth." I straightened, finding a bit of courage in the hope that the old man wasn't as grouchy as he'd have me believe. "I was... uh." I planted my feet and pushed aside any remaining hesitation. "My name is Elizabeth. I'm new in town, and I'm looking for a job." As many times as I'd practiced it on the ride into town, it still felt like a lie. Sure, I was new to town, but the way I'd said it, it sounded like I'd just moved in. There was no indication that "new to town" meant I'd just rolled in the night before and would be leaving town in a week.

"New to town?" he questioned. I figured I was caught for sure, but there was a hint of a smile on the old man's face.

"Well, new sort of, I mean, I'm not actually..." I really had no idea what I was going to say.

"You come in on that VW that was driving through town last night?" It was a question, but said in a way that made it clear that he already knew the answer.

"Yes." There was really nothing else I could say.

"Just passing through?"

"Yes."

"California plates on that VW," he paused, thinking, but I could tell it was just for show. I had the sinking feeling he somehow knew everything about me. "Probably coming from San Francisco. One of those hippies, I guess." I bit my lip. This was not going as planned. "Don't figure you'd be leaving the big city to tour the middle section of our country. Not much here to see, huh?" I shrugged my shoulders, and then, somehow, while trying not to lift my eyes from the floor, shook my head no.

"Going to Woodstock?"

My head popped up in surprise, and I couldn't hide my shock. "Yeah... I mean, yes. Yes, we're headed for Woodstock." I couldn't help but smile when I said it, even though saying it meant completely admitting to the lie I'd told when I first came in the store.

The old man gave a quick nod that brought a little smile to his face, and then he stood up. He moved quickly out from behind the counter, faster than I would have guessed he could. I thought he was coming out to shake my hand maybe, or worse open the door for me and usher a lying hippie out of his store. Instead he made a quick turn and stepped through a curtained doorway I hadn't noticed.

Before the curtain fell back into place behind him, I caught a glimpse of something that didn't fit the scene I was in at all. Trailing down the old man's back was a long grey ponytail. What I'd first seen as neat hair carefully combed back from the man's forehead, was actually longer than my own hair, neat only because a thin leather string held it tightly behind his head.

I stood alone in the store for a minute, wondering if I should just give up and leave. Maybe the old man going back behind the curtain was his way of telling me that our conversation was done. Maybe I should check behind the curtain? But that seemed too nosy. So instead, I moved closer, pretending to look at a shelf full of cereal, and I was able to make out what sounded like a teakettle.

A minute later, the man emerged from behind the counter holding two steaming mugs. He placed them on the counter and settled back into his chair. "I thought some tea might be in order," he said with a smile in his voice. "Sorry, I've just got this one chair, but com'on over and lean against the counter." He gestured toward one of the mugs, lifting the other to his nose and inhaling deeply before taking a tentative sip.

I treated my tea the same way. After discovering it was too hot, I stopped blowing on it and just took in its aroma. My mother mostly made coffee. When she did make tea, it just seemed like a watery version of her coffee, hot and light brown, but without any flavor. I had to load it with sugar and milk to make it drinkable. The old man's tea was different. It filled my nose with a scent that was both earthy and spiced, smooth and sharp. I began blowing it again, waiting for it to be cool enough to taste.

The man didn't seem interested in talking anymore. He sat with his eyes closed, occasionally bringing the mug to his nose and then to his lips. Like mimicking Emmie's meditation when I really had no idea what to do, I did the same with my tea, figuring that at least the old man wasn't going to kick me out of his store for lying to him, but for the moment wasn't interested in talking either.

Finally, the mugs were drained, and he pushed them to one side of the counter. "So, you and your friends are driving cross country, San Francisco to Woodstock, by way of all the backroads and little towns this country has to offer. And you got this far, but now your money's run out, and you need jobs for a week before you can keep heading east." He paused to smile quickly and let his eyes settle on mine. "That about sum it up, Elizabeth?"

I liked that he'd at least used my real name. It was certainly much better than the nickname he'd pinned on me, and I couldn't help but smile back. There was a weird sort of comfort in being caught in a lie and totally figured out. There was nothing left to hide, and I only had to nod and agree instead of actually needing to explain myself. So that's what I did. I just smiled and nodded.

"So you got any job qualifications, Missy?" He'd turned on his gruff voice again and soured his expression, but his nickname for me was no longer offensive. It had become a joke and his smile showed it. I told him about the job I'd had at Johnson's and let him know that I had my bike with me in town. He rubbed the stubble on his face and considered what I'd said for a moment. The stubble was intentional, I thought, maybe for the very purpose of having something to do while thinking.

"Not much call for grocery delivery in this town. You stand on one edge of town, you can look clear through to the other side. Folks here have so little to do, for some a trip to the grocery store is the most exciting part of their week. Wouldn't want to take that pleasure away from them. Besides, if they didn't come into my store once a week gabbin' about any matter of things, how would I find out about all the important stuff happening in town?"

He winked at me after saying the last part. The wink reminded me a little bit of my father, and I was left feeling happy and sad at the same time. I couldn't help but feel a little defeated. I'd only ever had one job, but that was more than a lot of the kids at my school could say. So I figured any job experience I had would count for a lot. I hadn't thought about some towns not really needing my unique grocery delivery skills.

"But I have been thinking about doing some rearranging in this store," the old man continued after he'd given me a second or two to hang my head in despair. "It doesn't make any sense for the canned vegetables to be in one aisle with the soups and such, while the canned fruits are clear over on the other side of the store with the baking supplies. And I'm embarrassed to say I'm responsible for the decision that put the cereals in one aisle while the pasta and rice are two aisles away." Most of what the man was saying didn't make a whole lot of sense, but I nodded knowingly anyway.

"I expect a job like that would probably take about a week." He paused again to smile and wink. "Wouldn't think someone in town would want short-term employment like that. But someone who was just passing through, someone who just needed about a week's worth of work... well, might be just right for someone like that.

The grin on my face was embarrassingly large. I nodded and tried to answer him five different ways at once. "Yes, absolutely, that sounds perfect. I'll take it! When do I start?"

Pausing

The storeowner's name was Gerald Chambers. Once I agreed to take on the job of rearranging the store shelves, he introduced himself, which I was glad for since calling him "The Old Man" just wasn't going to work. But he insisted that I call him Jerry. I shook my head and tried to explain a little about my father and how he would never allow me to call an adult by a first name, but it was useless. "Everyone in town calls me Jerry," he told me. "Doesn't matter what age. Mr. Chambers was my father." So, Jerry it was.

I reintroduced myself. My first introduction didn't feel right, like it was tainted because it had been coupled with a lie. I told Jerry to call me Bets, partly because I felt like he should be able to use my nickname if he was letting me call him by his first name, but mostly because it was feeling less and less like a nickname. It had started out as the special name my father gave me, and then I let Miss E. call me Bets because it just felt right, and now Emmie was using it. I had grown into the name, or it had grown with me, or something.

Jerry had only lived in Parachute for two years. He had been a lawyer in San Francisco until he decided to leave the job, leave the city, and find a simpler way of life. I asked him if he had retired, and he laughed. "Retiring is what old people do," pointing a stern finger at me but smiling while he said it. Jerry seemed to spend most of his time smiling, and it made me smile just being around him. "I prefer to think of it as quitting the rat race."

Jerry had worked for a law firm that mostly helped businesses buy other businesses. "Some days I'd be in my office and catch myself daydreaming about an earthquake, the big one hitting San Fran, and all the businesses I had to put up with just crumbling and sliding right off into the ocean." He said that with a dreamy smile on his face, and his eyes drifted toward the ceiling like he was imagining it happening right then and there.

On the side, Jerry had supported people and causes he believed in, helping them out in court when they got in trouble, people who had been arrested at anti-war demonstrations, people who had lost jobs and gotten kicked out of apartments because of the color of their skin or political ideas. They were trying to do the same things the crowds holding signs and shouting slogans were trying to do, except they were fighting in court instead of in front of City Hall.

I wasn't sure if Jerry had quit or retired or maybe been let go because his firm didn't agree with the stuff he was doing on the side. Whatever the reason, he'd left the city and settled in Parachute. I guess the town's name was a pretty good one for him too. He started out helping in the store for the previous owner and then bought it from her when she decided to move to the East Coast to live with her daughter. He still worked on some legal stuff when people needed help. Mostly he sold groceries to a couple hundred residents of Parachute, Colorado.

I was glad to have found a job so easily, but after learning Jerry's story, I wondered if the groceries actually needed to be reorganized, and thought that maybe he was just helping me out. Either way, I was looking forward to working with Jerry for a week.

For three kids coming out of nowhere and hoping to find jobs, we'd lucked out. Emmie and Seth had wandered around town for a while looking for possibilities and ended up at a diner. Seth still wanted to stick with his plan to tell people we were new in town, thinking no one would hire someone for just one week. But Emmie cut him off before he could start his story and told the man who ran the diner the truth.

It turned out that he had a waitress who had fallen while horseback riding and would have her arm in a cast and sling for months. He was good enough to let her work like that but she couldn't handle all the tables. He would have liked to hire Emmie on the spot to work the full two months but was happy to have her help for the week.

As for Seth, the diner was always short on kitchen help. The cook who was working when Emmie and Seth stopped by was looking at a week's worth of double shifts and no help during the lunch rush. Like Emmie, Seth could have landed a permanent job if he'd wanted it, but the diner owner and his busy cook would take Seth's help for as long as he was in town.

Stopping in Parachute was just what I needed. I didn't know it while we were on the road, but nearly two weeks of driving and camping and mostly seeing only Emmie and Seth had worn on me. The trip was fun and exciting at first, and still was, usually, but it was also monotonous, and at times because of Seth's shifting moods, caustic and stressful. Not what I had in mind when I'd daydreamed in school about the cross-country trip with Emmie.

But Parachute settled me. The week there was like a stretch after a long time sitting. I felt like I was breathing again. I was a little embarrassed by the feeling. I'd run away with Emmie because I needed a break from everything happening at home. The trip in the VW was all about freedom, but less than two weeks in, I needed a break from it, and I found just what I needed in a small town not unlike the one I'd left.

I rode my bike to the store. I could have walked into town with Emmie and Seth, but it felt good to be on my bike again, and the quick trip from the spot on the river where we were camping into town meant I had time to sit on the bench outside the diner and watch the town wake up each morning. The diner was the spot to do that. Jerry's store might get more traffic later in the morning and in the afternoon, but it seemed like everyone in town started their day at the diner, either getting something to eat or sharing conversation with someone who was.

The work in the store was easy. It was really just putting cans and boxes in one of the small carts Jerry had in the store for customers. I'd do the same with another shelf, and then most times I'd swap the carts and put the boxes and cans from one shelf onto another. There wasn't really a plan to follow. Mostly it was just Jerry telling me where to put one cart or another. Sometimes he helped me, sometimes he sat behind the counter and sipped tea. None of the customers who came in appeared to notice the work in progress. I'm not really sure how many of them actually bought groceries. I think most of them just came in to talk to Jerry, and I think that's how he wanted it. The occasional customer who bought something seemed like an interruption. Maybe after leaving the job he had in San Francisco, running the store wasn't really about making money and instead was about just being with people. I thought about that while filling a cart with cereal boxes and decided it was a pretty nice way to live.

When Jerry wasn't talking with customers or reading one of the books he kept behind the counter, he talked with me. I told him about Forestville, and about my parents and friends at school. I told him about our trip so far. I left out the part about leaving without telling my parents. Jerry didn't ask too many questions about my parents, and I was glad I didn't have to lie to him about how I'd left, because I was pretty sure I wouldn't have been convincing.

Jerry did ask questions about Seth. He'd met Emmie and Seth on our second day in town when they stopped by to bring me lunch from the diner. He didn't say anything right away, but then, in the middle of a conversation about something else, he'd jump to a question about Seth.

"So, what's Seth like?" he'd ask, or he'd say, "Seth seems like an interesting person. Is he a good traveling companion?"

"Oh, sure. Seth? Yeah, he's... yeah, he's interesting," I'd say, or something like that, then I would busy myself with the shelf I was moving. He'd give me a disinterested "uh huh" and turn back to his book, but I could feel him looking at me over the pages, and in the silence I felt like I had to say more. But I didn't.

Seth was better. Sort of. He was helping with meals and cleaning up. He even came up to me and Emmie the morning after our first day in Parachute and apologized for what he'd done at the gas station. While he did, I was thinking that an apology to me and Emmie wasn't really what was needed. What he needed to do was pay the gas station owner and apologize to him, but the fact that Seth was admitting that what he'd done was wrong seemed like a step in the right direction.

My work at the store was pretty flexible. Jerry never really talked to me about the hours he expected me to work or the time I should put in each day—a fact that added to my suspicion that he didn't actually need the job done and was just helping me out. I think I could have shown up at the store whenever I wanted each morning and ended my day the same way. But I liked routine.

Sleeping in wasn't an option in the VW. The screened windows in the pop-top could be zipped closed, but it never really shut out the light completely. When the sun hit the pop-top, it's orange canvas sides glowed with the light, and it only took a few minutes of sunlight before the temperature started rising inside. After that, getting back to sleep was impossible. So we got up with the sun and started our day.

I didn't waste much time hanging around the VW in the morning. Breakfast cooked over the camper's stove (or cold breakfast on some days) was fine, but since we were so close to town, I couldn't resist the ease and variety of breakfast in Parachute. I hit the diner each morning, ordering something different each day. And it was quick. Since there was no prep or cleanup, I was at Jerry's store before 8:00 most mornings.

He chuckled the first day when he walked up the sidewalk at almost 8:30 to find me sitting on the steps in front of his store. I raised my eyebrows and pointed at the sign on the door that listed the weekday store hours as 8:00 to 5:00.

"Anyone show up looking to buy something while you were sitting there?" he asked, chuckling again. I shook my head and got in line behind him as he opened the door. After he dropped his things on the floor behind the counter, he rummaged through a drawer and came out with a jingling set of keys. While I loaded cans of pears and peaches into a cart, I could see him out of the corner of my eye, sifting through the keys and occasionally holding one up close for inspection then comparing it to the one he'd used to unlock the front door of the store. He finally found one that he was happy with and made his way back over to the door to try it in the lock. After some grumbling, he went back to jingling the keys and searching for another. When he found it, he guided it off the ring, walked over, and handed it to me.

"What's this?" I asked, as he walked away.

"Key to the store. Let yourself in tomorrow if you're going to get here so early."

I marveled at someone meeting a kid from out of town one day and giving her the keys to his business the next. "Are you sure?" I asked, my amazement coming through in my voice.

Jerry only shrugged. "You going to steal all my peaches and pears?" Then he sat down, opened his book, and started reading. I slipped the key into my front pocket and got back to work. But I was smiling. Being trusted was a pretty good feeling.

Because I got to the store so early, Jerry kicked me out before 4:00 most days. He said I'd put in a full day's work even though he made me stop working for lunch and ended up sitting and talking with me long after I'd finished eating. But I left when he told me to, and I had a feeling he closed up shop right after that even though it was almost an hour before his official closing time. I used the rest of the afternoon to drift around town on my bike. There wasn't much of it, and I always ended up at the diner once I got tired of circling the same streets.

Emmie and Seth didn't have my same routine. Because they were working with others on a schedule, they were fit in where they were needed. One day they helped open the diner and were in town before I was. Another they worked the lunch and dinner rush and had a whole morning to kill before showing up for work. But whatever their shift, I knew I could stop by after I left Jerry's store and find them at the diner.

The first day I picked out a corner booth in back where I could read one of the books Jerry had lent me or page through the newspaper without being disturbed. But I realized there was really no need. They called it a lunch and dinner rush, but in Parachute there wasn't enough people to create much of a rush. I decided I might as well sit at the counter and have a conversation or two. After all, we were only in town for a week and then we'd be back on the road with no one to talk to but ourselves.

I was glad I did. If I hadn't, I never would have met Charlie. He was the other cook. Well, Charlie was the cook until Seth started helping out. They worked opposite shifts with some overlap, but each day while I was there, Charlie was either getting off work or taking a lunch break. He always sat at the counter.

Charlie was black, and like when I met the gas station owner, I wasn't sure if it was okay to include his skin color as part of how I thought about him. If someone asked me to describe him, what would I say? He worked at the diner. He was in his twenties. He lived on his own. He had a smile that made me want to smile, and when he laughed, I couldn't help but laugh right along with him. He was deliberate in all he did: how he shook someone's hand, how he told a story, how he looked at me while I was talking. I liked him immediately.

But I knew some people would only see him one way, would only see his skin color. So instead, I chose not to see that at all. Not because it was a bad thing or because I didn't want to see it, but because I'd firmly decided that it didn't matter. And if it didn't matter, why should I even notice?

"Nice to know you, Bets!" Charlie said with a smile when I first met him, and then he shook my hand as vigorously as I would have if I were meeting the president. I don't think of myself as shy. Being an army kid, we moved around a lot when my father got transferred from post to post. I could have kept to myself and spent half the school year as the new kid, but most places we moved I was able to make friends pretty quickly. And I give myself credit for being outgoing and friendly, but Charlie had me beat by a mile.

That first day, he spent his whole lunch break either asking me questions about myself or telling me his own story. With anyone else, asking so many questions would have felt invasive, and hearing so much about someone else's life would have become boring in no time. But the way Charlie talked with me, it didn't. He'd ask a question and then sit smiling with eyes wide while I told him about school, or our trip, or my parents. And if I said something funny he'd fill the diner with his laughter and practically fall off his stool. You pretty much have to be friends with someone when they laugh like that at the stuff you say.

Listening to Charlie tell stories was like reading a good book. No, it was better because when I read, it was just my own voice telling the story. With Charlie, the story was in his voice, on his face, moving with his hands. It came from his heart, and you could hear it in every word.

Most days, when he slipped off the stool to return to the kitchen or to head home at the end of the day, he left me thinking about all the things he'd told me and all the things I'd told him. By comparison, my life was pretty boring, but I would pick it any day over Charlie's.

He'd grown up in New York City, but he'd left home when he was only sixteen. My first reaction was surprise that someone so young would leave home, until I realized I'd done the same thing. Well, not really the same thing. I was going back. But I wondered if Charlie knew when he left home that he was leaving for good.

I tried to ask him politely why he left home, but there wasn't really any way to be polite about it, so I just asked. "Well..." he said, and then let his gaze drift to the ceiling while he thought about what came next. "I won't bore you with all the details. I guess I just knew things would be better for me on the streets than they were at home." Charlie didn't hide much with all the stories he told me, but his life before he left home was a big question mark.

It seemed like there wasn't anything Charlie hadn't done, hopping around from job to job and city to city. He washed dishes, paved roads, and emptied trash cans. He traded New York for Detroit and worked in an automobile factory. He'd gone to Chicago and hung from a rope twenty floors up washing windows. When I gasped at that, he laughed and shrugged. "I guess there's lots of things someone will do if the only alternative is standing on a corner holding your hand out for money."

He eventually left the cities behind to follow the seasons across the country, working on farms and picking whatever was growing. There wasn't a whole lot growing around Parachute, and I asked him how he ended up there. Another laugh and a shrug, "I suppose if you're lucky someday, you might be on your way somewhere and discover some in-between place that turns out to be what you were looking for all along. Parachute's about halfway between Nebraska corn and California strawberries. I never did make it out west to those strawberries. Been happy here ever since."

Charlie's life was a long story, and I knew he was only giving me pieces, the pleasant ones most of the time—but not always. Charlie told me about getting let go from a job when a white man came around looking for work. He told me about not getting served in restaurants, being told there was no work in places that had a help wanted sign in the window, and about towns that he just kept walking through even though he was tired and hungry.

The stories made me embarrassed, like I didn't know what I was supposed to say. I couldn't help but feel guilty, and at the same time I couldn't really figure out why I felt that way. I hadn't done those things to Charlie. But I felt guilty just the same, and angry, maybe because I wanted to fix all the things Charlie had told me about, but I didn't know how.

Charlie sensed the conflict in me, and brushed it away with a firm pat on the back and a smile. Then he'd say something like, "Got to take the bad with the good," or "Lots of good things in the world too." And that was that. He'd follow it with a funny story that would start me laughing again or a surprising story that would have me shaking my head and crossing my arms in disbelief until he could convince me that every word was true.

Stopping in Parachute gave me a much needed break from our drive across the country. Meeting Charlie and spending my afternoons talking with him made spending a week in the little town more interesting and a lot more fun. But if I could have guessed at what was coming next, I probably would have driven right through the town and left the people who lived there behind without even stopping to say hello.

Rage

70 E

W e'd decided that Friday would be our last day in Parachute. A week's worth of work would be enough to keep us in spending money for a while, and my work at Jerry's was mostly done anyway. The few shelves left to move yet were full of lighter stuff and bigger items—things that would be easy to move and wouldn't take much time. Jerry said he could take care of them, but I wondered if he ever would.

He put his book down around three o'clock and told me he closed up early on Fridays. I put a few remaining cans in place and then stood up, stretching sore muscles and surveying the work I'd done that week.

Jerry stepped out from behind the counter, sifting through a handful of bills. "I appreciate all the work you've done, Bets." Then he added with a smile, "And I enjoyed your company." I smiled back, took the money, and thanked him. Then, remembering the key, I dug a hand into my pocket and pulled it out.

"I don't suppose I'll have much need of a second key for this place," he said with a shrug. "Kinda pretty though, that little key, huh?" Then I could see an idea on his face, and he smiled again. He reached behind his head to untie one of the thin leather strips that hung around his neck, then held out a hand for the key. I gave it to him, confused, but then understood instantly when he slipped the key onto the leather strip and then tied it again.

"It's yours. A memento from your time in Parachute," he said, holding out the improvised necklace to me. I liked the idea immediately. The leather had been almost snug around Jerry's neck, but it slid easily over my head, and the key settled on my chest.

"It's perfect. Thanks, Jerry."

"Yep, looks like it belongs there. You've got some adventures ahead, Bets. It's a big country. Enjoy all the places you end up, and if you're smart you'll take something from each one, whether it's a key hanging around your neck, or a lesson learned, or a memory. You do that and the trip will be about a lot more than just the place you're going."

I nodded, told him I would, and shook his hand. And then, because the handshake didn't feel like enough and simply because I wanted to, I gave him a hug. He seemed a little surprised at first, but after a second he hugged me back. Then I was on the street, walking my bike toward the diner.

I spent the rest of the afternoon hanging around the diner and walking around town. Emmie and Seth both had afternoon and evening shifts, and while I was comfortable coming to town early without them, I never really wanted to head back to the camper on my own. There wasn't much on the fringes of Parachute, and it was a lonely place after dark.

Charlie's afternoon shift ended after the lunch crowd emptied out, but he hung around with me for a while. Friday was payday at the diner, but the owner was at a back booth totaling sales from breakfast and lunch, and Charlie was happy for my company while he waited to get paid. Once he had his wages for the week, Charlie got up from the stool to leave, and Seth poked his head through the window that separated the kitchen and counter area.

"Hey Charlie, it's our last night here. You want to head out to our campsite after Em and I finish up? Can't offer you much, except a fire to sit around, maybe something to eat." Emmie had heard the invitation from the other end of the counter, and we both looked at each other and then at Seth. His face was still framed in the window with a smile pasted on it.

Charlie hesitated for a second, maybe as surprised as Emmie and I were at Seth's friendliness. I wanted to shake my head no or say the word out loud even. Something wasn't right. Maybe Seth was just trying to be friendly. Maybe he was feeling the same way I did when I left Jerry's store, realizing that he was going to miss the town and the people he'd met. But that didn't fit with anything I'd seen from Seth up until that point. He'd gotten better since the gas station and since we'd stopped in Parachute, but better was relative, and friendly was easy to fake. He was still Seth.

"Sure, Seth." Charlie finally said. "That'd be real nice." Then he turned toward me and added, "Going to miss chatting with my pal Bets here. Happy to have her company for a little while longer." If he noticed the concern on my face, he didn't show it.

I don't really remember what Charlie and I talked about the rest of the time we spent in the diner. Whatever the conversation was, my mind wasn't on it. Inevitably, night came, the diner closed, and Emmie and Seth got paid for their week's work.

Parachute wasn't a busy place by day, but at night it was positively empty. The diner was the only thing open late, and once its lights went out we found ourselves in the dark. The circles of light cast on the road by the streetlights were like islands with only darkness between. We'd walked back to the VW at night before, but things seemed darker than other nights, and even with an extra person in our group, the stretch of road outside of town seemed lonelier.

I still wanted to say something to Charlie, but I didn't know what. Was I just being paranoid? Was I just a scared kid? It didn't matter. Seth was monopolizing Charlie in conversation, and anything I thought to say to Charlie I didn't have the nerve to say in front of Seth.

Emmie and I hadn't talked at the diner. She'd been busy, and there was always someone nearby. I wanted to know what she was thinking. Her glance in the diner had been enough to tell me that she was probably thinking everything that I was. She was walking behind Seth and Charlie, and I was a little bit behind her. I took a few quick steps to catch up, brushed her shoulder, and then slowed my walk. She understood and did the same, gradually fading back from Seth until we were walking next to each other.

"What do you think?" I whispered.

"Don't know." Emmie's voice drifted to me in the dark. "Not good."

Then Seth's louder voice cut through the dark with a shout. "Hey Em, you should tell Charlie about that protest you went to in San Fran."

"Yeah, I will."

"You should tell him now." And that was the end of our conversation. Emmie walked a little closer to Charlie, and I was alone again with my thoughts, left wondering about Seth's timing. It couldn't have been a coincidence that he picked the moment Emmie and I started whispering to call her into the conversation with Charlie.

The moon was up by the time we got to our campsite, but Emmie and Seth had picked the spot because of the shade it offered during the heat of the day. The same trees that blocked the sun made the campsite even darker than the road we'd just walked. So when Emmie pulled open the sliding side door, the lights that came on inside were a welcome relief.

But what they revealed made me cry out in surprise. Seth had been wearing a smile all evening in the diner, but he didn't have to pretend in the dark. The sudden flood of light fell on his true expression, highlighting features in the harsh black and white of light and shadow. Narrow calculating eyes shifted from me to Charlie and back again. His mouth was a snarl.

"Get in," he growled.

"Huh?" was all I could manage. My brain was still putting together the pieces, trying to figure out why Seth had invited Charlie out here in the first place, reading his face, wondering what the mood swing meant. I wasn't even sure he was talking to me. Emmie was already in the VW moving things around and getting ready to pop the camper top.

"Get in, girly girl," he said again, now clearly talking to me, but his eyes didn't move from Charlie. Then I saw it. Seth and Charlie were facing each other, and I was off to their side and a little bit behind Seth. So when he reached behind his back and lifted his shirt, I saw the knife before Charlie did. In one quick motion, Seth pulled it from the waist of his pants, pressed the button that flicked the blade out, and held the point toward Charlie.

Charlie's expression was confusion. "What's this?" he said, still smiling, like maybe it was a joke.

"The money." Seth pointed with the knife at Charlie's pocket then raised the blade back to his face. "Give me the money!" Then there was a tangle of shouting, some of it probably mine.

"Seth, what the... ?"

"Shut up, Em!"

"No, don't do this!"

"Get in the van, girly girl"

"Don't do this!"

"Put it down, Seth! Are you crazy?"

"Shut up!"

Charlie seemed to be the only one not saying anything. He just stood there, his hands slightly raised and a disappointed look on his face. I thought of the stories he'd told me, the jobs he didn't get, and restaurants he couldn't eat at. This was just one more story in a long list.

Seth shifted the knife to his other hand and then turned just enough to reach toward me and shove me into the van, his eyes still pinned on Charlie. I tumbled backward into Emmie and we both ended up in a pile on the floor. I had a second to see Seth and Charlie framed in the door. Charlie's eyes met mine, and there was apology in them. It didn't make any sense. He was sorry for me? Sorry I had to see this? Sorry I was tangled up with Seth? Then Seth grabbed the door handle and slammed it closed, shutting off the thought and my view of Charlie.

Emmie and I were still pulling ourselves off the floor when Seth's running steps crunched in the gravel beside the VW, and then his door was thrown open. He started the engine, and the VW sputtered forward, Seth's door still swinging wildly as we bounced over the edge of the road and veered between lanes. I'd gotten to my knees and had a chance to look through the side window into the darkness before the VW careened around a turn and I fell back to the floor, grasping for something to hold onto. I hadn't seen any sign of Charlie. I told myself it was just too dark, or he was already too far behind us, and I tried not to think that he might be lying on the ground, stabbed and bleeding.

Emmie was able to stay upright and pull herself into the passenger seat. "Seth, are you crazy? Stop, right now! Go back! Stop!" She kept shouting, but Seth ignored her. He just laughed and talked to himself.

"Stupid... gullible... so easy... those people... just so stupid."

Emmie wasn't done. "Seth, turn around!" She reached out and grabbed the wheel. Then there were four hands fighting for control. The wheel turned one way and then the other, while the VW veered between lanes, tires squealing. It was like a repeat of the gas station only worse.

Then the knife was back. I'd forgotten about it. I'm not sure where it came from, whether Seth had stashed it back in his pants or if it had just always been in his hand. Somewhere in my brain, I noticed that the blade was clean with no blood on it, and I was thankful. But there it was, pointing at Emmie.

There was no more fighting over the wheel. Emmie dropped back into her seat, her hands instinctively raised in front of her face in case Seth came any closer with the knife. He didn't. His arm dropped after a minute or two, getting tired I guess. Eventually the hand ended up back on the wheel, then resting on his leg, but he never let go of the knife.

"Why do you even have a knife? What made you think to bring a knife with you on this trip?"

Seth let out a disdainful laugh. "You're so naïve, Em. I had to. Did you think we were just going to cross the whole country without any problems? There's bad people all over, people who would steal from us, or worse. Chances are, if I hadn't gotten the jump on Charlie, he probably would have ended up robbing us all blind. I'm looking out for you, Em. Keeping you safe. You should thank me."

Emmie didn't say anything right away. I watched her, and I watched her, watching Seth. Her eyes slid from the blade, up to Seth's face, and back again. Then she let out a sigh. "You're right, Seth, I have been naive." Seth brought the knife back up briefly, like the sound of Emmie's voice reminded him that he needed to stay on guard.

"Hey, Seth, it's cool. Everything's cool." Emmie's voice sounded different, like she was relaxed even though she wasn't, like she wasn't frightened, even though she was. "That could have been a really bad situation. Thanks for taking care of us."

"Yeah?" Seth said, uncertainty in his voice at first. "Yeah, no problem."

"And you got some cash too? " Emmie sounded almost cheerful. I tried to make eye contact with her, tried to figure out what she was thinking, what she was doing, but her eyes never left Seth.

"Yeah... a bunch. Guy gets paid more than I did, and he worked more shifts. Here..." Seth dropped the knife to the floor beside his seat and reached into his back pocket. He pulled out a roll of folded up bills and tossed it onto the dashboard. Emmie picked it up and started counting. It took awhile.

"Sixty-seven dollars! I only came out of there with forty-nine. The tips there sucked." I squinted my eyes at Emmie. She never talked like that. She was up to something. I still couldn't figure out what her plan was, but she'd managed to get Charlie's money away from Seth. I grasped at the thought, wondering what we could do. If we could only get Seth to stop the VW, and we could hop out somehow. It was foolish, but I couldn't help thinking about it. Then, Emmie tossed the money back on the dashboard. What was she thinking? What was she doing?

"We're driving all night I guess, huh Seth? You want me to make you some coffee?" She was already climbing between the front seats toward the small counter. We'd never used the stove or anything in the camper's kitchen while we were driving before. I didn't even know we could. But Emmie lit the stove with no problem and put the little coffee pot on the burner. Then she half turned toward me and her finger went to her lips. Just for a fraction of a second, just long enough for me to see. Whatever she was doing, I should keep quiet.

I still wanted to know what her plan was. I still wanted to grab Seth, grab the wheel, grab Charlie's money. But it was enough to know that Emmie was doing something, that she wasn't just going along with Seth's stealing. Whatever her plan was, it was risky. Dealing with Seth was like putting her head in a lion's mouth. He was still mad enough at me that if I got involved, he might just bite. So I melted into the back seat and did my best not to make a sound.

It didn't take long before the coffee was hissing on the stove. Emmie poured a mug full and carefully brought it back up to Seth. I'm not sure if I slept. We were driving through darkness. If we'd passed a town, I didn't see it. Emmie and Seth talked. I must have slept. Emmie came back to make more coffee. She gave my arm a quick shake. The look on her face said it all. Be ready!

It was easier to stay awake then. My mind raced, trying to figure out what Emmie had in mind. I played through different ideas, but none of them seemed like anything that would actually work. The only thing I could do was wait. We'd been driving long enough that there was a faint glow in the sky to the east. If I looked into the darkness outside my window, I could just barely see what was outside, but there wasn't much.

"You want another cup?" Emmie's voice broke the silence.

"No, gotta go." With that Seth stomped on the brakes and jerked the wheel to the right so the VW skidded to a stop on the gravel shoulder of the road. Then he flung his door open and stumbled out on stiff legs, crossing in front of the VW to the high grass beside the road.

Then, it all made sense. Emmie making coffee—how many cups had she fed him while I was asleep? He'd have to stop sooner or later. My eyes flicked up front. Knife on the floor, money on the dash, key in the ignition and engine running. Would he have left all those things if Emmie had been yelling at him to turn around and give the money back? No way.

Emmie was already in the driver's seat. Gears ground as she moved the big shifter around looking for first gear. I heard a shouted "What the!" over the grinding sound before she found the right spot and jammed her foot down on the gas pedal. The engine roared, but the shouts outside were still loud enough to hear. "Hey! Hey, stop... nothing but a pair of scheming... I'm gonna..." I was glad for the darkness, glad I couldn't see his anger. But I could hear it.

Then, the passenger-side door opened, and the fingers of one of Seth's hands wrapped around the door-frame. Somehow he'd managed to grab the door handle as we pulled away and hung on long enough to get the door open. I wasn't sure how long he could run alongside the VW, but it would only take a second or two for him to pull himself inside.

I jumped out of the back seat. Somewhere I heard Emmie scream or maybe call my name. It was background. All that mattered was getting to the front seat and keeping Seth from getting in. He'd gotten his other arm inside and was clinging to the armrest. I half slid into the seat and kicked as hard as I could, my foot connecting with the door and Seth's hand. The force was enough to swing the door open wide and break his grasp on the armrest.

Seth disappeared from view, and I hoped for a second that maybe he was gone. But his hand still clung to the doorframe, and then it was joined by a second. I heard the engine wine as Emmie shifted gears and stepped on the gas again. There was no way Seth was running beside us anymore. I remembered the little step that was built into the side of the VW under the big sliding door. I felt a chill and understood. Seth wasn't running along beside us. He was standing on the step, riding right along with us.

Seth's pointy face appeared in the open door. "Come on, girly girl! Slide over and make room!" He was laughing wildly and the wind outside turned his lanky hair into an angry nest of snakes. "I'm coming in girly girl, whether you like it or not!" His right hand groped around looking for something to grab so he could pull himself in. He found my arm, and I screamed. Seth's long fingers dug into my wrist, but I pulled back violently enough to break free of his grip.

Then in one motion, I leaned out the open door and reached for the handle. The door was swinging with every bump and every turn. The tips of my fingers brushed it but missed. I thought for sure Seth would grab me again before I got it. Then my fingers wrapped around the handle, and I pulled with all my weight. The door swung closed hard, right onto Seth's hands still clinging to the door frame.

He screamed. Then there were shouted words, and there was rage in his voice that made me shiver. "You're dead, girly girl! When I get inside..." I slammed the door again and the words turned back into a scream.

Emmie turned to the left and the door swung open a little bit. My hand was still on the handle, so I kept it from opening all the way. But it opened enough for me to see Seth's face. Our eyes met. There was still anger on his face, but there was also pain. And there was fear. He clung to the door frame with just one hand. The other he held balled in a fist clutched to his chest. It wasn't light enough to see yet, but I imagine the fingers were bloody and broken.

"Girly girl, I'm going to..." he started to say through clenched teeth, but I didn't let him finish.

"My name! Is not! Girly girl!" I shouted into his face, slamming the door again and again like I was emphasizing each word as I said it. With the last one, Seth went tumbling off into the dark with a yell.

Then the inside of the VW was instantly still, as if he'd never been there. I sat for a moment catching my breath and staring out the window at the rising sun to the east. Then I turned to Emmie, and she took her eyes off the road long enough to look back. Her hair was a mess. At some point her shirt had been torn and one of her beaded necklaces hung broken, beads sliding off onto the floor. I was sure I looked just as bad or worse. I didn't care. Somehow, while still gasping for breath, I forced a smile, and she smiled back.

Detour

70 E, 6 W, 70 W, 70 E

We didn't really know what to do at first, so we just kept driving. Seth was miles behind. I guess we didn't need to worry about him, but he was really only one hitchhike ride away from catching up with us, so it felt better to keep moving.

It occurred to me at one point that we'd actually stolen Seth's camper. As horrible as his stealing gas and Charlie's money had seemed, we'd taken a car. And the car was full of stolen gas and Charlie's money! So we were as bad as Seth. I mentioned my concern to Emmie, and she just laughed.

"This isn't Seth's VW, no matter how much he'd like it to be. We bought it together, me and Seth, and my friend. When she dumped Seth and backed out of the trip, I paid her back the money she'd put in. So really, the VW is mine, mostly. We didn't steal it from Seth. He's just no longer in charge of driving." We both laughed, and I slumped back into the seat, feeling comfortable and at ease.

Having Seth gone was an obvious change, and the VW felt lighter without his sullen presence, but the mood change was more than that. Emmie was more herself, and I felt the same, like I could simply be me, without my guard up. Sitting up front with Emmie, I had an overwhelming sense of going somewhere. It felt, quite simply, like what I had imagined the trip would be like on the day the Woodstock ticket arrived in the mail.

Emmie turned south at the first intersection that looked like a significant road. I'd pulled out the map and tried to find a route back to Parachute that didn't take us the way we'd come. We'd both decided without even talking about it that we needed to return Charlie's money, and it didn't take much discussion to decide that we didn't want to risk driving back down the same highway where we'd left Seth.

I was glad he was gone, and I knew that if I hadn't slammed the door on his hands and knocked him off the side of the camper that he probably would have done a lot worse to us. But I didn't like to think about what happened to Seth after he hit the ground. There could have been broken bones or he could have been knocked unconscious. We'd been on a highway, but it was a lonely one. Even if he wasn't hurt, he was miles from a town with no food or water. But we still weren't going back to check on him. Emmie reassured me, told me that she hadn't really been driving that fast yet, and reminded me of how the ground had been sandy and soft beside the road. We also decided we would tell the police what had happened when we got back to Parachute. They could send someone up the highway to look for him. I felt better about that plan once I found out we hadn't really stolen a car after all.

The alternate route back toward Parachute led us up a twisting mountain road that seemed to get narrower with every mile. What looked like an easy loop on the map turned into miles of tight turns, stretches of road edged by steep cliffs, and long hills that made the VW's overworked engine sputter and groan.

Neither of us wanted to say anything at first, but I eventually asked Emmie if she thought we should turn around. She dismissed it, and I agreed, only to have her bring it up again a few miles further along when conditions got worse. The sun wasn't fully up yet and darkness still clung around each turn. We talked about turning around again, but then things finally started getting better. There were more downhills than ups, and the brightening sky lent its optimism to the road ahead. When we finally reached a stretch of highway that ran along a lake I had located as a landmark on the map, we knew we were close to getting back on the main road. Emmie slowed and pulled the VW onto the shoulder, as far off the road as she could without scraping the low, stone wall that bordered the road.

She shut the engine off and leaned her head back on the seat. Eyes closed, Emmie let out a slow breath and paused there for a few seconds. Then she sat up and turned to look at me. "That," she said with a tired smile, "was not cool." We both laughed and let go of the tension that had built up over the last two hours.

Emmie pushed open her door and hopped out. I started to open mine, but it bumped into the wall, so I climbed over the gear shifter and parking brake into Emmie's seat and out her door. The VW looked like it was glad for the rest as well. I circled in front of it, the thought still sinking in that it was no longer Seth's VW. Emmie owed him the money he'd put into it I guess, but for now, on all the roads between here and Woodstock, it was ours.

Emmie had already swung her legs over the wall and planted herself on its flat top. I thought for a second that she would somehow manage to balance herself there, pulling into a crossed-legged meditation pose. Instead she let her legs dangle over its edge toward the water below. I leaned over tentatively and then sat down and carefully worked my legs over the wall until I was in the same sitting position as Emmie. She didn't seem to be holding on as tightly as I was though.

We sat there for a few minutes in silence taking in the view, and then Emmie reached into her bag. She pulled out Seth's knife, pressing the button on the handle that made the blade instantly appear with a whispery click, and I nearly fell backwards off the wall.

"What the... Why are you..." I couldn't really finish the sentence. I guess I didn't have to. Emmie could tell I was surprised and confused. It wasn't that I'd forgotten about the knife. It would be a long time before I did. But with Seth gone, in a quiet place with a beautiful view, it couldn't have been more out of place. I hadn't seen Emmie put it into her bag, so it was the last thing I expected her to pull out of it.

She set it carefully on the top of the wall and it made little clinks and scrapes, metal against stone, as she shifted it to find a spot where it would stay without falling off. I felt the same way as I shifted my weight to turn and face Emmie. I looked at her, and then the knife, and then back at her again.

I finally found the simplest words I could come up with to express all the questions running through my mind. "Why do you have that?"

Emmie let seconds slip by like she was thinking about her answer. She looked down at the knife, and then shrugged a little. Or was it a shiver? She looked out at the water long enough that I thought she wasn't going to answer, then she turned and looked at me with eyes that said what was coming next was important.

"Seth walks through life thinking he can't trust anyone. From the start, he's decided that no one is a friend. He feels like he needs a knife in his pocket because he looks at everyone around him through a haze of suspicion and anger, and he figures that's the way they see him."

Emmie stopped to look out at the water, and I waited, knowing that she had more to say. "I have a different approach. The opposite approach. I start out thinking everyone's a friend. I trust everyone. Seth would call that naive. I guess maybe it is. But while Seth is fending off potential enemies, I'm walking through life looking for the good in people. I don't always find it, but most of the time I do."

Again there was a pause and a silence, this time long enough to make me wonder if Emmie was done talking. "Seth's not wrong, Bets. We're taking a trip across a country that's not always safe. I wish it were, but it's not. Soon we'll be going through cities and seeing more people. And they won't all be friends, no matter how much we want them to be. So you should know that, and then decide."

Decide. I looked down at the knife. I thought about how I felt around Seth. Would I have been more at ease if I had a knife in my back pocket? Would things have been any better if we both had a weapon? I thought about the feeling I had back on the dark streets of Forestville. Would a knife have helped me feel safe? I thought about the protest in San Francisco and the feeling of being closed in and crushed. Would a knife have protected me? Would simply holding it out in front of me have kept people away, or would I have had to use it? Could I ever use it, and if I did, would it make anything better?

That thought made the decision easy. I flicked my fingers at the knife and let it skitter off the top of the wall. It spun once as it dropped through the air and then cut through the water with a small plunk. Sunlight sparkled off its edges for a split second before it sank into darkness.

"Cool." Emmie looked intently at the ripples spreading out from where the knife had entered the water. "Yeah, cool." Emmie nodded and lifted her legs over the wall as she turned so she could plant her feet back on the ground. Then she walked back toward the VW.

I was still nervous about what lay ahead. I'd already witnessed two robberies and hate toward people simply because of their race, and all that was from our traveling companion. What could we expect from strangers? But I knew Emmie's approach was the right one. So far, two strangers, Jerry and Charlie, had turned into friends. I wanted to believe our country was full of more people like them.

The rest of our trip back to Parachute was uneventful. Now that we were back on the main highway, the VW cruised along happily. It felt funny driving back into Parachute after just having left, but I realized our trip across the country wasn't going to be a straight line, and I didn't want it to be.

Emmie pulled up right in front of the diner. Two hippie girls climbing out of the camper drew some stares from folks in town. Maybe some people recognized us from the week we spent working there, others were seeing us for the first time. Either way, we weren't easy to miss.

Charlie was working back in the kitchen, but he saw us as soon as we came in. He was framed in the window that separated the kitchen from the rest of the diner, and I immediately saw the disappointment on his face. We'd robbed him the night before and now we were back, bold enough to come walking right back into the place where he'd earned the money we stole. That thought gnawed at me, and I replayed the events of the night before frantically searching for something I said or did that would have shown Charlie that I wasn't going along with what Seth was doing. The possibility that he could have watched the VW driving away into the night thinking I was in on the whole plan brought a flush to my face.

But Charlie's eyes went from me to Emmie and then to the door. When he didn't see anyone walk in with us, a smile grew on his face, and he nodded. He emerged from the kitchen and came out from behind the counter. There was still a question on his face, and his gaze shifted between Emmie and me.

All I could do at first was stand there foolishly and just smile at seeing Charlie again. Then I remembered and quickly dug into my pants pocket for his money. I held it out to him, and he took it slowly, still looking to me for an explanation.

"You knew right? You knew it wasn't me? That I wasn't in on what Seth was doing?"

Charlie's laugh filled the diner, and people sitting at the counter turned around to see what was going on. "Of course I knew! I was just worried for you both. What happened? How did you...?"

"How did we get away from Seth?"

Charlie nodded.

A call from the waitress made him jump and he hurried back into the kitchen. Emmie and I found spots at the counter and ordered coffee and breakfast while we filled Charlie in on everything that had happened.

He stifled giggles when we told him how Seth had to pull over after Emmie filled him with coffee, and concern grew on his face when I told him about Seth chasing after us and holding onto the side of the VW. "He's out there somewhere, Bets. Guys like Seth have a way of coming back even when you think you're rid of them for good.

Emmie and I waved him off and assured Charlie we'd be fine, but I thought back to the mountain road we'd taken because we were afraid to drive down the stretch of highway where we'd last seen Seth. We were driving, he was walking, and we'd leave him in our dust with just a few hours of driving. But he knew where we were going, didn't he? We were driving a vehicle that was pretty easy to spot. And hitchhiking would let Seth catch up with us eventually no matter how fast we drove.

We lingered awhile after we'd finished eating, sipping coffee and enjoying the snippets of conversation we had each time Charlie had a chance to step out of the kitchen. But as the morning came to a close, we knew we had to move on. We weren't sure where we'd be stopping for the night, but we wanted to make sure we were far from Seth when we did.

We said our goodbyes to Charlie, and he thanked us again for returning his money. I gave him the sort of hug that doesn't seem like it's going to ever end, and you don't want it to, but then it does and you're left feeling happy and sad at the same time. Emmie gave Charlie a big hug as well. I was a little surprised, not realizing that they'd gotten close over the last week, but then I smiled, remembering that Emmie saw everyone as a friend.

Once we were back on the road, we decided quickly to avoid the mountain detour, reassuring each other that it was silly to worry about Seth, that he certainly wouldn't be hanging out in the spot where we left him, waiting for us to come back. And even if he was, we could just drive by him. He couldn't make us stop.

Still, Emmie and I both became quiet the further along we got. I'd catch myself scanning the scenery, looking for something I recognized. Then I'd remind myself that it was dark during most of our ride with Seth, and that we'd been traveling through an area that was mostly flat and featureless. I squinted ahead, wondering if I'd see a hitchhiking figure silhouetted on the horizon. I never did. Nothing familiar, no hitchhikers, no Seth waiting beside the road.

Emmie checked the mileage. I checked the map. We both finally convinced each other that we were far beyond the place where we'd left Seth. We let out a collective sigh of relief and relaxed a little. There was open highway ahead of us. There were new towns and new people out there waiting, and whatever was ahead, we were in it together. Just the two of us. At least that's what I thought.

Shifting

70 E, 36 E, 183 N, 136 E

I slept late the next morning. We'd found a good camping spot on a small side road that branched off from the highway and probably lead toward some small town. We had already stocked up on food, and I think after spending a week in Parachute, we were both happy to just be in the middle of nowhere again. Emmie had found a level spot nestled between some trees with branches that seemed to entwine each other, and it was their shade that had let me sleep long after the sun was high in the morning sky.

I lowered myself from the camper bed and onto the floor. Emmie had left the sliding door wide open, probably not wanting to risk waking me by closing it. I padded onto the ground in bare feet and scanned the surroundings. Emmie wasn't anywhere nearby, so my eyes searched further away, trying to see between and beyond the trees. Nothing.

Then my eyes caught a flutter of color in the otherwise solid green canopy of leaves. Emmie sat about ten feet up on a wide branch. She somehow managed to balance there cross-legged, hands resting on her knees. She faced away from me, but I was certain that her eyes were closed and her mind was far away.

I didn't disturb her. I knew if I tried to join in, my struggle to climb the tree would only distract her. Instead, I ducked back into the VW and pulled some fruit out of one of the cupboards. I sat in the open sliding door, not really watching Emmie, but taking in the whole scene. Emmie uncrossed her legs and slid down from the tree about the same time I'd finished eating.

"Hey sleepy, you ready to go?"

I smiled and nodded, "Yeah. Ready." I hopped up and together Emmie and I lowered the camper top and locked it in place. Then I dug into my bag for a change of clothes, finding what I wanted easily. We'd taken the time to wash everything in Parachute, so my bag was full of clean and folded laundry. I lifted my bag onto the back seat where it would be out of the way, a little bit embarrassed at its weight. Clearly, I'd brought too many clothes. After weeks on the road, I hadn't even gotten to the bottom of my bag, and now it was filled to bursting again with clean clothes.

But with Seth gone, we certainly weren't cramped for space. We'd left his things in a used clothing box back in Parachute. It didn't feel right just tossing them beside the road, but we didn't want them with us in the VW either. Someone could get some use out of them. Maybe that would make up for some of the crummy things Seth had done.

By the time I'd finished changing and put my bag away, Emmie had already closed the sliding door and moved up front. I followed and was surprised to find her settling into the passenger seat.

"What are you..."

Her only answer was to hold out her hand with the key dangling from a finger. I reached for it because it was being handed to me, but my brain was still trying to figure out why Emmie wanted me to have it.

"Emmie, I can't drive. I don't know how." I really didn't. At sixteen, I'd already had my hands and feet on the controls of an airplane as it cut smoothly through the air a thousand feet above the ground, but I didn't know the first thing about driving a car. My parents had never shown me. Heck, I rarely even got it sit in the front seat.

I was old enough, but there hadn't really been any reason for me to get my license. I could ride my bike anywhere I needed to go, and if I was going anywhere much farther than school or home, I was probably going there with my parents anyway. I knew some kids at school who drove, and I knew lots more who wanted to, but I was happy to ride my bike or sit in the passenger seat.

"Emmie, really. You drive, okay?"

She smiled and sized me up, probably trying to figure out what I was afraid of. "You can totally do this, Bets. It's fun, like riding your bike... just faster." I made a face. "OK, it's not like riding a bike, but it is fun." Her smile faded a little and her voice got more serious. "Besides, with Seth gone, we need another driver. I can only drive so far each day. If we're taking turns, we'll get a lot farther." I thought for a second that Emmie's reasoning was just a made up excuse to persuade me, but I felt myself giving in, wanting to make sure that I was doing my fair share. But I still must have looked hesitant. "Come on, try it. It'll be cool."

I took the key from Emmie's finger and slumped into the driver's seat. "Yeah, cool," I said with a sigh.

I was immediately surprised at how different the driver's seat felt compared to the passenger seat. I felt the need to sit up straight, instead of slouching back relaxed like I was used to doing. Maybe it was the steering wheel, making me want to lean forward and hold it tightly or the pedals on the floor that seemed to be taking up all the legroom. But I think most of all, the seat felt different because everything was reversed. The door was on my left, the aisle on my right, and the view out the windshield shifted slightly to the side. It was just a few feet from one seat to the other, but the perspective was entirely changed.

I put my hands on the steering wheel and then realized I was still holding the key. I shifted my feet on the floor trying to find the pedals, then tilted my head to one side so I could take a look, only to discover there were three pedals and only two feet. I fumbled with the key, trying to insert it one way and then the other and then switching back to the first when it still wouldn't fit. I finally gave up and turned toward Emmie with a frustrated growl.

"What do I do?" I shouted in a voice that immediately sounded too big for the inside of the VW. I tried to turn the angry face I was wearing to one that pleaded for sympathy instead, and then apologized. I wasn't angry at Emmie after all, but I was frustrated.

"It's cool, Bets. No worries... okay, here... put your left foot down on that pedal. Yeah, all the way to the floor. Okay, the key... put it in this way." Emmie talked me through each step, pointing and gesturing, and doing her best not to simply grab the key and start the VW for me. Somehow it slid into the ignition smoothly with Emmie's coaching, and turned easily once I had it in place.

The VW's engine sputtered to life, and I jumped a little, pulling my hands off the steering wheel when I felt the vibrations in it. My foot hopped off the pedal, and it popped back into the upward position with the thunk.

Emmie coached again. "OK, Bets. Cool. You got the engine started. Now, foot back on that pedal. That's right. Alright, one hand on the wheel, other hand move the shifter." There seemed to be more controls than I could cover. Three pedals, a steering wheel that I felt compelled to hold tightly with both hands, and now the shifter. It stuck up from between the two front seats with a cryptic diagram of numbers and the letter "R", far enough away that for a second I thought I'd ask Emmie to work it for me. But I knew that was silly.

I forced myself to pull my right hand off the wheel and reached out to move the shifter into the 1 position.

"Good. Alright, Bets, now right foot on that pedal, no not that one. The other one." I pushed the pedal to the floor like I had the first one, and I heard the engine scream in the back of the VW. I yanked my foot off and shot Emmie a look of angry surprise.

"Be cool, Bets. It's okay. So, that's the gas. Don't push that one all the way down. The middle one's the brake, and the one on the left, the one your other foot is on, that's the clutch.

"The what?"

"It helps you shift gears."

"Well, why do I need to shift gears? Can't I just step on the gas?" Clearly all the time I had spent in the back seat of my parents' car had taught me nothing about how a car actually worked. Emmie explained each pedal again and told me how I'd need to use both feet together to push in on the gas pedal while slowly letting out the clutch. It reminded me a little of putting my two feet on the rudder pedals of Miss E.'s airplane, but the memory was useless. This was nothing like flying an airplane.

I tried what Emmie told me. At first I was too fast pushing in the gas and too slow letting out the clutch. The engine revved again, and we went nowhere. Then I had the opposite problem. The engine coughed and sputtered while the VW lurched forward once and then twice before the engine stalled and we came to a shuddering stop.

At sixteen, I hadn't encountered a whole lot that I couldn't do. I was a good student and pretty much got all

A's in my classes. I sometimes think adults all need to spend some time walking through a high school just to see everything kids are doing. Working on math problems, experimenting in science, toss in a musical instrument or the school play, write a story in English and research in history. All in one day. Repeat five days a week. We grow up and become adults and decide we can't do any of that stuff anymore, but for a few years at least, we feel like we can do everything, which sort of sets us up for embarrassment when we have to learn how to drive a car.

I tried again, and again. I alternated between revving the engine and stalling it, but each time I tried I came a little closer to finding that place right in the middle where the engine had enough gas to move the VW forward. Finally I found it. I felt it before it actually happened. One pedal pushed in, the other came up, and somewhere in between the VW started moving, not jumping forward and then coughing to a stop, but rolling smoothly like it was meant to do.

As soon as it happened, I panicked. What do I do next? I had to steer, and control the speed, and the VW was rolling onto the road where I'd also need to actually drive it, paying attention to where I was going and what I was doing. For an instant, I wanted to remove my hands and feet from all the controls and simply give up. Instead, I shouted at Emmie. "What do I do? What do I do!"

"It's cool, Bets." Emmie's calm voice seemed out of place in the VW at the moment, but somehow it helped.

"Just go slow at first. Keep it in the lane, and don't worry about the next gear."

"The next gear?" I hadn't even thought about the next gear until Emmie mentioned it, then I worried. With as much trouble as I'd had getting the VW moving, I couldn't imagine going through the same process all over again while steering and trying to keep from driving right off the road. So I took Emmie's advice and just went slowly at first, staring straight ahead at the road in front of me without blinking and doing my best to steer. Thankfully the road was straight and there were no other cars for miles.

It wasn't long before I felt comfortable enough to go faster than a crawl, and I could hear the engine starting to whine. Emmie talked me through shifting gears, pushing in the clutch, letting out the gas pedal, shifting, and then finding that balance again, letting the clutch out while starting to push the gas pedal in. There was a frightening grinding sound as I shifted gears, and Emmie shouted something about keeping the clutch pushed in. But shifting from first gear to second was a lot easier than getting the VW moving from a standstill. We picked up speed. The engine was whining again, and I shifted into third gear, this time without making that horrible grinding sound.

At some point while I was driving, I started to doubt Emmie's skills as a driving instructor. Sure, she'd gotten me on the road and talked me through shifting gears, but I realized that she'd taught me how to manage the clutch and gas pedals, with only a passing mention of the brake pedal. The road we were on was empty, but I really had no idea what I'd do if I saw a car coming in the other direction or if I encountered a stop sign.

Maybe she'd guessed that the road ahead of us that morning would be mostly straight with only a couple intersections and very few cars. There were a couple frightening moments—at least for me. A pickup truck and two cars came toward us in the other lane, and I cringed as they passed, moving the VW as far to the right as I could without driving us off the road. At one point, a tractor trailer truck slowly gained on us from behind. My eyes flicked to the rear-view mirror, checking its progress. I willed the VW to go faster, but before long, the truck was so close the view in my mirror was filled entirely by grill and headlights. Then the truck changed lanes and rumbled up beside the VW. I gripped the wheel tightly, not wanting to breathe for fear of making a wrong move and veering into the massive truck. It was ahead of us and over the next hill before my breathing returned to normal.

The intersections forced me to stop, although I contemplated just slowing down and rolling through. But the fear of causing an accident was greater than my concerns over working the pedals properly and getting the VW rolling again. I struggled at the first two intersections, stalling twice at the first one and letting the clutch pedal out so slowly at the second one that another car caught up to me, paused for a second and then roared past me in the other lane. But I pulled away smoothly from the third intersection. From that point on, getting the VW moving started to feel natural, and the timing of shifting through the gears while working the pedals became intuitive.

We'd left Colorado behind and were straddling the border between Kansas and Nebraska, south of it at first and then eventually on a diagonal heading northeast into Nebraska. But it was hard to tell when we crossed from one state to the other. They looked the same. The whole world around us was nothing but flat and wide open.

The roads we were on were straight and empty, and I could see for miles ahead of me as I drove with plenty of time to prepare for a passing car or a bend in the road. But it wouldn't be long before we were through the plains and cornfields in the middle of the country and driving into bigger towns, eventually cities with more traffic. I wasn't sure I was ready for city driving, but by the time we stopped for lunch, I was feeling confident and excited about my new-found skill. When my time in the driver's seat ended and Emmie took over driving for the afternoon, I missed the feeling of being in control, and I wished for a few more driving days on the plains to practice.

When Emmie pulled to the side of the road that evening, we'd just passed a sign advertising a diner two miles ahead. After the stressful morning I had learning to drive, I could have used some time meditating next to Emmie, but instead I pulled my bike down from the top of the VW. It felt funny riding it after driving. The thought that I might be getting too old for it crossed my mind, but I pushed it away and enjoyed the wind in my face as I rolled into town. It was a pretty small place, and it didn't take long to find the post office. I coasted up to the mailbox, put both feet on the ground to come to a slow stop, and dropped my postcard in.

Tranquility Base

The town felt too empty. It was small, with barely any houses on the fringes, but even small towns have some people walking around or cars driving down the streets. There was no one. The sun was getting low in the sky, and the dusky half-light made everything feel a little bit like I was in a movie, which made the empty town start to feel creepy.

I was swinging a leg over my bike and was ready to push down on a pedal when I heard it. There were voices. Muffled, quiet, but definitely voices. I decided just to ride out of town, but then turned and pointed the front wheel of my bike in the direction of the sound instead.

There was a restaurant, a bar, I guess. The sign above it was faded and unreadable. The shades were pulled closed, but as I got closer, the voices got clearer. There was one, louder than the others, that shouted for quiet. And then it was quiet for a minute, until the other voices crept back like someone turning up the volume on a radio.

I leaned my bike up against the wall of the bar or restaurant, or whatever it was. Then I wrapped my hand around the doorknob and pulled it open. Noise flooded out. With the door open, my ears could pick out individual voices, the man who had shouted, and others. An old lady? A younger woman? I heard two kids, a boy and a girl, I guess, and men's voices, lower than the others. But mixed in with all of them were voices that sounded different. They were scratchy and hard to understand, like they were coming from a record player with an old needle. Voices that sounded like they were a million miles away.

I stepped out of the dim dusk light into a place that was almost completely dark, except for a rectangle of light. Huddled around a TV screen was a crowd of people, maybe everyone in the whole town. On the screen, dark, black and white images moved. One minute rocky terrain glided by, the next, faces too close to the camera to be in focus.

I watched, drawn like the others to the images on the screen, even though I had no idea what I was seeing. There was more rocky terrain and garbled voices, and then a voice could be heard above the static, above the murmurs in the room, "Houston, Tranquility Base here. The Eagle has landed."

"They did it! I can't believe it, but they did it!" There was just one voice at first, but then they all joined in, everyone shouting their own disbelief, their own excitement. I couldn't take it any longer and had to know what was happening on the television and what all the excitement was about.

"What's going on?" I finally found my voice. A couple faces turned back toward me, the rest just stared at the TV.

"Young lady," an older man stepped toward me, "You been in a cave the last week?" I could only shrug. I thought of all that had happened in the last week. I certainly hadn't been in a cave, but I hadn't really had the opportunity to sit around watching TV or reading the newspaper either.

"They're on the moon, sweetie," a woman said. She didn't seem old enough to be calling people sweetie, but that didn't stop her.

"Kiddo, sit yourself down and start watching. Armstrong will be getting ready to take his first steps soon." That voice was a man's, louder, with a hint of frustration, like I was interrupting and he just wanted to get back to the TV.

I marveled at the number of names I'd been called in less than a minute and could only stupidly mumble, "Uh, my name's Bets." Then it finally clicked. There were astronauts going to the moon. Had we totally missed it? Were they already there?

I let the faces turn back to the TV and just stood there watching. It suddenly made sense. The rocky landscape, the grainy black and white images, and the static-filled voices. Everyone in town had gathered around what was most likely the only TV for miles, so they could watch Neil Armstrong and Buzz Aldrin land on the moon.

I had to get back to Emmie. It didn't even occur to me to stay in front of the TV and watch for myself. I had to tell her. I burst outside, back into the light, and hopped on my bike. I pedaled hard, not even sitting down on the seat for most of the ride.

My ride into town had been leisurely, a substitute for sitting down next to Emmie and meditating. I'd pedaled slowly, taking in the scenery and getting lost in my thoughts. My ride back was the opposite, furious and focused. I didn't stop to even consider why it was so important to me. It was important to everyone it seemed. People had been talking about it for months, for years I guess. It was important. I felt a pang and pushed aside the thought that what I really wanted, what I really should have been doing was sitting at home between my parents, watching the moon landing with them.

I got back as the last light was fading from the sky. Emmie was still off at the edge of the field we'd parked in. I called out to her in a voice that was too soft to get her attention. I called again, louder, not wanting to interrupt her, but needing, desperately needing, to tell her the news.

Emmie stood and ran toward me. I remembered, for one brief second, the way she ran toward me in City Hall that day in San Francisco. But I pushed the memory away and brought myself back to the present.

"The moon," I shouted, "We landed on the moon! They're going to walk on it!" Emmie had reached me in a whirl, her hair and dress flowing out behind her. She was as confused as I must have looked back in town, and I did my best to fill her in between excited gasps for breath.

"It's cool Bets," she said in a calm voice. "We'll tune in. It's cool." I tried to absorb some of Emmie's calm and make it my own, but it was impossible.

Emmie opened the passenger side of the VW, and I followed close behind, expecting her to slide over to the driver's side so I could hop in after her. Instead she stopped with her feet still on the ground, and I nearly lost my balance trying not to run right into the back of her. She leaned into the VW and turned on the radio.

A blast of music came out of the open door, but she quickly changed the station. There were bursts of static separated by snips of voice or music as Emmie turned the radio dial and scanned through stations. She paused at a couple, listened for a second, then moved on. Finally she found it, and I heard the same static voices I'd heard on the TV in town. Emmie adjusted the dial, losing the station for a second, and then tuning it in perfectly so that the voices seemed like they were right there with us in the VW.

"Columbia, Columbia, this is Houston. One minute and 30 seconds to L-O-S. All systems go. Over."

"Columbia. Thank you."

"Stay where you are a minute, Neil. "

"Okay. Need a little slack?"

"You need more slack, Buzz? "

"No. Hold it just a minute. "

"Okay. "

I had no idea what they were talking about, but we were listening to voices from another world. I looked at

Emmie, and she just looked back and smiled. We listened for another minute, neither of us saying anything, just looking at each other, then looking at nothing, the way people do when they're listening to something that they can't see while their minds are busy imagining it.

"We might be able to make it back to town in time, Bets," Emmie said with a smile, "but watching from here is better." Her eyes shifted up toward the sky and she giggled a little. My eyes followed hers and then settled on the glowing white crescent hanging far above us. The moon. I giggled with her and smiled back.

Then, without a word, Emmie turned toward the VW, stepped up onto the back tire, grabbed the roof rack, and pulled herself up onto the camper top. We hadn't raised the top of the camper when we'd parked, so she was able to crawl onto the large flat roof and lie down.

I wondered for a second if I'd be able to pull myself up to the roof with the same ease that Emmie had, but I didn't care. I repeated her steps, onto the tire, grabbing the rack, and then I was beside her. The roof was uncomfortable at first, flat and hard, and I felt with my right hand for the edge, not wanting to fall off. But once I had settled myself and put my hands behind my head like a cushion, I felt my body relax, and my eyes settled on the moon far above us.

It was perfect. I felt foolish for thinking that we needed to rush into town to watch on TV. There was complete darkness around us, the only light came from the stars and moon above us. The voices on the radio drifted out the open door and filled the night. I felt Emmie's hand brush mine, and I reached out to hold it. My mind relaxed. I knew I couldn't possibly see the astronauts just by looking at the moon up in the sky, but I was overwhelmed by the sensation of hearing their voices on the radio while I was looking up at the new world they were exploring.

"Roger. We copy."

'It takes a pretty good little jump."

"Okay."

"I'm at the foot of the ladder... I'm going to step off the LM now."

There was a short silence on the radio, but we were still listening, knowing that the silence we were hearing was coming from far far above us.

"That's one small step for man, one giant leap for mankind."

And just like that, people from Earth had walked on the Moon. Emmie and I lay there, listening to the voices on the radio and watching as the moon traced its path across the sky. It was a path it had followed every night since forever, but tonight it would be moving through the sky with two passengers on it.

We listened long into the night. We heard the astronauts describe the surface of the moon, heard Huston call up questions and directions, heard the silence in between conversation when our imaginations took over.

At some point, my thoughts drifted back to Earth and everything that had been on my mind for weeks, for months. Our trip across the country and Seth, the war, my father—somehow all of that seemed a little less important. How could it matter now? We'd walked on the moon!

No, that wasn't right. It did matter, and it was just as important as it was an hour ago, or a month ago. The difference was that all of those things were now happening in a world where people had figured out a way to send astronauts to the moon. And if we could do that, if we could send people all the way to the moon, then anything was possible.

Our trip across the country? That's easy. We've gone to the moon. Ending the war in Vietnam? Of course, we've gone to the moon. My father... well, that was different.

I pictured him at home, watching the moon landing on TV. Could he be thinking the same things that I was? Feeling the same possibilities that the moon landing opened up for us? Was he realizing, right along with me, that we had landed on the moon and now anything was possible?

I was hoping so.

Dodging

In an instant, I was completely awake. We'd been on the road long enough that my mind didn't need to push through the slow remembering of where I was and what bed I was in. Something wasn't right.

There was no soft glow of morning sunshine on the camper's sides. The sound of birds didn't fill the air. Instead it was dark except for a silvery moonlight that turned the world black and grey. Everything was silent and still. I lay motionless for a few seconds, staring at the ceiling of the camper and wondering why I was completely awake in the middle of the night. Then I heard it.

The clunk of a pot being moved, picked up, and set down. It was quiet, quieter than it would have been if someone had done it while making dinner. Quiet, like someone was setting it down carefully, trying not to make any noise.

My mind flooded with memories—the way Seth glared at me, Emmie locking the VW's door that night after he'd gotten so angry, the things Seth shouted at me as he clung to the side of the VW. The air in the camper was suddenly hot and close, and I felt sweat cover my body. Seth was back.

I held my breath, not wanting to be heard, thinking maybe, foolishly, that if he didn't hear me, he would leave us alone. Then my hands balled into fists, and I shifted my weight, slowly rolling onto my side and then onto my stomach. I was pretty quiet, but he'd probably heard me. There were no other sounds, so he must have heard what little sound I'd made. But I was hoping it mostly sounded like someone shifting positions in their sleep. After all, he knew we were up in the camper, but he didn't need to know that I was awake, didn't need to know that he wouldn't be surprising us.

I thought about nudging Emmie, but I worried about how she would wake up. I had made no more noise than it took to open my eyes, but I was pretty sure Emmie would grumble and moan at being disturbed in the middle of the night. Instead, I raised myself onto my elbows and inched forward toward the opening that lead from the camper's top to the floor below.

I don't know how many minutes it took—long enough that my eyes had adjusted to the darkness. There were more noises from below, and I thought that they might hide the few noises I made. I held my breath and slowly pulled myself to the edge of the opening and peered over.

The space below was darker than up above, but even waiting another minute for my eyes to adjust didn't help much. I could just make out the shadowy movements of

Seth's body, a dark shape in the dark. He was hunched over, like he was looking for something in the cupboards. Now that I was watching him and had a visual to go with the sound, the quiet noises were more obvious. The soft shift of something on the cupboard shelf, the click of metal touching metal, the rustle of coat fabric.

I couldn't imagine what he could be looking for. Had he left something in the cupboard, something important enough that he would walk miles to find us again, something that he would search for instead of taking revenge on Emmie and me? Then it hit me—knives. There were knives in the cupboard. As soon as the thought entered my brain, I knew what I had to do, and it scared me almost as much as the thought of Seth with a knife.

Again, as slowly and quietly as I could, I moved. Not just rolling over this time, but sitting up, and then turning slowly, so slowly, until I faced the opening again. I could still see down into the blackness, could still see Seth's shadowy movements. I slid my feet over the edge and let them dangle into the space below. They were just above him. If Seth had straightened up from rummaging in the cupboards, he would have bumped his head on my feet. Then I pushed myself forward and slid off the edge of the opening and into the darkness below.

My feet connected squarely with Seth's back and my weight falling on top pushed him to the floor. He let out a high pitched yell of surprise, and I crumpled on top of him. There was a tangle of arms and legs, and even though my eyes had adjusted somewhat to the darkness, it was still impossible to tell what was what. I pushed away an arm only to discover it was a leg. I grabbed for his hair and instead came away with a scrap of torn shirtsleeve. When I felt Seth trying to push me off of him, I swung a fist hoping to connect with his jaw but instead met empty air.

I managed somehow to keep him on the floor and eventually pinned his arms behind him. I remembered how tall Seth was compared to me, and even though he was thin, he must have been twenty-five or thirty pounds heavier than me. Still, I was able to stay on top of him, twisting an arm until he cried out again in a high-pitched voice.

I was surprised at how easily I'd overpowered Seth, or more accurately how easily he'd given up. He was so controlling, always doing whatever he wanted, intimidating and threatening. But now, all that seemed to disappear. The oily, gravely voice had been replaced with a whining one, and even though he still struggled, physically I'd easily gotten the better of him. Had I thought for a second, I would have wondered what had changed, what wasn't right. But I was still too full of my victory to care. Seth had come back for us, and I had beat him.

Emmie had heard our struggle and was awake. Her voice called down to me, and I shouted back up at her trying to explain everything, but our voices mixed in the darkness and there was only confusion. She finally reached an arm around the edge of the opening and flicked on the dome light, flooding the VW with a warm glow.

Below me was a face covered with three or four days worth of stubble, light colored hair cropped shorter on the sides and back, bangs hanging over blue eyes that stared back at me in surprise. There was no glare, no snarling smirk, no greasy black curls tumbling to his shoulders, no angular features or pointed nose. The man beneath me was not Seth.

Emmie lowered herself from the bed above, somehow avoiding the two of us still tangled on the floor. Her eyes took in everything at once and then focused on the man. He wasn't really a man, I guess. I mean, he was older than me, but just Emmie's age, or maybe not even.

"Who are you?" Emmie asked, and then spoke again without giving him any time to answer. "What are you doing in our van? Stealing food?"

"I... no. Sorry. I was just..." His voice wasn't as high-pitched as the surprised yells I'd heard him make in the dark. But it certainly wasn't threatening like Seth's. If my heart wasn't pounding so hard, I might have even thought it was... pleasant. In fact, he did seem pleasant. Boys didn't have pretty faces, but handsome was too old sounding. Cute fit better. If I'd seen him in town or at school, instead of sneaking into the VW in the middle of the night, I might have waved, said hello, maybe even smiled.

Emmie's accusing voice brought me back from my daydream. She questioned him again, sounding angrier, "Why were you stealing our food?" Even though he'd denied it, Emmie had clearly decided her first guess was correct.

She grabbed a backpack from the floor that I hadn't noticed. I guess it had been knocked out of his hands when I landed on him. She pulled it open to reveal cans and boxes, all taken from our cupboards.

"Sorry. Yeah, yeah, I was. Sorry, I was so hungry. I just... I needed..."

"Are you a dodger?" Emmie interrupted his chain of half-broken sentences. I looked at her and made a face. A what? I looked back at the man, or boy, or whatever he was. I could tell by the downcast look on his face that he was guilty of whatever Emmie was accusing him of. She zipped up the backpack and tossed it at him so it hit him in the chest before landing with a thump on the floor in front of him. "Go, take it, get out of here, dodger."

"Wait!" I shouted, not really meaning to, but feeling the urgency of the moment. "What's... what's a dodger?" I grabbed Emmie, pulling down the arm she was pointing toward the door and then turned to him. "Who are you?"

Emmie didn't give him a chance to answer. "He's a draft dodger," she said with a hiss. "He's running away instead of going to Vietnam to fight. And he's stealing our food. Go!" He cringed at her shout. His hands went for the backpack, but then he thought better of it and moved toward the door without it.

"Wait!" This time I grabbed his arm instead of Emmie's. He was already out the door. "What's your name?" He only shrugged, his eyes flicked toward Emmie and then he tried to pull away from my grasp. "What's your name?" I repeated. I realized as soon as I asked the second time that if he was running away from the draft, he was probably afraid of us turning him in, but I was only asking because I wanted to know who he was, and I didn't want him to go.

"Jake," he said to the ground, then he looked at me with a shrug. "My name's Jake." Then he turned and walked away.

"Hey, Jake." I heard his footsteps in the gravel stop. "Here." I dug in the backpack, pulled out an apple and tossed it to him. I couldn't really see him in the dark, but I didn't hear it hit the ground, so I figured he must have caught it. "Just stay there a minute, okay? Don't go."

"Okay." His confused voice drifted back from the darkness beyond the light filtering out of the VW, and then I heard him bite into the apple.

I turned to Emmie. "I don't get it. What happened to everyone being your friend? Trusting everyone? What's wrong with dodging the draft? If the war is wrong, if you want to stop the war, isn't it a good thing if someone runs away instead of going over there?" Questions spewed from my mouth, and I gave Emmie no time to answer, but she didn't wait for me to pause.

"Why should he get to avoid it?" she interrupted. "Why shouldn't he have to go to war? Why should my father..." Then it all clicked—her father. Emmie's father was killed just a month after he'd left for Vietnam. Emmie was clearly against the war. She went to anti-war demonstrations. She encouraged me to shake things up in my own small town by organizing a protest, and she seemed to have peace signs attached to everything she owned. So it didn't make sense that she'd be angry at someone who was actually avoiding the war. But fathers? I understood that the rules changed when it came to fathers.

I spread my arms at the same time that Emmie moved into them. By the time I wrapped her in a hug, she was already shaking with sobs. I just held her and let her cry, knowing that saying things like "It's okay" and "It'll be alright" was just stupid.

I'd gone to Emmie when I was upset and confused about my own father being in Vietnam, and her story and her experience had helped me find my way through it. But we never sat down just to talk about how she felt, to focus on her and let her share her feelings about her father. She was older than me, had seen more than me, knew more, had done more. I never thought I'd find myself comforting her and helping her, but I was.

I also knew I didn't agree with her reaction to Jake. Sending someone else to fight in a war wouldn't bring her father back. Emmie had gone to the protest in San Francisco with the hope of keeping other people's fathers, and brothers, and sons from dying in the war. Now someone had come to us, someone who we could actually help stay out of that war.

"We need to help Jake," I said. I wanted to use a stronger voice, wanted to shake Emmie and look her in the eye and ask her what the heck she was thinking. But I knew she was vulnerable and hurting, so I simply told her what we needed to do, hoping she would see it and understand. There was a long silence. I kept holding her, not knowing if she was thinking about what I'd said or angry at me for saying it. Then she pushed herself away from me and turned toward the open door.

"Hey, dodger," Emmie called to the silhouette that was hovering just outside the circle of light from the VW. "We'll see you at breakfast." Then she closed the sliding door and pulled herself up into the camper bed.

Drafted

I woke up wondering if Jake would still be outside the VW. He'd left his bag full of food on the floor where Emmie had tossed it. But after the way Emmie had treated him, I wouldn't have been surprised if he'd spent the rest of the night putting some distance between us and looking for someone else's food to swipe instead

I slipped down from the bed and landed softly, remembering the leap into darkness I'd made the night before. Emmie was still in bed, on her side and facing away from me. She could have been sleeping, but I didn't think so. She always woke up before me and was usually outside meditating before I even crawled out of bed. I figured she was still trying to sift through her feelings, and that was something she needed to do on her own.

I grabbed a couple pieces of fruit and a loaf of bread, and then when I couldn't find the jar of peanut butter in our cupboard, I dug through Jake's backpack and found it there. I somehow managed to grab a plate and knife and then push the sliding door handle up with an elbow. I slipped through the open door using my hip to push it closed as best I could. I didn't want it to slam in case Emmie really was still sleeping, but I was pretty sure she wasn't.

Jake was there, sitting crossed legged in the grass, staring at the ground as if he were sitting next to a campfire, even though there was nothing there. He lifted his head when he heard the sliding door open, and he smiled. Jake had a smile that showed in his eyes. It reminded me of my father's smile when he was really happy about something. I smiled back.

"Morning," Jake said in a mumbled half-whisper. Maybe he was thinking about Emmie still sleeping in the VW, but probably it was the stillness of a day that wasn't fully awake yet. That was one thing that surprised me my first few days on the road—how quiet it was in some of the places we camped. Even close to a road, the sun came up long before cars rolled down the pavement, and there were sounds in a town that you just stopped noticing, until they were gone and you realized how quiet the world was without them. It didn't seem right to talk in a regular voice and ruin the silence.

So I whispered back, "Good morning." Jake smiled again. I felt my cheeks blush, and I was glad for the still dim light of early morning. It wasn't like I'd never talked with a boy before. I went to a school that was full of them. But there was something different about Jake. Maybe because he was older, or just because we were out on our own in a beautiful place and weren't stuck sitting next to each other in a classroom.

I walked by boys in school every day, watched them do stupid stuff in the hallways, and grumbled when they cut in front of me in the lunch line. But even though I'd caught him stealing our stuff, I felt like Jake was polite and kind, someone who would hold a door open instead of pushing past to be the first in line. And his eyes—for some reason I wanted to look at them, but I didn't want to get caught looking at them. They were bluer than they had any right to be that early in the morning.

His eyes met mine, but before they did, I caught them flick down to the food I was carrying. I remembered how hungry he must be. He was hungry the night before, hungry enough to try to steal from us. I'd tried not to think about him trying to take our food. I just wanted to sit down next to him and talk. The night before was years away.

"Hungry?"

"Yeah," he said in a hesitant laugh, like he wasn't quite sure if I was being friendly or taunting him. I sat down as close to Jake as I dared and spread the food out in front of us, hoping he'd see that I wasn't holding any grudges over last night's events.

"Thanks." The word had barely left his lips and his hands were already grabbing. He was nearly done with an apple by the time I pulled out a slice of bread and spread peanut butter on it. He devoured that in four bites and was starting on a banana while I made him another sandwich.

I thought about how hungry he must have been. Still he left the VW when Emmie told him to, spent the night outside knowing that there was a backpack full of food just inside the sliding door, and had the patience to smile and offer me a cheerful greeting when I came outside. I couldn't imagine any of the boys in school doing that.

"How old are you?" The question was out of my mouth before I could catch it. I wanted to ask him so many things. I wanted to know everything about him. I tried to think of the best question to ask, one that would make conversation without making me look like I was overly curious about him, and that's what came out instead.

He laughed a little, and then stifled it, maybe realizing that to do more would make things more embarrassing than they already were. "I'm twenty-two," he said in a voice that sounded a little apologetic. My heart sank a little, but my brain did some quick math, subtracting sixteen from twenty-two and then counting up in years. When I'm eighteen, he'll be... when I'm twenty-two... It was foolish thinking, but I thought it anyway. Then I desperately tried to think of another question to make up for the last one.

"How long have you..." I hesitated, feeling like I was just going to embarrass myself all over again. "How long..."

"How long have I been running away from the draft?" Jake finished my thought with harsh clarity. Then he just looked at me, maybe trying to figure out how I felt about what he'd done. He already knew what Emmie's opinion was. I somehow tried to appear curious and disinterested and non-judgemental all at the same time. I think I failed miserably.

The sound of the sliding door opening broke the awkward silence, and Emmie stepped out of the VW. Her eyes scanned the scene, taking in Jake, and me, and then the improvised breakfast that was spread out around us. Then she looked toward the horizon, and I half expected her to just walk past us without saying anything and go off to meditate somewhere. Instead, her eyes came back to us, and then settled on Jake.

"You still here, dodger?" she said in voice that tried to be spiteful, but sounded playful underneath. My eyes swung between Jake and Emmie trying to figure it out.

"Yep, still here, flower child." Flower child? I'd heard the term before. Older people used it to refer to kids who were against the war the same way they used hippie or beatnik, most of the time accompanied by a disapproving eye roll. But there wasn't disapproval in Jake's voice; there was the hint of a teasing laugh. I thought about Seth calling me girly girl, and how much that bothered me. But I didn't think I would mind so much if Jake decided to call me flower child too. I pushed my hair behind my ears, wishing I had put a few thin braids in it or maybe a string of tiny beads like Emmie.

"Wanted to stick around a little while to see how far into the day we'd get before you pulled yourself out of bed." Again, there was a laugh in his voice. Jake's words could have been an insult, but his tone said otherwise. And he was different. Maybe it was because he'd finally gotten some food in his stomach, or just that he was fully awake now, but he seemed like he was sitting up straighter, more attentive, his words less hesitant.

Emmie sat down across from us. Again, I felt like there should be a campfire between us since we were sitting on the ground in a circle. But there was only grass, some fruit, and half the loaf of bread. So instead, it just felt awkward.

"OK, dodger," Emmie said in that same voice, a sharp edge hiding the softness beneath. "Let's hear your story." She reached for the bread, pulled out a slice, and then carefully dipped the knife into the peanut butter and spread a perfectly even layer. Jake and I watched in silence, neither of us knowing what to say and using the time to think.

Finally, Jake broke the silence and started his story.

"Lots of people would call me a coward. They'd be right I guess. For some reason we've all decided that going off to a war to shoot at people and have them shoot at you is a brave thing, the right thing to do. Maybe sometimes it is, but it sure doesn't feel like it."

I realized immediately that so far I'd only heard him say a few short sentences, so the flood of words felt strange on my ears. I couldn't help but hear his accent, although I really had no idea where to place it. Was it midwest or southern, or was it from a certain state or city? I hadn't lived in enough places or met enough people from other places to be sure. The way he blended words together or chopped certain syllables had a lazy feel to it, and if he was talking about anything else, I would have thought that he didn't care much about what he was saying. But somehow it was clear that he was thinking about every word and choosing carefully.

"My father fought in Korea. I was just old enough to barely remember, only five or six. It's hard to know how much I remember myself and how much is stuff people told me. I remember my father being gone though. I remember what my father was like before he went away, and I remember what he was like when he came back. It wasn't the same.

"It could have been worse, right? Lots of kids' fathers didn't come back. So I should feel lucky I guess. But when you're just a kid, you don't really think that way, you don't compare yourself to what others have. You just know what you have or don't have, and what you're dealing with."

Then he just stopped talking. Emmie was carefully spreading peanut butter on another slice of bread. There was a second where I watched, waiting for her to put it into her mouth, and then instead, she passed it to Jake. He smiled, and their eyes met. I watched them, part of me happy that they were getting along, happy that Emmie hadn't sent Jake away. But with it, came a sinking feeling that I had a hard time understanding. Jake started talking again, but the feeling didn't really go away. Instead, it settled in, nagging me as I half listened, my eyes wanting to stay on Jake, but now and then shifting to Emmie to watch her watching him.

"As I got older, my father told me more about the war, about Korea. I guess he figured I was old enough to understand, or maybe he could only keep the stories inside so long." Jake paused. He'd mostly been looking at the ground, tugging on blades of grass until they snapped in half and then tossing them aside. But he gave Emmie and me a long look, and then his eyes dropped back to the ground. "You don't need to hear the details. There were two types—stories about my father killing people he didn't want to kill, and stories about people he knew getting killed."

I watched Emmie, trying to read her face. Was she thinking about her own father and what had happened to him, or was the sadness I saw all for Jake. She caught me staring then looked away, grabbing an apple from the ground between us. She made a show of pushing her hair out of her face, but I thought maybe she was wiping her eyes instead.

"This would be an easier story if I could tell you about how bad things were at home," Jake continued. "But even with my father struggling to deal with all that had happened to him and all that he'd seen in Korea, home was still a good place. The only place I really wanted to be. So leaving home wasn't easy, but my number came up."

Again, there was a long pause. It was clear that this part of the story wasn't easy to share. I wanted to stop him, to tell him he didn't need to go any further, tell him that we knew how it ended. But I thought about what he had said about his father, about how maybe he'd started telling

Jake war stories because he couldn't keep them inside any longer, and I thought that maybe, even though it was hard, telling me and Emmie his story was something Jake needed to do.

"My mother got the mail the day the letter came. My father was at work. She knew what it was before she handed it to me. It was easy to see from the return address. It was probably something she looked for every day, flipping through the day's mail, hoping not to find it.

"She let me open it. Maybe carrying it in from the mailbox was all she could manage. We both just sat at the kitchen table, the letter unfolded between us. I hadn't really read it. There were important details I'm sure—when to report, where to go, what to bring. But I didn't need to read it to know the only thing that mattered; I was going to Vietnam."

I tried to remember the day we found out my father would be going to Vietnam. I'd come home from school to find my mother and father sitting at the kitchen table with an official-looking letter between them. Jake's description painted the same picture in my mind. I was used to my father getting orders to move to a new base. Moving from town to town was something I knew how to do. But I could tell right away from my father's expression that the paper on the kitchen table was somehow different.

"My mother told me that I better go pack my things." It hurt just to think of it, a mother sending her son off to a war. But from the look on Jake's face, I knew there was more to it than that. "She looked me in the eyes, and then she slid the letter toward her, carefully refolded it, and put it back in the envelope. She kept looking at me as she made the envelope disappear into her apron pocket. I thought for a second that I'd need the letter when I reported to the Armed Forces office, then I realized what she was trying to tell me with that long stare.

"I didn't say anything else. I just got up and went to pack my things. It wasn't like she was forcing me to run away. I thought about that while I stuffed things into a duffle bag. I already wanted to, had probably decided when the war started heating up and I saw other guys in town getting drafted. My mother wasn't telling me to run, but she was giving me permission.

"It was a fast goodbye. Maybe that was better. We both knew my father would be home from work soon, and that would add complications. He could come down on either side. We hadn't really talked about Vietnam, and I had no idea how he felt about it. He could have been proud to send me off to war when he saw the letter, or he could have reacted the same way my mother did. I'll never know. I was on a bus out of town long before he came home."

That was really the end of the story. Jake filled us in on a few details between his leaving home and his rummaging through our cupboards, but it was his decision to run that really mattered.

His mother had given him all the cash she had in the house. It was enough for a bus to Chicago, but after that he would have been penniless. Instead, he rode the bus as far as the next town, and then walked or hitchhiked. He started out with a bag full of food from home, but that had run out after the first week, and his money ran out after that. We could guess at the rest of the story and how he came to be rummaging through our camper, stuffing food into a backpack.

The three of us sat there in silence for a minute or two, picking at the food that was left between us or pulling on grass blades like Jake had done while he was telling his story. The sun was already high in the sky. Jake was done talking. I really had no idea what to say. It was still sinking in—my father going to war, Emmie's father getting killed, Jake's father changed by the war he fought in, and Jake. I tried helplessly to sift through the right or wrong of it.

I glanced hesitantly at Emmie. For the first time since we'd left Forestville, I didn't know how to read her. I still had that sinking feeling inside me that turned into a pang when I looked at Jake, but I thought back to Emmie catching me staring at her and didn't want it to happen again.

Emmie was the first to stand up. She unfolded her legs and brushed the dirt off her pants. "Well dodger, it looks like we're making a detour to Canada."

Crush

136 E, 61 N, 34 E, 80 E, 94 E

Just like that we were three again. We'd really only been without Seth for two days, but it felt like much longer than that, maybe because things were so completely different without him. The tension in the VW had left with Seth. Emmie and I were free to laugh and tell stories or just enjoy each other's company in silence when we felt like it. With both of us driving, things felt equal, like we were making the trip together, rather than me just tagging along.

I was happy that Jake was traveling with us, but it did change how things felt. Maybe it was a boy thing. Conversation was different when it was just between girls. Maybe there was leftover tension from Emmie's initial reaction to Jake, although after that first morning they seemed to be nothing but friendly toward each other.

Most likely it was just the difference between two and three. When there's just two people, you only need to pay attention to one person, there's no dividing your attention or leaving someone out. There's no figuring out who to look at when you're talking.

There were other differences. One of us had to sit in back. We took turns, mostly. But Jake was older and more comfortable driving, and he seemed happy to stay behind the wheel most of the day. Maybe he felt like we were doing him a favor and he should do what he could to help out. Whatever the reason, it meant I wasn't driving much at all. I didn't mind really. At least that's what I told myself. Emmie had to talk me into it in the first place, so I shouldn't care, but I did.

Being a trio with Jake was much better than having Seth around. When we settled down for the night, Jake made himself comfortable in a sleeping bag on a flat spot of ground near the VW. Emmie had offered to move things around in the back of the VW so the back seat could be folded down into a bed. I didn't even realize the back seat did that and wondered briefly why Seth had ended up sleeping outside from the start, but then I thought again about Seth and was glad he had. Regardless, Jake refused the lower bed, saying he was happy to sleep outside.

Beyond sleeping arrangements, Jake was unlike Seth in every way. He helped make meals and cleaned up afterward. He was soft spoken, but was able to fill the better part of a day with conversation, telling us about himself and his life before he ran away, but also asking us questions and listening as we shared our own stories. He was polite, and kind, and pleasant to be around.

I wondered how different the beginning of our trip would have been if we'd started out with Jake instead of Seth. But that line of thinking only reminded me that Jake wasn't really a traveling companion. He was a passenger, a hitchhiker, only catching a ride with us as far as the Canadian border. But I was happy to be spending time with Jake, so I pushed any thoughts about him leaving out of my mind.

After our first day traveling together, I woke to the sound of the sliding door opening, then the soft clinking of a pan and utensils and the shifting of items in the cupboard. I immediately thought of the night Jake tried to rob us, but knew what I was hearing was harmless. I turned to nudge Emmie and found her eyes already open. We smiled silently. When Emmie pointed toward the space below where Jake was doing his best to keep quiet and then dramatically rolled her eyes, I covered my mouth to keep in a giggle. We both pushed back the covers, and then slowly slid toward the opening to peer over the edge at Jake.

"You planning on robbing us again, dodger?" Emmie said in a voice loud enough to make Jake jump. He dropped the food he had cradled in one hand and knocked a pan off the cupboard and onto the floor. He tried gathering everything up again in a frustrated huff, grumbling defensively under his breathe, then he gave up and joined in the laughter. After he composed himself, he looked up at us with his hands on his hips.

"I figured I'd make you breakfast, flower child. After that horrible stuff you made last night, I guess the only way I'm going to get something edible is to make it myself." He laughed after he said it, and Emmie threw a pillow down at him. She slid down through the opening, and Jake dashed through the sliding door, dropping half the stuff he was carrying.

I wanted to chase after him too, but I didn't. I still had that funny feeling, like my stomach was sinking or like my lungs didn't fill up all the way when I took a breath. I forgot about it sometimes, like when I was laughing with Emmie, but then it crept back in when I saw Jake, or I guess mostly when I saw Jake with Emmie.

They were outside somewhere. I lowered myself down to the floor and took in the view through the VW's big sliding door. As we got farther and farther east, it was getting harder to find a space to camp that wasn't near a house or a town, but today the door framed a grassy hill that ended in a line of trees, just barely touched by the morning sun.

I didn't really want to follow Emmie and Jake. Well, I guess I did, but I didn't think it would make me feel any better. It was fun, what had just happened: surprising Jake, seeing his reaction, sharing that laughter. But he'd said, "flower child." Singular. No matter how much I felt part of a trio, Jake was talking to Emmie when he joked about making breakfast. Just Emmie. I shrugged it off and stepped outside. Emmie had made dinner last night, so I told myself it made sense that he'd looked at her when he made that joke. But I couldn't shake the thought that what I wanted, what I really wanted, was for Jake to talk to me and look at me. Just me.

Emmie and I had been heading for Chicago when we met Jake, not that we really had any plans to go into the city. The camper was pretty self sufficient, and I guess we could have spent the night in a parking lot as easily as we could in a field, but it just felt better to be out in the open. I thought back to the conversation Emmie and I had before we tossed Seth's knife into the water. Crossing the country wasn't without its dangers, especially for two girls on their own. The fewer people that saw us, the less attention we attracted, the better. So we were headed in the direction of Chicago, but not planning to go into the city.

Once we picked up Jake, I checked the map and decided that Detroit was the best place to cross into Canada. We would be able to keep going east without making much of a detour north. But we got there faster than we thought. Maybe it was Jake's willingness to drive for most of the day, or maybe it was just that we'd left the big wide-open spaces of the west behind, and places in the east were closer together. Whatever the reason, we were seeing signs for Detroit with miles listed in the double digits much sooner than we'd expected.

Neither of us wanted to say it, but we didn't want Jake to leave. And I don't think Jake was ready to leave either. He was taking a turn in the back seat, and Emmie was driving, so I was sitting up front with the map unfolded in front of me.

"What about Buffalo?" My question hung there, unanswered. Emmie took her eyes off the road long enough to glance over at me, and I could hear Jake shifting in his seat, maybe sitting up straight after being pulled out of a half-sleep.

"What about crossing at Buffalo instead?" I clarified my question, realizing I was the only one looking at the map. "It's a day away," I added, knowing what we were all thinking. Emmie glanced over at me again, raising her eyebrows.

She shrugged, pretending she wasn't interested even though I knew she was. "I guess. Does it take us very far out of the way?"

I looked back at the map, but I didn't really need to. I'd studied it enough before I'd said anything. We'd just passed by the southern tip of Lake Michigan and we were pretty much heading due east. We were on a major highway, and it was easy to make good time. Whether we went to Detroit or Buffalo, we'd need to take a detour north, but it wasn't much, and we'd need to do it wherever we crossed.

I explained all that, and then added, "It looks like there's a national park or something nearby. We could camp there tonight." I let the idea float in the silence, knowing that the three of us understood it would mean another day together, another day before we had to say goodbye. "And then we could go on to Buffalo."

Not knowing what else to do, I passed the map back to Jake and then watched his eyes scan the route I'd described. I got that sinking feeling, but it was mixed with something else, something that felt better, something warm and positive. It was good to have him with us.

"Yeah, Em. Bets is right, it looks like a better route." I felt good that he liked my idea, that he'd given me credit. I liked that he'd said my name. But... Em, he'd called her Em. When Seth called her that it sounded insulting, like when he called me girly girl. But when Jake called her that, it sounded casual. It sounded close, like he'd gotten to know her and was comfortable being around her. I didn't know what made my stomach hurt more, Jake pinning the flower child nickname on Emmie or hearing him shorten her name to a single syllable.

Emmie shrugged again, like she didn't care, "Yeah, sure, whatever you think. How do I get to this park?"

I took the map back from Jake and became the navigator, following road signs and telling Emmie where to turn. We weren't far from the park. If I'd waited another ten or fifteen minutes to suggest the route change, we would have already passed it.

It felt strange being in a park with a designated camping area. We'd been on the road so long and had gotten used to just stopping and camping wherever we found a spot we liked on the side of the road. But once we were in our camping spot, we went through our usual routine of popping the top on the VW and sifting through the cupboards to decide what we wanted to eat.

The park was a beautiful place. We camped among sand dunes, and the lake—big enough to feel like an ocean—could be seen between them. After eating, we sat just enjoying the sound of the waves and the wind. I thought about sitting on the beach with Jake, watching the ocean together, and I imagined him reaching out and taking my hand. Then Emmie's voice cut in.

"Go for a walk?" I looked up and turned toward her, but as soon as I did, I realized she wasn't talking to me.

"Yeah, sure," Jake said, a little hesitantly, but only to hide the eagerness that had become a part of who he was around Emmie. They both stood up and brushed the sand off their jeans.

Emmie looked at the dishes they'd left and then turned to me. "This okay?" she said apologetically.

"Sure. Yeah, go ahead," I forced a smile while the bottom dropped out of my stomach. Then I watched them walk away toward the shifting surface of the lake. They found their way through a low spot between two dunes and then, just before they were hidden on the other side, I saw them reach out and take each other's hand.

I looked back at their plates on the ground and tossed mine down with them. I couldn't figure out how I felt, but I knew I wasn't doing their dishes. I dragged myself into the VW and up into the bed. Each movement was an effort. When I finally made it into the pop-top, I couldn't be bothered with changing into pajamas. My feet still hung over the edge, and I let my sandals slip from my feet and fall to the floor below.

I don't know how long I lay there. It was still light when Emmie and Jake went walking off toward the lake. It was dark when I heard their hushed voices return. There was a long whispered conversation. I tried to hear the words but couldn't. Instead I could only pick up the emotions. Sad, happy, urgent, hesitant, calm, pleading. None of them felt good, and I felt wrong listening, but couldn't stop.

Finally the whispers ended and there was a long silence, long enough for me to wonder what was happening. Then the sliding door opened, and the sounds of the lakeshore drifted in. I heard Emmie pulling herself up into bed, and I held my breath. I wasn't sure I wanted to talk with her, and I had no idea what I'd say if I did.

I lay there motionless, as Emmie shifted and wiggled and got herself settled under the blankets. There were so many thoughts in my head, but I didn't dare say them. I held my breath. I let it out silently through my nose. I tried not to move. I wondered if Emmie could hear me, not breathing, not moving.

And then, "Do you love him?" My question hung there in the dark.

Emmie let out a sigh. "Oh, Bets. I..." She paused and I felt her searching for words in the small space. It was hard to breathe while I waited for her to say more.

"He's going away, Bets. How could I... I just met him... I'll never see him again." My silence asked the question again. *Do you love him?*

She hesitated. I could feel it in the dark. Her, right there, only breathing, and then finally, a whispered, stuttering breath, "Yeah." Silence and hesitation, and then again, "Yeah, Bets, I think I do." There was sniffing or tears or something. "Oh gosh, I'm sorry, Bets. I know that... that you... I do, I love him. It's silly. I barely know him, and he's going away, but I love him."

I could have turned away. I could have just rolled over, turned away from her and gone to sleep, thinking angry thoughts, alone in my own hurt. Instead, I turned toward her and opened my arms.

I don't know how long we both lay there, one crying, then the other, then both. After a long time, we cried ourselves to sleep, each for different reasons.

Crossing

90 E, 2 E, 20 E, 5 E

I'd carefully measured the distance on the map between the lakeshore where we camped and Buffalo, New York. I held my index finger to the map scale, and then traced the route, twisting my wrist to line my finger up with the highway as it turned this way and that. I estimated the trip was about five hundred miles.

The day before when I'd suggested the detour, the extra travel time seemed like nothing. The VW struggled to go much over the speed limit, but even at that speed it would only take us eight hours, maybe nine if we stopped a few times along the way. Then we'd have to say goodbye to Jake.

But when I woke up, the thought of an entire day spent in the VW with Emmie and Jake was unbearable. Every emotion seemed amplified. That funny feeling—a crush? I guess that's what it was. Why would anyone ever want one? I was embarrassed. Emmie knew how I felt. She must have, or she wouldn't have been apologetic last night, and if she knew, did Jake know? Maybe that was part of their whispered conversation. I was angry at Emmie. Why her instead of me? I was angry at Jake. Why come into our lives only to leave again in just a couple days?

So I ate a silent breakfast and then climbed into the back seat. If we could have driven with the pop-top open, I would have crawled up there and gone back to sleep. I silently hoped Emmie or Jake would offer me one of the front seats. Then I was determined not to budge, even if they did offer to trade seats, hoping they would feel guilty for excluding me. But they didn't offer.

I tried to sleep. The camper was great for sleeping when the top was up and I could spread out head to toe along the length of the VW. I'm sure it would have been the same if we'd moved all our bags out of the way and unfolded the back seat into a bed. But otherwise, the back seat was unfit for the job. I could stretch my legs out, but was forced to lean my back and head against the sidewall. Or I could lay down flat, but only if I pulled my knees up to my chest, otherwise my feet would press against one wall and my head would eventually slide into the other. So I gave up on sleeping. The only alternative was to sit up and watch the world go by outside the windows. Emmie and Jake hadn't turned on the radio. Maybe because they thought I was trying to sleep. I wasn't about to ask them to turn it on, so I just sat, looking at the highway coming toward us through the front windows.

Watching the scenery eventually got boring, so I started watching Emmie and Jake. Jake did all of the driving that day. Maybe he'd guessed that Emmie hadn't gotten a good night's sleep, or maybe he figured he should help out now, since after he left, Emmie would be doing most of the driving to Woodstock and then clear across the country back to California. It didn't matter; he was driving.

So I got to watch Emmie watching him. She was trying to be sly, but she was really bad at it. She would casually look out the windows and then gradually turn like she was looking at something passing us on the left. Then she'd stop turning and look at Jake. When she wasn't doing that, she was stealing little glances toward him. All of it was easy to see from the back seat. Jake wasn't much better. He had to keep his eyes on the road, so he couldn't take the long leisurely gazes that Emmie was, but he still turned toward her when he could.

I watched, and I thought. I did some quick math and decided that Emmie was a lot closer to Jake's age than me. Was that difference in age important? I guess it was, even though I didn't want it to be. But it was how we felt that really mattered. I'd spent two days figuring out that the sinking feeling I got in my stomach whenever I thought about Jake was just a crush, but Emmie had used the word love. Was she really in love? I sat, and thought, and watched some more. Did she keep looking at Jake like that because she was in love with him? She was hesitant the night before when she told me, but even just to say the word seemed worlds away from how I felt. Had she said it to him? I remembered how quickly I had gone from stranger to good friend with Emmie. Maybe she had said it. Did he say it back?

And suddenly all the things I felt seemed small and unimportant. I still had an empty feeling in my stomach, like something that had never been there was somehow missing. But I realized that would go away, that somehow it would be replaced, maybe when the next boy came along. Would Emmie's feelings get replaced so easily? I didn't think so.

And just like that, a thought that should have been there all along swept over me. I needed to be doing everything I could to make this easier on Emmie, and instead I was making it harder. She needed a friend, not someone sulking in the back seat.

"You two look cute together," I said, and as the words left my mouth I could feel the smile growing. They did look cute together. I was just too busy thinking about myself to see it. Emmie turned around. There was relief on her face, and then a smile. She tried to say something, but looked like she couldn't find the right words. She finally just looked at me again and mouthed the words, "Thank you."

Jake took his eyes off the road long enough to glance back at me. "Actually, she looks cute. I'm just along for the ride." Emmie made a face and then looked at me, rolling her eyes and shaking her head. I put my hand to my mouth, but it was useless. Giggles slipped out, and then a full laugh.

Jake looked at both of us, feigning shock and offense, but only for a second, and then he joined in the laughter too. "That has a lot of potential," Emmie stopped laughing long enough to say, "Either a bumper sticker or a t-shirt." There was another round of laughter, and when it was over, Emmie turned back toward me.

"C'mon, Bets. Your turn to sit up front." Then, like it had never been there, the tension between us was gone. I'm sure there will be a lot of things in life that I look back on and regret. Thankfully, holding a grudge and losing my friendship with Emmie would not be among them. Emmie and I traded places, and Jake and I spent the rest of the trip chatting while the road signs counted down the miles to Buffalo.

Buffalo was really the first city we stopped in since we left California. We'd driven through Denver just because that was the shortest way east, and we'd passed by the southern edge of Chicago, close enough to see the skyline, but we didn't go into the city. Those places were just scenery, but when Jake pulled off the highway and the VW rolled down the exit ramp onto a busy street, we became a part of the city of Buffalo.

It felt like there was work happening in Buffalo. We'd passed some industrial buildings on our way in, white smoke billowing from their chimneys, and the streets felt alive. Not just cars or people window-shopping, like I'd heard about New York City. Buffalo was filled with people on their way somewhere. Coming from jobs probably, since we'd arrived in the afternoon, or going to jobs I guess, if they had the late shift. Buffalo seemed like a place where people worked the late shift.

I don't know how Jake knew where he was going, or if he knew. The lake was north of us, on our left coming into town, and I could see on the map that there was a bridge that went right from the edge of the city and into Canada, crossing the water where the lake narrowed and turned into the river.

The streets were full of cars, and we kept getting caught behind them at red lights, so there was lots of time to look around and figure out where to turn. Jake would take a left turn and head in the direction of the water, and then take a right and drive further east. On the map, it looked like a pretty big bridge, so I thought maybe we'd see it poking up above the buildings.

At one point, we pulled up at a red light beside another VW. We'd driven through a lot of places where we didn't see any other cars, but when we were on busier roads, we usually saw a VW or two. We'd only seen one other camper and that was while we were still out west. It had been painted all over with a swirling colorful design that made me feel a little embarrassed about our plain two-color paint job.

The VW next to us was two-tone like ours, red on the bottom and white on the top, but it wasn't a camper. I could see it was full of stuff: tools, lumber, and small boxes of all sorts of hardware. I guess if we could use a VW as a place to live, someone else could just as easily use one to haul around stuff for work.

We ended up even with it at the stop light, me sitting in the passenger seat, and just a few feet away the driver of the other VW. It felt wrong to just sit there and ignore him. After all, he was driving the same car as us practically, and even though we'd seen a lot of them on our drive cross country, the boxy Volkswagens were still rare compared to all the other cars on the road. So two of them sitting side by side was pretty cool.

I turned and looked at the driver. He wore sawdust-covered overalls and a baseball cap pushed back on his head. He must have seen me out of the corner of his eye or felt like he was being looked at, because he turned and looked back. I raised a hand, making a peace sign, and he raised his own hand, smiled, and waved. Then the light turned green, and we pulled away. The red and white VW took a right at the next intersection, and we kept going straight.

Jake finally found the bridge. Emmie noticed its greenish blue steel girders as we crossed a side street. We made a left turn at the next intersection onto a street that ended in a small park at the base of the bridge. Jake pulled the VW into a parking spot, and we opened the doors and climbed out. None of us really wanted what came next, but we'd also been driving all day and were ready to be outside in the fresh air.

Emmie had left the sliding door open, and after stretching and walking around for a few minutes, the three of us sat down with our legs hanging out the door. We took in the view as the water flowed past in front of us and a line of cars crossed the bridge overhead.

I'd noticed on the map that it was called the Peace Bridge. I wasn't sure when it was built. It looked like it had been there a while. The name seemed hopeful, maybe from another time after a war had ended, or from a time like ours, when peace seemed far away, but was all that we wanted.

Canada was just across the water. It didn't look that far away really. I watched the cars and trucks for a minute and wondered who was in them and where they were going. For most of them, I'm sure crossing the bridge was no big deal. Some of the people, maybe the ones in the trucks, might do it every day, crossing one way, and then crossing back. Easy.

While we were still miles from the city, I tried using the map scale and my finger to measure the length of the bridge. A mile maybe? Probably less. But whatever the distance was on the map, however close it looked across the water, it still felt far away. It was another country, and it would mean a completely different life for Jake.

"Don't go," I stood up and faced him.

"Bets, what are you..."

"Don't go," I said again, cutting Emmie's question short. "Don't go to Canada."

"Bets?" Emmie said slowly after a few seconds of silence. "We talked about it. Jake told us. He told us why he doesn't want to go to Vietnam."

"No," I jumped on top of the word just as it left her mouth so she couldn't say anymore. "I'm not saying you should go to Vietnam. But I don't think you should leave for Canada either. You had to leave your home, now you're leaving your country. I understand you wanting to run away, but that means that you will always, always need to run. Don't let the war make you do that. Don't let it change your life. Stay here and fight it." I was talking in short little sentences like that was all my brain could put together at one time.

Jake just looked at me with his mouth open, like he didn't know what to say. Emmie sat silently, eyes wide, taking in everything I'd said. She was able to speak first. "Bets, Jake has to. He... he could go to jail, Bets."

"Then stay here and hide. Stay with us. Who's going to find you with us? No one even knows where we are."

"Bets, I know you're going to miss him, but.." Emmie said, misunderstanding.

I had to correct her, make her understand. "No, Emmie. It's not about me missing him." I clenched my hands into fists. "It's about one more person's life being changed by the war. Forever, don't you see?" My eyes narrowed with the question. "Whether he goes over to Vietnam and dies like your father or comes back like mine, or runs away to Canada, he'll never have his old life back, ever."

Emmie tensed at the mention of her father, but then I could see her eyes fill with thought, and I knew she got it, that she understood too. My words hung there in the silence, no one really knowing what to say. For what seemed like a long time, there was only the sound of water passing us by in the river and cars crossing the bridge above us.

I sat back down between Emmie and Jake. I tried to let my feet swing, but they only scuffed across the ground and stirred up dust. The three of us sat there taking turns looking at the water, or the bridge, or the ground.

"You could stay," Emmie said in a hesitant voice, like each word required thought and took effort.

"Em..." There was frustration in Jake's voice, even in that single syllable.

She got up and walked away. She was sitting beside me one second, and the next her silhouette was moving off toward the river, not running, but fast enough that her dress and long hair flowed out behind her.

Jake lingered for a second, looking toward Emmie, then at me. There was almost too much to read on his face: the frustration I had heard in his voice, anger toward me and the conflict I raised, a plea for support, but most of all confusion. My expression must have offered no help, a mix of slack-jawed surprise at Emmie's reaction and raised eyebrows that put all the responsibility for what came next on Jake.

He finally stood up in a huff and stomped off toward Emmie. I cringed a little, guessing what sort of reaction that attitude would provoke in Emmie. I wasn't wrong. They'd walked as far away as they could. If they'd gone any farther they would have been splashing in the river, but I could still hear Emmie's voice like she was standing next to me. She shouted, she scolded. I didn't need another reason to admire Emmie, but she gave me one.

Jake's posture immediately changed. He put his hands up defensively and lowered his head a little. The rest of the conversation was low enough that I couldn't hear it. I felt funny just sitting there watching it all, but I didn't want to look away. I wanted to know if he would be staying.

Jake looked like he was trying to explain. At first Emmie just shook her head and crossed her arms in front of her chest; eventually she softened. Her arms dropped. She stopped shaking her head and just looked at Jake. Then she threw her arms around him, and her knees bent, like all her weight hung from Jake's neck.

I watched longer than I should have. I'd already guessed at his decision, and any more time I spent looking at Jake and Emmie was just intruding on their privacy. I knew things weren't going to end the way I wanted, but I needed something, some positive in what suddenly seemed like a completely negative world.

Then Emmie pulled away from Jake. She raised her head a little and Jake lowered his. Then he pulled Emmie toward him and their lips met.

I stood up and turned back toward the VW so I could step up on the rear tire and reach the roof above. I started pulling at the knots in the rope that held my bike to the roof rack, not really knowing why I was doing it, but just needing something else to do.

By the time I was lowering my bike to the ground, Emmie and Jake were walking back toward the VW holding hands. I could see the remnants of tears on Emmie's face, and Jake twisted his face into a forced smile when he noticed me looking at him and then just gave up and lowered his eyes to the ground.

I busied myself with my bike, pushing a thumb into the tire to see if it needed air and brushing road dust off the seat. Emmie put a hand on my shoulder and then pulled me into a hug.

"Jake's going to go, Bets." The words were flat, forced.

"It's... it's the best way," Jake added.

My eyes flicked to Emmie's, and a quick head-shake along with her tight-lipped expression told me that arguing the point was useless.

"We were thinking..." Emmie scuffed her feet and turned to Jake for help.

"We were thinking it might attract less attention if it was just the two of us. Uh... me and Emmie, I mean. You know, so we don't look like a car full of hippies."

I shrugged and looked down at my bike, wondering why I'd instinctively pulled it off the VW while I waited. "Yeah, that's cool," I shrugged. "I get it." I forced myself to say the words as my heart sank. I didn't want to say goodbye at all, and being set aside made it all the worse, even if what Jake had said made sense.

Crossing into Canada wasn't like going to a far away country in Europe of Asia. You didn't even need a passport to go to Canada, but there was still a customs inspection station on the other side of the bridge. Really not much more than a toll both, but someone was there to ask questions. Where are you going? What are you bringing into the country? How long are you staying? Those are easy questions if you're crossing the border to go on vacation or make a delivery, but questions get tricky when the answers are lies.

Jake and Emmie would need some reason for crossing the border. Without me, they were a couple. They could be going to the beach for the day. They could be visiting a friend for the weekend. If I was along, there might be other questions. Was I a younger sister? Where were my parents? Did they know I was leaving the country? I didn't like it, but they'd have an easier time without me.

"It's cool. I have my bike. I'll go exploring." I tried to smile when I said it, but I'm pretty sure my voice gave away how nervous I was. I was far from home. How many miles? I'd lost count. There were times when I felt homesick, when all I wanted was to be with my parents. Through it all, Emmie had been a constant, always there, always calm, always smiling, and now she was leaving me in an unfamiliar city all by myself.

"It'll be okay, Bets." She must have heard the tremor in my voice. "Don't go far, okay? Just find a place to hang out, a diner or something. I'll meet you back here. We won't be long. Just an hour, maybe a little more."

All I could do was nod. I knew this wasn't a plan my parents would like, but I reminded myself that this whole trip, starting with the night I snuck out of their house, wasn't a plan my parents would like, and every mile of the trip had taken me farther from them.

I leaned my bike against the VW and hugged Jake. It's wasn't a hug I wanted to let go of, so I didn't. We both just stood there, arms around each other, not saying anything. I was glad for that. There wasn't anything that Jake could say that I really wanted to hear, and I couldn't think of anything worth saying. Secretly, I knew if I tried to say something, I'd just start crying. Jake gave me one last tighter squeeze, and then his arms drifted away from me. I did the same, not because I wanted to let go, but because I didn't want to feel stupid for hugging him after he'd stopped hugging back.

"This'll be okay, Bets. You'll see," he said with a thin smile on his face.

For a second, I thought he was talking about me being on my own while Emmie took him across the border, and I almost said something about me being totally fine riding my bike around town. I realized just in time that he didn't just mean me, he meant all of it. My crush, Emmie, his going away, everything I was feeling, including the war.

"Yeah, I hope so." I raised a hand to wave, and Jake climbed into the passenger's side of the VW and slid over to the driver's seat. Emmie told me again to stay in the area and assured me she'd be back soon. Then she climbed in.

I watched them drive down the street until they disappeared around a corner. I looked back up at the bridge and thought about waiting until I saw the VW crossing it. Its boxy shape and two-tone paint would be easy to spot. Instead, I hopped on my bike and rode away. There was a postcard in my bag, and I had a mailbox to find.

Parkside

Emmie had told me to stay close to the spot where we'd parked, but after I found a mailbox and dropped in my postcard, I just wanted to keep riding. A lot had happened in the last few days, and it felt good to be out riding with the wind in my face. One street led to another, and before long I was miles from the river. Pedaling my bike all around Forestville delivering groceries had kept me in good shape, and it was easy to cover that distance without much effort.

I did follow Emmie's advice about finding somewhere to eat. The growling in my stomach reminded me to do that at least. I found a place that looked like they made good sandwiches, and then I wandered down the sidewalk, holding my sandwich in one hand and trying to steer my bike with the other as I walked beside it. I wasn't moving very fast, but I didn't care. I really had no place to go and just time to kill until I felt like it was late enough for Emmie to be coming back.

While I was stopped at a crosswalk waiting for the light to change, I looked around at the city that surrounded me. I'd ridden far enough from the center of town that the bigger buildings and busy intersections had faded to streets lined with two or three story buildings, most of them with a shop or restaurant on the first floor and what must have been apartments on the second and third.

A place across the street caught my eye. A sign in curly script traced with pink neon lit up the corner in the late afternoon light. "Parkside" was all it said. The building looked a little shabby around the edges, and I could see the same word painted on the wall, faded and chipped enough that the bare brick was showing through. I wondered about the name and looked around, but didn't see any park. Curiosity got the best of me though, so I crossed the street to check it out.

I leaned my bike up against the wall beside the door. Buffalo felt like it was a place where I could do that and not worry about someone taking it. At least, I wanted it to be a place like that. A bell above the door jingled when I opened it, and I was immediately taken in by my surroundings, the world outside forgotten.

The space was shared between glass-fronted cases of candies and tables full of customers. A few people sat sampling chocolates, but most sipped at milkshakes or held ice cream cones in various stages of melting. I looked around for an empty table but there were none.

The crowd was made up of couples who looked like they were on dates and parents who'd taken their kids out for a treat. I immediately felt self-conscious, looking down at my sandals and torn jeans. I pulled my arms in close, like they could hide my flowing multi-colored shirt and the strings of beads hanging around my neck. I might not have looked like a hippie when we'd started out from California, but a month on the road had soaked into me. I fit right in next to Emmie riding along in the VW, but we hadn't been in a real restaurant since we'd left Parachute, and that one didn't really count.

A couple people looked up. I was probably just imagining it, but it felt like when they turned back to their table, there were whispers and pointing. I was imagining it, I told myself. Who cared what I looked like?

There was a large table by the window that seemed like it was full of college kids. I remembered seeing signs for a university when I was biking, so there must have been one nearby. I thought for a second that one of them might offer me a chair at their table, but then I hoped that they wouldn't. It was easy to see they were years older than me, and I didn't feel like being a kid at the grownups' table.

I stood behind a few people who were already at the counter and waited to order something. I just figured I'd take it outside. Better not leave my bike on the street for too long anyway, I told myself. But it was a pretty cool place. As uncomfortable as I felt, I did want to stay. Being there was a little like stepping back in time. The walls were painted mint green, the arched ceiling was carved in intricate designs, and all the tables and chairs looked like they could have been antiques, except they were perfectly clean and neat. Most of all, it was the smell that made me want to stay. The air was filled with chocolate. I took a deep breath through my nose and savored the smell.

I turned around slowly while keeping my place in line, taking everything in. My eyes settled on a boy at a table in the very back of the shop. The half-round booth was set into the wall, and a small, circular table was pushed up close to its curved seat. I guess I didn't notice it at first, but once I did, it seemed like the little curved booth was the focal point of the whole place, almost like it was there first and the rest of the ice cream shop had been built around it. It was small, really just big enough for a couple. Two people in the curved seat would end up sitting next to each other rather than on opposite sides of the table, and maybe that's what most people wanted. Couples on dates surely came through the doors on Friday nights hoping to find it empty, but it probably never was.

As full as the shop was, the boy was sitting there all alone. A boy? That wasn't quite right. He was older than me for sure. Emmie's age? Maybe, but probably younger. He didn't seem as old as the college kids sitting at the table by the window.

He looked out of place, like he didn't quite fit. It wasn't just the size of the booth or the odd curve of the cushioned seat. I had a feeling the boy would have looked out of place wherever he was. His elbows stuck out on either side of him at awkward angles, and he moved his hands from table to knees to lap like he was searching for a comfortable place for them that he never quite found. He stuck out his neck a little and tipped his head to one side like he was ducking under a low ceiling, even though it was far above his head.

I giggled a little, and quickly put my hand to my mouth when I caught myself, hoping he hadn't heard me. If I had seen him in the school cafeteria while I was sitting with my friends, I probably would have had the same reaction. But I was a long way from the school cafeteria. Instead, my giggle turned into a smile, as I twirled one of my necklaces. He was cute in spite of his awkward elbows and the funny way he tilted his head—or maybe because of it.

He was cute. Or he would have been I guess, if his expression wasn't so serious, like he was thinking about things way more important than the things people normally thought about in ice cream parlors. I caught myself wishing I could see him smile or laugh or talk, so I'd know what his face was like when it wasn't so serious. I gave myself time to wonder what he was thinking and why he was sitting all by himself, while I tried to look like I was doing something other than watching him.

I looked longer than I should have, and when he shifted in his seat, he caught me staring. I looked away too late and tried to act interested in the carvings on the ceiling and then strained to see the list of ice cream flavors on the counter at the front of the line. But after a minute, my eyes drifted back and I caught him staring at me, or maybe we caught each other staring.

"Miss?" he called and raised his hand before I could look away again. I'd never been called Miss before. Not ever. He pointed toward the empty space next to him in the booth and then his eyebrows raised a little bit in an expression that was both inviting and shy at the same time. When I didn't respond, he stood up and took a few quick steps toward me. During one of those steps, my eyes flicked toward the front doors and my mind raced toward them. But instead of running away, I took a step forward.

"There's room in my booth. Uh, I mean in the booth. If you'd like to sit. You look tired." I felt my face flush and looked down again at what I was wearing, comparing it to his neatly pressed pants and collared shirt. "Sorry, I just meant you could sit, if you want to... with me. If you want." He spoke in a voice that seemed too loud for the space we were in, like he could make up for what he'd said by the volume of his apology.

"Hi, I'm Bets," I smiled and held out my hand, figuring I could dwell on his awkward invitation and my shabby appearance, or I could appreciate a kind gesture and enjoy some pleasant company in the nicest seat in the shop.

"William. I mean—uh—I'm William." He took my hand and shook it. "Or Bill, friends call me Bill. Mostly, they do. You could, if you wanted to."

"Hi, Bill. My name's really Elizabeth, but I like when friends call me Bets." I hesitated, wondering if he'd understood. "So, you should call me that too," I added, and then I smiled. He relaxed a little and smiled back, gesturing toward the booth.

"If you want to sit there, we better go back before someone else grabs it." I nodded, and he led the way, stepping aside to let me slide in first and then sitting down next to me. There weren't really menus, just a list of ice cream flavors. I scanned it for a minute or two, trying to think of what to say next.

When a girl from behind the counter came over to take our order, I asked for marshmallow fudge and Bill ordered chocolate. He wrinkled his nose a little at my order, and I kicked him under the table. He cried out in surprise, but he wasn't really hurt and we both ended up laughing. What started out as awkward, somehow, suddenly felt comfortable and sort of fun.

I caught myself wondering if all dates started out feeling awkward. I pushed the idea out of my mind, but not fast enough to keep a warm blush from rising on my cheeks. We weren't really on a date, were we? Was that what he was thinking when he invited me to sit with him? I looked across the table at Bill and tried again to guess his age. He was older than me, but not that much older. I tried to imagine seeing him at school or walking down the street in Forestville, wondering if I would pay any attention, wondering if I'd sit down with him if he'd called me over to a table at Sonny's. But Forestville felt far away. It was far away, and Bill was sitting right there next to me.

When the ice cream came we ate a few bites in silence, and then because I didn't really know what else to say, I started talking about our drive cross country. I didn't tell him everything. I left Seth out of the story, even though he was a big part of everything that had happened since I left home. I just wasn't ready to talk about him, wasn't ready to relive those parts yet, and certainly not with someone I'd just met.

Bill listened with an expression of wonder on his face. He let me talk without interrupting, only slipping in an occasional "Wow!" when I said something that impressed him. Then when I'd said all I had to say, he asked, "So you just left home?" like he'd gotten stuck on the first thing I'd told him and hadn't heard the rest.

"Yeah, I just left. I told you..." I immediately felt defensive, like I had to explain my reasons for leaving.

He put a hand up. "No, I get it. It sounds like you had some good reasons. It's just, it had to be... it must be hard being away from home." I just looked at him. I tilted my head and my eyes narrowed a little. There was something to his reaction. Something more than surprise at the story I'd told.

"So what's your story?" I leaned back in the booth and crossed my arms in front of my chest. His eyes caught mine and then looked away, but I didn't let him get away with it. I looked at him until he looked back, and then he started talking.

"I'm going to Vietnam, Bets. That's my story." And that's all he said for a little while. I just sat there, wondering if he was going to give me more or just leave it at that. I would have understood if that's all he had to say. It seems like most boys who got called up felt like that was the end of their story—at least their mothers did.

"My father fought in Germany, World War II. He doesn't talk much about it. I asked him a few times when I was young. Stupid questions. Was he scared? Did he kill anyone? Questions that seemed like good ones to a kid, until you realize that everyone in a war is scared, and everyone probably kills someone or gets killed. My father's got a uniform hanging in a closet somewhere. He used to pull it out on Veterans Day and for parades. I don't think it fits him anymore, because he doesn't ride in parades now. He just stands on the sidewalk watching.

"I'm proud of my father. Don't get me wrong. I learned about the war in school, read the books. I know it was a big deal. I know it was war we had to fight, and I'm proud of him for fighting it. Just not sure I'm ready to fight in this one."

He didn't say anything for a minute, and I tried to think of something to break the silence. "So, when's your birthday?" It was just a random question, something to fill the empty space of no one talking, or maybe I was still wondering about his age and if he was much older than me. But I wanted to take it back as soon as I'd said it. There was a draft lottery planned that would assign people a number based on their birth dates, and people were already talking about which dates might end up being the unlucky ones, meaning the ones that would send boys to war the soonest. Given the circumstances, it was the stupidest question I could have asked.

"My birthday doesn't matter, Bets. I signed up."

My heart sank.

After a couple days on the road with Jake, I couldn't imagine just volunteering to go, but then I remembered my father. He didn't volunteer necessarily, but he went willingly because it was his job, his duty. I wrestled with that thought while Bill continued. "Guys are getting drafted, I know. My number probably would have come up anyway sooner or later. I'm the right age. I'm healthy. But I was going to college. That would have kept me out of the war I guess, but it didn't feel right. The way my Dad would look at me, ask me questions about what I was learning in school, what sort of job I thought I'd get. Then he'd talk about what he was seeing on the news, which was mostly about the war."

He must have seen the shock on my face and shook his head quickly. "Oh, he didn't make me sign up or guilt me into doing it. It was my decision, but thinking about my father and what he'd done in World War II helped me see what I had to do. So I dropped out, and signed up."

I had a million questions but I didn't ask any of them. I thought of my father, going away to war because it was just part of his job. I wondered what he would think of Bill's decision and what he'd think of me helping someone leave the country because he didn't want to fight. I thought of mentioning Jake, thought of telling Bill that there was another way, a choice that didn't mean fighting in a war, but I didn't.

Instead I reached across the table, found his hand, and held it. I said something. I don't remember what. It couldn't possibly have been the right thing. What do you say to someone who's going away to war? Somehow, my father going away was different. He was older. He was an adult. Adults did things like fighting in wars. Kids didn't. At least, they weren't supposed to.

We just kept sitting there holding hands across the table. Dishes were cleared. The check was brought. Bill paid. I let him. Out of the corner of my eye, I saw the waitress watching us. There were people waiting for the table probably. So, we finally stood up and walked toward the door.

I waved Bill out and held up a finger letting him know I'd just be a minute. I stopped by the counter and grabbed a pen and a pad the waitresses used to take orders. One of the girls looked at me surprised, but I didn't care. I scribbled something on the top sheet, tore it off and stepped outside.

Bill was standing on the corner looking up at the Parkside sign. I stepped up to him and slipped the piece of paper into his hand. He unfolded it, read what I had written, and then looked at me, confused.

My parents' address. My address. I hadn't thought about it when I was writing it down, but it sank in by the time I was stepping out onto the sidewalk. I'd spent the last month driving away from home. We were almost to our destination, but then what? We'd listen to some music and have some fun. And then? And then we'd go home. I left home. I desperately needed to get away from home, but I was never really running away from home. I knew that after this trip, I'd be going home again, and that meant dealing with all the things I'd been trying to get away from. I knew all that, but putting my address on a piece of paper made it real.

"Write me."

And then I kissed him. I don't really know why. Maybe it was because I'd seen Jake and Emmie kiss, and wanted the same. Maybe it was because Bill was leaving, and I was leaving, and there was only a little bit of time left. Maybe it was because he was cute in an awkward sort of way. Or maybe kisses didn't need reasons.

It was just a quick kiss, but while it was still happening I already wanted another. I pulled away, or he pulled away, or I guess we both did. We were just far enough apart that I could look him in the eyes.

"Don't die, okay?" Bill looked at me with confusion in his eyes. He scowled a little, but there was a half smile on his face. Maybe from what I'd just said, or maybe from the kiss. "Write me while you're over there, okay? And don't die. And come back, and..."

"And?" Bill turned my sentence into a question. I didn't really know. There didn't need to be a next or a what if. At the moment, all I wanted was for him to come home again. I couldn't bare the idea of someone I knew dying, even if it was someone I'd only just met.

"Just come home safe. I want to know when you're home again." He just looked at me like he was still sifting through everything. I guess that was understandable since less than an hour ago, he was sitting at a table by himself figuring out what flavor ice cream to order. "Write me, okay? And come home again. Please?"

The urgency in my voice snapped him out of whatever thoughts he was having. "Yeah, I mean, yes. Yes, I'll write you. I would really like that, and I'll do my best to come home again." I thought of my father on the day he left, not promising to come home, but promising to do his best. That seemed like a very careful choice of words and a very grown-up promise, too grown-up for the boy standing in front of me.

I kissed him again. It was different than the first time. The thrill of a first kiss had passed, but without that in the way, it was somehow more exciting. It was almost like wanting the first kiss was mixed up in wanting something I'd never had before, and with the second, I just wanted to kiss and be kissed. I don't really know what to say about the third kiss, or the fourth, or fifth. They mostly just blended together.

I finally took a step back, not really wanting to. Bill took a step forward, but I took another step back. Common sense told me that there wasn't really any other way for things to end. He was still going away to a war. I was still, sooner or later, going home.

I walked the few steps over to my bike, rolling it away from where it had been leaning against the wall. I threw one leg over it and turned to face Bill. I felt better on the bike, like I was ready to say goodbye, ready to leave even though I didn't want to. "Write me," I fixed my eyes on him, and he returned my gaze, nodding. Then I pushed my foot down on a pedal and rolled down the sidewalk.

Painting

Emmie was angry when I got back. She was already there, waiting by the river. Had she been there a long time? How long had I been gone? I had no idea; I'd totally lost track of time. The sun had set. It was still light out, sort of, but the sky was starting to have a nighttime look. I had been too distracted to notice as I biked back to the river and thought about everything that had happened, but Emmie's face told me how badly I'd messed up.

There were questions before I even rolled to a stop. Where was I? Why was I so late? What was I thinking? I answered them all with a shrug. I knew there were no answers to the first questions that were a good enough excuse, and the answer to the last question was easy. I wasn't thinking.

Apologies streamed from my mouth. What I said wasn't nearly as important as how I looked. My face, my whole body said I was sorry. I wasn't faking it. I knew I'd screwed up and was really sorry about it.

There was silence after I'd said everything I could think to say. Emmie looked like she still wanted to be angry, still wanted to yell at me and ask me questions that didn't really have answers. Instead, she just looked at me, silent, pleading. And then I realized that only part of what she was feeling was panic and anger over my being late. Under that was something else. I'd left her alone when what she needed most was to be with a friend.

"I kissed a boy." The words fell out of my mouth. I'm not sure I would have said anything if I thought at all about it. Emmie was upset about Jake leaving. How was my story any comfort? But I felt like those few words summed up the whole time she had been gone, made my excuses for being so late, and inserted something positive and hopeful into an otherwise depressing situation.

"What?" Emmie said with laugh in her voice. She sat down in the VW's open sliding door and called me over, patting the space next to her. I knew that telling any less than the whole story was not an option.

We talked late into the night. First me telling Emmie all about meeting Bill, ice cream, and first kisses. Then she told me about crossing into Canada and Jake leaving. Neither story was anything to be happy about, other than the two of us being back together and now having something else in common.

We ate. We went to bed. At some point while I was falling asleep, I heard Emmie crying. I put a hand on her shoulder so she'd know I was there, awake, ready to listen.

But there wasn't really anything left to say. We'd already talked about all of it. It seemed silly, sort of. Emmie had just met Jake a few days ago. How could his leaving be so upsetting? But I still understood. I eventually fell asleep. I'm pretty sure Emmie was awake long into the night.

☮ ☮ ☮

Waking to sunlight drifting through the window screens of the camper pop-top now felt normal, part of a routine, like it had always been. My arm immediately shifted toward Emmie's side of the bed and found it empty. That wasn't really a surprise. Neither was finding her meditating by the river's edge after I'd lowered myself from the bed and emerged from the sliding door. I made breakfast and smiled a hello to her once she unfolded her legs and returned from the river.

After we'd eaten, we packed everything away in the cupboards, collapsed the pop-top, and tied my bike to the roof. Again, these things felt like a routine that had always been, and there was comfort in that. We were away from home, and somehow at the same time, doing the same things day after day made the VW feel like it was our home.

We were on the road before the sun was high enough in the sky to be seen over the buildings that hugged the river. I unfolded the map and traced the route we'd need to take to Woodstock. It seemed like such a short distance compared to what we'd already covered. I placed my finger along the map's distance scale to estimate the miles—a few hundred. That seemed like nothing. We'd crossed mountains, a desert, plains, practically the whole country. We only had one state left to cross.

I looked up from the map and watched the city roll by. Parked by the river, we'd only been a few blocks and a couple turns from the highway, so I was surprised that the view out the VW's big front window showed we were in the middle of the city with no highway in sight. Emmie took a turn here and there like she knew where she was going, but after a few turns, it was easy to see that she didn't.

"We going somewhere?" I asked, trying for a sleepy sounding voice that made it seem like I didn't really care.

"Yeah," was the only response I got. After a few more turns, Emmie leaned out the window at a red light and talked to someone in the car next to us. I couldn't really hear, but her turns seemed to be more deliberate after that, and I felt more like we had a destination and less like we were lost. Emmie finally pulled the VW over to the side of the street in front of a small store that looked like it sold nothing but paint and painting supplies.

"We need some paint?" I asked, trying to sound only mildly interested.

"Yeah," was again the only response.

When Emmie climbed out her door, I did the same. I waited on the sidewalk until she rounded the front of the VW and then followed her into the store. She had a quick conversation with a man behind the counter, and then walked down an aisle pulling different colored cans off the shelves. I didn't even bother asking questions. Whatever

Emmie was up to, I'd find out eventually. Emmie ended up back at the counter with an armful of cans and a few brushes.

She put a handful of bills on the counter. It was less than I expected after seeing the load of paint she was buying, but it still seemed like a lot of money to be spending on something that until a few minutes ago I didn't know we needed. We'd made a good amount of money working for a week in Parachute, and we'd been careful about spending less and not wasting food. We were hoping to get to Woodstock early and avoid stopping in another town to work, but now I wasn't so sure.

Emmie pocketed the change, and the man behind the counter loaded the cans into two boxes. I stepped up and grabbed one before Emmie had a chance to struggle with both. She thanked me for the help, nodded at the man behind the counter, and then headed out the door. We set the boxes down on the floor of the VW, closed the sliding door, and hopped in. I still had no idea what we were doing.

Emmie pulled back into traffic and once again seemed to be deciding which turn to take as she came to each intersection. I went along with it the first time and put up with the detour to the paint store, figuring she had a good reason for all of it, but I'd reached my limit. Something was going on, and I needed to know what.

"Hey, Em? What are we doing? What's up with all the paint?" Emmie seemed like she was thinking about what to say, but there was only silence between one intersection and the next. So I asked another question that lumped all the others into one. "Is something wrong?"

Emmie shrugged and took her eyes off the road long enough to turn and look over at me. Then she turned back to the road. "Yeah, Bets, so many things. Think of all that's happened to us, just since we left California."

I didn't know what to say, so I said nothing and instead did exactly what she'd asked me to do. We had had a lot happen to us. I thought back to the day Emmie's letter arrived with the Woodstock ticket and an invitation to join her. I had no idea what the trip would be like, but I certainly didn't expect some of the things that had happened. Would I have gone if I'd known? I hoped so. Because the truth was, the trip came with a lot of good things as well. But I got Emmie's point.

"Ok, I get it. We've been through a lot." I paused, ready to catalog everything out loud, but I knew I didn't really need to. "So do you want to tell me about the paint?"

She laughed, and the sound of it immediately made me feel better. "You didn't think we were going to roll into Woodstock looking like every other VW on the road did you?" My mouth hung open, but it all made sense. I thought back to the other camper we'd seen while crossing the desert. Once Emmie put the idea in my head, I was actually surprised we'd made it this far across the country without painting the VW.

"What are we going to paint on it?"

Emmie shrugged again, but this time it felt different. The first time had made me feel like the answer to my question was obvious, like it wasn't worth asking. This shrug made me feel like my question had limitless answers. "Whatever we want," Emmie said with a smile.

I hadn't been paying attention to where Emmie was driving since we'd started talking, but somehow we ended up back at the little riverside park near the bridge. We climbed out of the VW, pulled out the boxes of paint, and spread them out on the ground. I helped Emmie shake each one to mix it, and then we pried off the lids.

It was an amazing palette spread out in front of us. I couldn't think of a color that wasn't there among the little glossy circles of paint that filled the cans to the edge. The effect was doubled by the the lids we'd set to the side. The flat empty side of the VW in front of us was a stark contrast, inviting us to cover it in color. I picked up a brush and tried to decide which color to start with.

"Wait!" I was surprised by the urgency in Emmie's voice. "There's more to this than just painting a picture, Bets. It's about all that stuff we've been through, all the things that have happened to us." I must have looked confused, paused with a paintbrush in my hand, mid-step toward the paint cans.

"Meditation's good for dealing with all the stuff that comes our way, letting go of thoughts that would otherwise create stress or distraction, but it can only do so much. At some point, you need another way to deal with it, a way to let go. Some people blow off steam by getting angry or drinking or drugs. They think that works, but it really doesn't. Other people take the feelings that are bothering them, the stuff that's making them worry or stress out, and they put it into art, writing, poetry, painting, sculpture. When someone is really good at doing that, you can see their feelings in what they created. But people seeing it afterwards isn't really the point. The important part is letting the feelings out."

With that, Emmie picked up a brush and a can of brightly colored paint, and walked to the other side of the VW. I stood speechless, more than a little embarrassed at how carelessly I was about to start splashing paint around. So I thought about what she said, thought about our trip, about why I'd wanted to make the trip in the first place. Then I dipped my brush in a color and started painting.

Emmie walked back to my side a few times to exchange colors. We both stopped occasionally to wash out brushes. Without really talking about it, we both somehow decided the cans of paint would be easier for both of us to get to if they were at the back of the VW. We didn't move them all at once, just picked them up from my side, used them, and then set them down in the new spot.

We worked for a long time. It was morning when we started, but the sun was getting low in the sky when I began to feel like I was finished. Neither of us had walked around the VW to see what the other was painting. Maybe we didn't want to show our own work until it was finished and figured the other felt the same, or maybe we were just too focused on painting to think about what the other was doing. Whatever the reason, we stayed on our sides except for a few short breaks we took back by the paint cans.

I was putting the final touches on my painting when Emmie stepped around the corner. We must have finished at the same time. I stepped back so I could see the whole side of the VW at once, and Emmie joined me.

To someone watching the VW drive by, my side would have simply looked like a sea of flowers, and that's what I wanted. They were every color and burst out all over. Leafy vine-like stems curled from front to back and crawled up the space between the windows to sprout flowers along the edge where the side of the VW met the roof. But there was more to it than that. On the bottom edge, the paint grew darker, like the flowers and leaves were shadowing it. That's where I'd hidden all the stuff that had been bothering me. I didn't really care whether people noticed. It was there that silhouettes of soldiers marched toward a battle, an endless column of army trucks drove toward war, and a thin white figure pulled a knife on black man who helplessly raised his hands.

You'd never be able to take it all in just watching the VW drive by. To see it all, you'd need to stand in front of the painting long enough to notice the details, because there was even more to the painting. The flowers had thin roots that snuck in twisting circles around the figures of the soldiers, built up roadblocks in front of the army trucks, and stood ready to entangle the knife wielder before he could do any harm. Taken all together, it was easy to see that the flowers were choking out the darkness that lurked below in their shadows.

I knew what Emmie was going to say before she said it. "Cool," she nodded and smiled. "Yeah, cool." We stood there for a couple minutes just looking. Emmie walked closer and crouched down to take a more careful look at the figures at the bottom of my painting, then she craned her neck to look up at the flowers towering above her. She nodded again as she turned around and looked at me, "Cool."

Then Emmie led me around to her side. I made myself take a few steps away from the VW before turning around to see it. I wanted to be able to take it in all at once. Then I turned and soaked in the scene in front of me.

Emmie had filled the big square sliding door with faces. They we all facing toward the back of the VW. Behind them, on the passenger side door, billowing clouds seemed to blow toward them, and the faces' long hair streamed out as if caught by the wind. The hair was painted with such detail that it really did seem like it was blowing in the wind, and when the VW was traveling down the road, I was certain that people would look twice, tricked by the illusion of motion Emmie had created.

Toward the far back, more faces hovered, their hair also blowing, some of it long enough to wrap around the back corner. Between the two groups of faces, there was empty space, except for a thin graceful bridge, its arches connecting one side with the other—or I suppose, depending on how you looked at it, separating them. I looked over my shoulder at the painted bridge's twin, the one Emmie had driven across with Jake just the day before.

I looked again at the faces. One of the ones in back had to be Jake, another was probably Emmie's dad. Some others I didn't know. Maybe they were grandparents. It was easy to pick out Emmie on the other side of the bridge, and me. Some others I could guess at. Her mom had to be one of them. Just like I'd done, Emmie had woven meaning into her painting. She was separated from some people that were important to her.

A few steps toward Emmie's painting revealed the same careful detail I'd hidden in my own. The hair of all the people in the painting was actually tiny vines, each individual hair sprouting leaves all along its length. And flying among the vines and leaves were even tinier butterflies.

"Em, this is beautiful, absolutely wonderful." She was covered in paint—her clothes, her face—but she smiled as her eyes slowly moved from one side of the painting to the other. "Did it help? You know... with, getting your feelings out?"

"Yeah, I'm cool." She nodded. Then she stepped forward and revealed one more hidden treasure in her painting. She opened the sliding door. As the big square door moved backward, it started to cover the back half of the painting. Slowly the bridge disappeared and the faces on the door moved closer to the ones in the back corner, and then the door stopped. The bridge and the empty gap between the faces was gone. The two groups were joined, and even the hair seemed to tangle together.

I laughed at the surprise and at the perfection of it all. "Emmie, it's magical!" I hugged her and then just stood back and admired what she'd done.

We started gathering up the cans of paint, and then realized that the front and back of the VW looked plain and boring compared to the sides. The paint and brushes came out again and we worked together painting the front and then took care of the back. There was only fun in the painting, no hidden meanings, no feelings to pour out, except for whatever we we feeling at the moment. Joy, happiness, friendship, mixed in with a bit of silly. More than once, a loaded paint brush was flicked by one of us toward the other.

When we were finally done, most of the paint cans were empty. We gathered those up into one box and put the ones that still had paint left in the other. I took the empties to a garbage can while Emmie put the box of leftover paint in the back of the VW. Maybe someone would show up at Woodstock with a car in need of painting. I smiled at the thought.

As I walked back to the VW, Emmie called me over to her. I was surprised when she sat down next to the front wheel instead of sitting in the open sliding door, but I sat down next to her anyway. She reached a hand into her bag and pulled out a bottle opener. She seemed to have everything she needed in there, and I often wondered how she managed to carry all of it around with her since the bag rested on her shoulder so effortlessly.

Emmie stuck the bottle opener under the edge of the front wheel's shiny round hubcap and wiggled it around, prying at it in one place and then moving to another spot and prying there. I was about to ask what she was doing when the metal disk popped off and fell to the ground with a clang.

Something else fell from behind the hubcap when it came off, and Emmie picked it up. A small bag. It looked like it was made of leather with a drawstring that pulled it closed. Emmie played with it in her hands, letting it slip from finger to finger and fall from one hand to the other. I couldn't help but lean in closer with curiosity when she finally held the bag in one hand and tugged the drawstring with the other.

When it finally opened, sand poured out of the bag and sifted through Emmie's fingers. I was full of questions. What was the bag even doing behind the hubcap? How had it gotten there, and what was it? Just a bag filled with sand? The flow of sand out of the bag slowed to a trickle until only a dusting was left on Emmie's hand. Then something else slid out.

It caught the sun as Emmie moved it in her hand, then she reached out and dropped it into mine. Somehow I knew what it was as soon as I held it. It was smooth, like it had been polished, and it was translucent, almost clear. It had an irregular shape, like parts of it had been thicker or thinner, and I could still remember where the sharp edges had been. It was the piece from the broken glass, the one that I had dropped on the kitchen floor on a day that seemed like years ago but suddenly felt like only yesterday.

"Where did you? How...?" I remembered Emmie keeping the glass after it had fallen from my bike basket and hit me in the head. Keeping it when all I wanted to do was throw it away. What had she said that day? There's a weight to it. And something about not throwing away a bad memory.

So Emmie had hidden it away. I'd forgotten about it, and at some point she'd snuck it into the little bag filled with sand. For thousands of miles it had been tossed around, spinning, falling, turning inside the hubcap as we rolled down highways and crossed the country, the sand rubbing against its edges and wearing them smooth. It was beautiful. It was amazing. But what was the point? It just brought back a memory I'd been trying to forget.

"My old memory come back to haunt me?" I raised the polished glass and let its surface catch the sun, admiring it, enjoying the smooth feel of it on my fingertips, but also wanting to toss it into the river.

"Don't you get it, Bets? Memories change over time. The parts that hurt the most start to hurt a little bit less. You don't forget that they hurt, but you eventually start to heal. The sharp edges get worn smooth, and you're left with something that reminds you of all the good parts, even if they were mixed in with the bad."

With that she stood up and left me sitting on the ground turning the piece of glass over and over in my hands, remembering the sharp edges and jagged points and running my fingertips over what was left, smooth and beautiful.

Dirty Hippies

5 E, 90 E

Driving in the newly painted VW, I felt like we attracted attention wherever we went. People turned their heads as we rolled through small towns and cars beeped their horns as we cruised down the highway. I didn't feel self conscious about it; I soaked it in.

Maybe some of the adults back home thought I was a hippie before I left, but if we drove through Forestville in the VW now, there would have been no question, and it wasn't just because of the new paint job.

I'd been a little embarrassed standing in the ice cream shop, but now that seemed silly. I was who I was. I liked how my favorite skirt hung on my hips and drifted in the wind as I walked. Back home, I never went a day without brushing my hair morning and night. Now, I could hardly even remember where my brush was. My hair was longer than it had ever been. Putting tiny braids into it gave me something to do on long stretches of highway, and Emmie sometimes did the same while we sat by the fire at night, feeding strands of hair into little beads and then entwining them in braids. More beads hung around my neck and wrapped around my wrists on thin leather laces.

I'd taken a thin wire from a broken necklace and carefully wrapped it around the piece of glass that Emmie had given back to me. A piece of leather fed through a loop in the wire turned it into a necklace, and it now hung from my neck. Emmie was right; it did have a weight to it that couldn't just be thrown away. But its smooth edges were comforting against my skin.

Spring had turned into summer while we were on the road, and I left my window rolled down most of the time. I'd wave to passing cars that beeped and then stretch my arm out the window holding a peace sign high above for them to see. Not all the cars that beeped were happy to see us. Sometimes my peace sign met with angry faces, shouts, or hand gestures that were not peaceful at all. But most of the time people smiled and flashed back peace signs of their own.

When we rolled into a town, people paused to look as we passed, and lots of times there'd be a small group of people standing around wherever we stopped for food or gas. Sometimes people would just stand there and smile at the paint job we'd given the VW, and sometimes they'd gawk at us or say an awkward hello just to be polite. More than once people asked if we were heading to Woodstock. I got excited just hearing the question, knowing we were finally close enough that people assumed that's where we were headed.

Some towns were different.

"Dirty hippies!" someone shouted from behind us as we walked along the sidewalk looking for a place to eat. My breath caught in my chest, but my legs kept walking on autopilot, mostly because I was too afraid to turn around.

"Hey! Talkin' to you!"

Emmie stopped and turned. I didn't want to, but I did the same. I wasn't going to keep walking without her, and I wasn't going to leave her by herself. She stood there with her hands on her hips, angry, defiant, daring the voice to say more. There were more than a few people behind us. Not enough to make a crowd, but enough that I felt intimidated standing there just the two of us. So Emmie's stance was impressive in every way. I tried to mimic it but was certain I'd failed miserably.

"You hippies don't want people fighting to protect our country?" It was the same voice as before, but now it had a face. I'd heard that argument before, but I never understood it. The soldiers we were sending to Vietnam were fighting to keep the North Vietnamese from taking over South Vietnam, but I was pretty sure the North Vietnamese wouldn't be piling into boats to cross the ocean and attack the United States any time soon. So when people talked about soldiers protecting our country, I didn't get it.

The group was mostly boys, older than me but probably still in high school. Not old enough to be drafted, but maybe some of them had brothers in the war, or fathers? Blue jeans and t-shirts seemed to be the dress of choice. Not a tie-dye or beaded necklace to be found.

"Just peace and love for you two, huh?" This was a new voice. The comment was followed by snickers and a couple loud laughs.

"Something wrong with Americans fighting for what's right?" This from a girl who stepped forward and pointed an accusing finger at us.

"No, nothing wrong with it," Emmie said in a voice that was calmer than I could believe, since I was ready to jump out of my skin. My eyes had been darting here and there since I turned around, trying to figure out where we could run to if things went from bad to worse. There wasn't much around, and I didn't see anyone else on the street. But once Emmie spoke, my eyes jumped back and forth between her and the faces of the crowd gathered in front of us.

"My father fought for what people are saying is right," Emmie continued, "and he died for it." A couple faces in the crowd dropped a little, and a few others suddenly became interested in something across the street or up in the tree branches. "Her father was in Vietnam too." Emmie jerked a thumb toward me but never took her eyes off the girl who'd spoken last. "You're right, we don't really want people fighting, especially if it means more people dying. And yes, we'd be happy with a little bit more peace and love in the world."

With that, Emmie turned around and continued down the sidewalk. I hesitated long enough to see the group's reactions and then turned as well, leaving behind stunned silence.

We'd walked half a block when I heard a voice calling at us again. "Hey! Hey, stop!"

We didn't.

"Hey, wait up," the voice again, this time a little closer. Our steps slowed, and out of curiosity I turned and looked over my shoulder. It was the girl who'd stepped forward and pointed accusingly at us. I nudged Emmie and then turned around and stopped.

"Hey, sorry," the girl said in a puffing breath as she caught up to us. "That wasn't right, what we did back there. Sorry for how my friends acted. Sorry about what I said."

"Thanks," Emmie kept walking a few steps, like it wasn't a conversation worth stopping for. She had changed too since we'd been on the road. If the confrontation on the sidewalk had happened a month ago, I think she would have welcomed the girl and her apology with open arms, introduced herself, and sat down to listen as the girl told her story. But now I wasn't so sure. Emmie had been through a lot. Enough that her always friendly, always positive attitude was a bit of a surprise, one that I hadn't really been able to figure out but admired just the same. So if she let that positive attitude slip occasionally and didn't want to make friends with a stranger who'd insulted her just minutes ago, I got it. But after a few steps, she stopped and turned, not saying anything, but ready to listen if the girl said more.

"My brother's over there." I let out a sigh. There were lots of brothers and fathers and husbands over there, but it was never easy to meet someone with family in Vietnam. "I guess that's why I said what I did. I don't like people saying things that make me feel like what my brother's doing is wrong." I knew how she felt, but I stayed silent. Something told me this was between Emmie and the girl. Emmie didn't say anything either, and for a minute there was an uncomfortable silence. "Did your father really get killed?"

"Yeah."

Another silence. "Sorry about your dad. I don't really like that people are going over there to fight. I... mostly I'd just like my brother home again."

"Yeah," Emmie said with a far-away look in her eyes, "I hope your brother comes home safe." Then she raised a hand in a wave, turned back the way we were heading, and continued down the sidewalk. I smiled an uncomfortable smile at the girl, feeling guilty somehow for already having my father back home with me and then leaving home to get away from him. Then I said goodbye and caught up with Emmie.

Daisy Cutter

90 E, 28 S

We heard the motorcycle long before we saw it. We'd set up camp in a quiet spot beside a small road we'd followed off the highway. It was easier again to find places to camp. We'd left the bigger cities along the Great Lakes behind. I'm not sure if Buffalo counted as big city, but it seemed like once we'd left there, we were in the country again. There were mostly farms on either side of the highway and miles and miles between towns, which also meant I got to drive again.

The empty, wide-open spaces made it easy to hear the motorcycle. If we'd stood still and listened carefully, maybe we could have heard the sound of trucks back on the highway, but I'd driven a while before Emmie pointed to a spot that looked good. The motorcycle was closer than the highway, too loud to be that far away, and it was getting louder.

I don't really know why I paid attention. Sure, it was easy to notice in the quiet, but I could have just gone back to getting dinner ready. Instead I stopped, and I listened. I looked at Emmie, and she was already looking over at me to see if I'd noticed. Lots of people rode motorcycles, so it didn't really make sense for us to worry. But I had seen a newspaper story about motorcycle gangs and the trouble they were causing in some cities, and I'd heard about a big concert near San Francisco where a motorcycle gang was in charge of security and ended up beating up a bunch of people when things got out of hand in the audience.

We'd seen a few groups of motorcycles as we crossed the country. I guess they were gangs. What makes a group a gang? Maybe there was a better word for it. One gang was so big, it reminded me of the army trucks passing us by. We had stood and watched as motorcycle after motorcycle thundered by us. The men riding them looked intimidating, dressed in black leather and torn blue jeans, some wearing sleeveless shirts and showing arms covered in tattoos. The field we were in suddenly felt very far away from any place we could get help if we needed it.

There was no question the sound of the motorcycle was getting closer, and I figured it had to be on the same road we'd taken. I looked expectantly at Emmie, wondering if maybe we should do something. Get in the VW and lock the doors, maybe drive farther off the road so we wouldn't be seen, or just get in and drive away.

We were in the middle of making dinner. She'd stopped cutting up vegetables and tilted her head, one ear turned toward the approaching motorcycle. The sound grew louder and louder, until it seemed like the motorcycle should be right on top of us, but I looked down the road and still didn't see anything. Then it came around a turn, leaning into it, faster than I'd want to go on just two wheels.

I held my breath as it roared by, filling the air with aggressive rumbling. We were just standing beside the VW, right where we were when we first heard the sound, like we were frozen there. I tried to make myself small, willing the rider not to see us, not to pay any attention, to just keep going. And he did. I emptied my lungs in one long sigh and looked at Emmie. She only raised her eyebrows, which could have meant anything, and then went back to chopping vegetables.

The sound of the motorcycle was fading into the distance, but then it changed. Now that I was driving, I was more aware of all the sounds an engine made. There was the higher pitched whining when it was time to shift to a higher gear, the low grumbling that told me I'd shifted too soon, and the puttering that came when I took my foot off the gas pedal and the engine started slowing down. That was the sound I heard from the motorcycle.

The sound of the rumbling engine changed to a putt, putt, putt like it was barely getting enough gas to stay running, and then it revved again and got louder. He was coming back.

I watched Emmie's eyes shoot down the road and then toward the open sliding door of the VW. I could see her calculating. How far had the motorcycle gone down the road before turning around? How long would it take to get back? How long would it take us to get into the VW and drive away? Too long.

Emmie had stopped chopping, but she hadn't put the knife down. I watched in disbelief as her fingers nimbly turned the knife in one quick motion so that the blade pointed up and rested neatly along her wrist and forearm while her hand firmly grasped the handle. I was standing behind her so I could see it, but someone standing in front of her would just see a clenched fist.

I thought of Seth's knife and what Emmie had said to me before I'd pushed it off the wall and into the water below, what she'd said about going through life like everyone was your friend. I'd seen Emmie do that over and over again, and it always surprised me how trusting and welcoming she could be to people she didn't know—until now. Something was telling her that now was not a time to be a friend, not a time to trust.

"Bets, get in." I knew what she meant, but I had no time to act. I was five steps from the VW. I would have had to climb in the side door and get up to the driver's seat—one second gone—fumble with the keys then start the engine—two seconds, then three seconds gone. Add to that my hesitation; I wasn't sure if Emmie meant to climb in after me or cover my escape. Either way I wasn't leaving her on her own, so I stood there, frozen. It was too late anyway. A second after she'd said it, the motorcycle thundered into view and came to a stop in front of us, followed by the cloud of dust it had stirred up. For a second the air was full of choking sound and grit, then the engine thundered one last time and stopped.

I didn't know what someone in a motorcycle gang was supposed to look like. Two years ago, I didn't really know what a hippie looked like, and then somehow, I became one. I suppose lots of people who saw me made assumptions about the person I was based on the way I looked, and I knew a lot of those assumptions were wrong. But I couldn't help doing the same to the man who stood before us.

He wasn't wearing a leather jacket. I guess I thought everyone in a motorcycle gang wore one. But he was wearing torn up jeans and worn leather boots and a black t-shirt, so he definitely seemed like he could be in a motorcycle gang. There was some sort of symbol on the shirt. Maybe it was a skull with crossed bones, or maybe they were machine guns. Something was rolled up in one shirtsleeve that looked about the size of a pack of cigarettes. I didn't even know anyone who smoked.

The man's hair hung to his shoulders. It was unkempt and tangled and flowed right into his beard, which was just as messy. There were streaks of grey in his hair and beard, but I thought his face looked almost too young for that. It was hard to tell. He wore mirrored sunglasses that made it seem like he was looking everywhere at once.

"We're camping here tonight," Emmie said in a firm voice that didn't sound like hers. If I didn't know her, if I hadn't spent the last month listening to her voice, I probably wouldn't have noticed the hint of a nervous tremor. But I did, and hearing it made my stomach turn. "This is our spot," she continued. "Lots of places along this road, but not much room left here. So, probably best if you just keep going."

He pushed the kickstand down with the heel of a boot, learned the motorcycle to one side, and climbed off.

"Hey, listen," Emmie said, taking a step forward. "We don't want any trouble."

"Young lady," the man said in a slow voice that would have sounded stern if there wasn't the slightest hint of a laugh beneath it. He took off his sunglasses and revealed bright blue eyes that didn't seem to fit with the rest of him. "Someone with a knife hidden in their hand usually ends up with trouble whether they want it or not."

My mouth hung open, and my eyes darted to Emmie, wondering how she would respond. She hesitated, just a second or two, probably just as surprised as me. Then she flipped the knife back around, its blade no longer hidden, and held it up in front of her.

"OK, it's not hidden any more. So now get out of here," Emmie said in that same firm voice.

The man just laughed and took a step away from his motorcycle and toward Emmie's knife. I glanced toward the camper door, wishing I'd run for it when Emmie told me to and wondering if we could still get away somehow. But the man raised his arms like he was surrendering and then smiled and laughed again.

There are different kinds of laughs. Sometimes people laugh and it feels like they are laughing at you. Other times it feels like you should be laughing too but you missed the joke. When Seth laughed it made my skin shiver and my stomach turn. But this wasn't like any of those laughs. It was the kind of laugh that made me want to join in and laugh right along with it. It was hard to tell, but I'm pretty sure Emmie lowered the knife just a little bit.

"I don't mean you no harm, young lady. Saw you back in town. Was standing on the other side of the street. I heard everything that bunch of idiots said to you. Didn't hear what you said back, but I figured it must have been good." I watched his eyes while he talked, again surprised at how they didn't fit the rest of his appearance, and then I felt a little embarrassed for letting myself judge the man on his clothes and hair, before I knew anything about him.

"Wasn't following you, understand." The man shook his head then shrugged his shoulders, putting his hands back down. "Just saw your VW as you were leaving town. Hard to miss." I giggled a little at that, and the man looked at me and smiled. "Was just heading down this road looking for a place to stop for the night and saw it again. Figured I'd turn around and say hello. Was also curious to find out what you said to shut the mouths of that group back in town."

He laughed again, and this time I laughed a little with him, remembering the faces of the crowd when Emmie spoke to them. I'd been watching him while he talked and hadn't been paying attention to Emmie. So I hadn't noticed when she lowered the knife. Her arm hung down next to her hip, and she held the knife loosely in her hand. If I hadn't seen the exchange over the last few minutes and just walked into the scene, I would have thought Emmie was just chopping vegetables, pausing for a minute to chat with the man.

I made a decision. I stepped forward and put out my hand, "Hi, I'm Bets." I saw him take a quick look at Emmie, like he was making sure it was okay, then he put his hand out too.

"Pleased to meet you, Bets. Name's Teddy." There was a second when the name didn't feel quite right, like when he first lifted his sunglasses and I saw his eyes, like it didn't fit the person I was seeing. Then it fell into place and felt right. The bright eyes, the easy laugh, and the name. I liked the way he left off the beginnings of sentences, and I was glad I'd stepped forward to shake hands. The tangled hair and beard, the dirty clothes and motorcycle, those were the things that didn't fit.

Maybe Emmie was seeing it too. She put down the knife she had been holding and shook Teddy's hand as well. There was an awkward moment when Emmie started to apologize. I could tell she was embarrassed, so I cut her off. "We were just getting ready for dinner. You could join us."

Teddy glanced at Emmie again, looking for approval. He'd decided she was in charge I guess—because she was taller, older, more sure of herself than I was, or maybe because she was the one who had been holding the knife. "Yeah, you should join us. Dinner's almost ready."

"That'd be real nice. Thanks." Teddy stepped away from his bike and took a look around. "Looks like you picked out a good spot. Be okay if I make a fire?" I nodded before Emmie had a chance to respond. I knew a fire would mean we'd stay up longer. Mostly we went to bed when the sun went down just because there wasn't much to do after dark. But having the light of the fire nearby made it feel right to stay up. There was something about a fire that made people want to sit around and talk, and I was curious about what Teddy had to say. Something told me he had stories to tell.

I helped Teddy gather wood and then watched him start a fire, carefully feeding it twigs and then larger and larger branches. Emmie divided up the food she'd made onto three plates and brought it over. Maybe there was a little bit less because it was divided three ways, but none of us seemed to care. We ate in silence, just watching the flames as they grew higher, and then when our plates were almost clear, Teddy turned to Emmie and mentioned again the crowd we'd run into back in town and what she'd said to silence them.

So Emmie told her story. I knew it already, but I listened like it was the first time. She talked about her father going to Vietnam, the one letter that he sent home, and then the two soldiers that had come to her home to tell her and her mother that he had been killed. Teddy seemed to straighten a little when she got to that part. He pushed the hair back from his face and ran his fingers through his beard as if combing the tangles out. I think if he'd been wearing a hat he would have taken it off.

When Emmie finished, Teddy stood up, stepped around the fire toward her, and then crouched back down so he could look her in the eye. "I'm so sorry for your loss." He put one hand on Emmie's shoulder and the other to his heart. Then, just for a second or two, he bowed his head. It wasn't like he was praying. More like he was showing respect, not for Emmie but for her father. When Teddy raised his head, their eyes met, and I saw Emmie mouth the words, "Thank you."

Then he settled back into his spot by the fire. He picked up a longer stick and poked around in the coals, shifting pieces of wood that hadn't caught fire yet, and moving burning pieces toward the center where the fire caught again and grew. I watched the fire for a few minutes as he tended it, and then I felt Teddy's eyes on me and looked up. He had heard Emmie's story, and he was waiting for mine.

I shrugged and looked back to the fire. My father had been gone for a year. I missed him and was afraid for him while he was away, but he was home again. That was nothing compared to Emmie. I said as much in a few short sentences, and then went back to watching the fire, trying not to make eye contact and waiting for it to be Teddy's turn to talk and not mine. But he just kept pushing coals around with his stick, and the feeling that he was waiting for more didn't go away.

"What?" I said in a tone that was more accusation than question.

Teddy didn't react, just kept looking at the fire. Then he lifted his eyes. It was totally dark by then. The three of us were just shadows to each other, features occasionally highlighted by the flickering flames. But I could see Teddy's eyes clearly, and they were uncomfortable to look at and hard to turn away from at the same time.

"That's a good story with a happy ending, but I have a feeling there's more to it than that." His sentence lingered in the smoke above the fire, and I let it, stubbornly silent and waiting to move on from my story. I wanted to sit back and let my mind drift while someone else talked. I wanted to just go to bed. But I didn't want to talk. And then I did.

Once I started, the words came out like a flood. I talked about what happened after my father came home, not the happy reunion at the airport, but what came next. The afternoons that I'd come home to find him staring at nothing and the nights when I'd wake up to his nightmares and his screaming.

War was frightening and horrible. It made sense that he would need to sort through it all after he came home, that he couldn't just forget it. But it had been a long time, long enough that I'd almost forgotten what he was like before he went away.

I talked about all of that and more. I think I cried. I probably did. How could I not? I didn't care. Who could see me in the dark? I talked at the fire and at the dark space around us and sometimes at the two faces watching me. I let everything spill out. I'd gone on the trip with Emmie to get away from it, but I hadn't really, not at all. I'd brought it with me, without even knowing it. I'd carried what I had been feeling all the way across the country. I'd kept it hidden somewhere inside me, but I couldn't stop it from pouring out all at once. If it had been water, it would have put out the fire.

Teddy made a humph sound and went back to poking at the fire. I wiped my face on a shirt sleeve, irritated at the wetness on my cheeks and the smoke that stung my eyes, angry at myself for saying more than I wanted, and angry, suddenly, at Teddy for seeming to judge me. There were words with sharp edges in my mouth. I took in a quick breath, ready to spit them out. Then he started talking.

"Not going to say that I understand what your father's going through, 'cause I think anyone who's been over there has their own stuff to deal with, has seen and done different things, and everyone has their own way of dealing with it. I won't make excuses for him." He paused, stirring the coals. "But I won't judge either."

I swallowed, but it got stuck halfway down and seemed to block off my breath. Teddy had been in the war. Pieces fell into place: the t-shirt with the skull and crossed machine guns, the tattoos, the way he'd responded to Emmie when he found out her father had been killed in Vietnam, and the crumpled khaki jacket tied to the back of his motorcycle. Lots of hippies wore army surplus, torn and worn, but light and warm. I figured it was just one of those, but realized it was Teddy's own jacket, brought back from the war. It all made sense.

"You were in Vietnam?" It sounded funny coming out of my mouth. I'd heard people say the same to me while my father was over there. *Your father is in Vietnam?* Some people said it with surprise in their voice, like the news stories they'd seen on TV had come to life. Some said it with a touch of sympathy. Most said it like they didn't know what else to say.

"Yeah, I was in 'Nam," Teddy said in a voice that was half whisper, half grumble. "Went over when the war was just getting started. Did two tours before I got discharged. Went back home again for a spell, but it didn't last. Family and friends seemed like they'd just gotten used to me being away. Oh, they tried to put up with me, but most just didn't understand what I was going through." I dropped my eyes to the fire, then looked off to the side, into the distance and into the darkness, anywhere but toward Teddy. I thought for sure he was looking at me, and I wasn't ready to meet his gaze.

"Then there was the folks in town who didn't agree with the war. Can't blame 'em really. Not a big fan of war myself," he laughed a little, but it wasn't the kind that made me want to laugh with him. "But, seemed like most of 'em forgot that the soldiers they were yelling about were people just like them, only we got called up to fight in a war, and they didn't. Anyway, didn't care for being called things like baby killer and vagrant in the town I grew up in, so I up and left."

"Left?" Emmie broke the silence that had moved in around the fire after Teddy stopped talking.

"Yeah. Didn't really have much family back home, a brother, and a sister with some kids. Friends all had other things to do by the time I came back, or they seemed to. So I left. Felt better on the road anyway, at first least ways. Seemed like I was leaving my problems behind. If I moved fast enough, thought I might even be able to out-run the problems, and the memories, and the dreams I was having." He stopped like he was thinking about what he'd just said, or giving us time to think about it. "But that doesn't work"

I wished I had a stick to poke around in the fire. Something, anything to do other than talk, or listen to Teddy, or look him in the eye. Too much of what he was saying felt like he was telling my story from the opposite perspective—my father's story. He'd stopped talking, and I didn't know if that was because he was done or because he was waiting for Emmie or me to respond or ask a question. There were lots of things I wanted to say, and I had lots of questions, but I wasn't ready to hear any of the answers.

"What happened?" Emmie finally broke the silence. Teddy made a dismissive sound but didn't say anything in response. "You said you had memories and bad dreams?" Emmie pressed. "What memories? What happened in the war? You said you were running from some memories when you left town." I marveled at Emmie. Maybe she was curious or maybe she wanted someone else's perspective to help make sense of what happened to her father; but that was secondary for her. I could see it in her questions, gradually stronger, probing, nudging. She knew Teddy needed to talk, knew he would be better off reliving his story in words instead of in dreams. She was caring, and selfless, and wonderful. I thought back to our first conversation, when I needed so badly to share how I was feeling about my father being away, my conflict over the right or wrong of the war, and how much better I'd finally felt after talking with Emmie.

Teddy stopped poking the fire and looked carefully at Emmie. His eyes bore into hers, and he tilted his head to the side, rubbing a hand across the rough hair on his cheeks. He saw the kindness and love in her, but didn't know what to make of it. He also saw what she was doing. He'd been doing the same to me, saying things that he knew would dig at me, framing his story to fit with mine, getting me to talk. I spilled my story before I realized what he was doing, but he'd caught on to Emmie quickly, and I wasn't sure if he was going to tell us more.

"We were trying to take some hill north of Saigon," Teddy finally began. I was so lost in my own thoughts, I might have jumped when he started talking, except that his voice started off so low, he was halfway through his sentence before I realized I was hearing it.

"Can you figure that out? People fightin' over a hill?" He paused and just shook his head for a second. "Right from the start, nothing went the way it was planned. We fell back and called in for air support. We thought for sure we were all goners until we heard the C-130 coming with a daisy cutter." Emmie and I must have both looked confused. "You wondering what a daisy cutter is?" He laughed a little. "You like cuttin' daisies, flower girl?" he asked looking at Emmie, and she bristled at the nickname. Too similar to what Jake had called her, and at the same time, said in a tone that couldn't have been more different from Jake. "A big old C-130 Hercules brought it in. That plane's so big it looks like it has no business being up in the air, and a daisy cutter was the biggest bomb you ever seen. Designed special, so it would explode just before it hit the ground. 'Stead of making a big hole in the ground, the blast would travel straight out, cuttin' everything down in its path. Used 'em for clearing the jungle away to create a landing spot, but if it took out some Viet Cong along with the trees and vines, we didn't mind.

"After the dust cleared, we all hid out at the edge of the clearing waiting for the chopper we knew would be coming for us. Didn't dare head into the clearing until it was landing, because the Viet Cong knew just what we were up to and were hiding out just like us, waiting to pick us off one by one as soon as we left the jungle.

"Once it landed, we all made a break for it." He paused, thinking about how to continue. "The thing about running for a helicopter is that some people will get there first, and some won't. I was one of the first ones there, and I did what I was trained to do. I climbed aboard and then turned right around to help pull the next guys in. One after another, we climbed in. But that chopper pilot, he's playing a waiting game, see? He's watching out those big ol' windows he's got up front, watching the stream of soldiers running toward him, but also watching the edge of the clearing for the ones shootin' at 'em. He's sittin' up there wondering how many men he can get aboard before the other guys come out into the clearing and start shooting at him.

"Because he's got his orders too. Rescue as many men as you can, not necessarily rescue all of 'em. You see, Uncle Sam wants his soldiers back. But gettin' a chopper back half full is better'n havin' a chopper that's full get shot down and no one coming back.

"So we pulled guys in as fast as we could, but we knew when we heard the motor rev up and those chopper blades started spinning faster that the guys still running weren't going to make it. They knew it too, but they ran faster anyway."

We were off the ground while men were still trying to climb in. Had my hand on the arm of one, trying to help him up. All the sudden his feet were hanging in midair and there's nothing but the grip I got around his forearm keeping him from falling back to Earth. Guys in back were holding onto me, making sure I didn't get pulled out. We were hand in hand, looking at each other, and then he was gone.

Emmie and I didn't say anything. We just sat there, letting Teddy decide if there was more to the story or not. I'm not sure what Emmie was thinking about, but I was wondering about my father. I'd never really talked to him about what it was like for him in Vietnam. At first I was just glad he was home. Back then, being in the war only seemed to have two outcomes. You either came back, or you didn't. Listening to Teddy, I realized there was something in between.

"That chopper we was in got far enough away from the clearing, and then the planes could come in. Figuring there was a whole bunch of enemy soldiers that missed their chance at shooting some Americans, they'd do a quick fly by and drop some napalm. Looked like the god Vesuvius swooping in spreading death and..."

"Vulcan," Emmie corrected. Teddy stopped mid-sentence and raised his eyebrows. "I think you mean Vulcan," Emmie explained. "He's the Roman god of fire." She hesitated, like she wasn't sure she should continue, "And Hephaestus is the Greek god of fire. Vesuvius is just the name of a volcano."

Teddy eyed her, maybe not sure what to say at first. "Okay college girl, let's go with Vulcan. It's easier to say." We laughed a little, which seemed strange after all that had been said, so we stopped quickly, like we were doing something disrespectful.

After it got quiet again, Teddy continued, "It's that man's eyes I see each night when I close mine. Not the desperate eyes while he was still clinging to me, but the hopeless ones that came after his hand slipped from mine." He sighed, but it seemed like more breath was coming out of him than his lungs could possibly hold. "That's what I see at night, before I go to sleep, and after."

Long Distance

We doused the fire after Teddy finished his story. There was really nothing left for anyone to say. We didn't dare ask more questions, and I could think of nothing to say that wouldn't sound meaningless and flat. Emmie put an arm around Teddy, and they held each other for a moment, both seeming to get something from the hug. Teddy had gone a long time without anyone to pull him close and comfort him, and Emmie, I think—though we never talked about it, and I never dared to ask—saw a little bit of her father in him.

Then it was off to bed. The fire was out; the darkness had closed in. We climbed into the VW and settled into bed while Teddy pulled some things from his pack and made himself comfortable on the ground. We were happy to have a companion again.

There were a million things to think about as a lay in bed. Jake, Bill, my father, Emmie's father, Teddy's story, and the story I would ask my father about when I returned home. But it was beyond late, and I was tired not just from the long day but from the cross-country trip that seemed to pull so much from me.

At some point during the night, I woke from a dream, a nightmare. Emmie and I sat around the fire talking, at first with Jake, and then somehow in the sort of transition that can only happen in dreams, we sat with Teddy. As the firelight faded, so did Emmie, first from the conversation, and then from the dream, as if she'd never been there. Then, as the last flames sputtered out, I realized Teddy had stopped talking. I turned to see if he was gone too, and there was Seth, the last light of the coals glinting off angry eyes and his knife.

I must have screamed. I gasped for air, my eyes flicking around the dark camper. Emmie was still asleep beside me, her breathing slow and steady. I could hear Teddy snoring outside. So my scream was only in the dream, but the fear I'd felt had come back with me into real life. I thought for a minute about waking up Emmie. I wanted to check the camper. I wanted to search the fields around us and, like a frightened child checking for monsters under the bed, I wanted to peer under the VW to make sure Seth wasn't hiding there.

Instead, I lay in the dark, my heart still racing, replaying the last seconds of the dream. I thought about Teddy's story and the dreams he described. I remembered the first time my father's dreams woke me in the middle of the night. I remembered how frightened and confused I was. My father had always seemed so strong, so sure of himself. It didn't make sense to me that he would have bad dreams. But that seemed like a long time ago, and I felt embarrassed thinking back to my reaction. Sure, Seth was frightening and creepy and dangerous. But my father had been in a war. I figured if I could wake up in the middle of the night screaming, he'd earned the right to a few nightmares.

Those thoughts replayed on a loop in my mind: my dream, Seth, Teddy's story, my father. At some point, I must have fallen asleep again, although after I woke from the dream I was certain I'd be awake the rest of the night.

When we woke the next morning Teddy was gone, leaving nothing behind but tire tracks in the soft dirt where the grass-covered ground turned into paved road. It felt funny not being able to say goodbye, but at the same time, I wasn't really sure what I would have said. Maybe he felt the same way and that's why he left.

It was exciting packing up our things that morning and collapsing the camper's pop-top. We were within a short day's drive of Woodstock. That night, we knew we'd be camping on the farm that was being turned into a gigantic outdoor concert space. We were early. The music wouldn't start for a few days, but we didn't want to wait. We'd seen enough towns and had driven on enough roads. We were ready to finally see our destination, even if it wasn't ready for us.

I was the last to drive the day before, so Emmie offered to start the day in the driver's seat. I tossed our things on the floor, closed the sliding door, and climbed in the passenger door. I noticed Emmie's ticket on the dashboard, and I felt my face go white.

As much as I'd thought about our destination over the last month, over all the miles we'd traveled, I'd not once thought about the ticket that would get me into the festival. My mind raced back to the night I'd packed and snuck out of my house. I remembered taking it out of my desk drawer, I remembered grabbing my bag, but I had no memory of where I'd put the ticket. Was it in a pocket? Was it in my bag? Had I put it somewhere in the VW?

I must have made some sort of sound when the shock hit me—a gasp, a cry of surprise.

"What! What?" Emmie shouted. She'd been pulling onto the road when I remembered my ticket, and she quickly slammed on the brakes. The engine stalled and a cloud of dust from the skidding wheels hung in the air outside the windows. It made it feel like the world around me had been frozen in time while my mind raced backwards through a month of changing clothes, packing, and unpacking. In none of those memories was a ticket.

"My ticket," I finally said to Emmie. "My ticket!"

She let out a sigh. "Jeez, Bets. The way you screamed I thought I was pulling out in front of a truck, or about to run into someone, or something else horrible." She started the VW's engine again and moved it off the road. "Where's your ticket?"

"I don't know!" I said in a voice that I realized was too loud as soon as I spoke. "I don't know," I said again, this time in a choked whisper. I looked at Emmie with panic on my face and then dove between the front seats, ready to search every bag and cupboard.

I started with the clothes that were already out of my bag. Once Seth was no longer with us, we'd turned the back seat of the VW into a clothes closet of sorts. Not bothering to pack our clothes away every day, we just folded stuff we'd worn and put it on the seat. It was easier than digging in our bags every time we needed something, and it kept things from getting so crumpled. Having Jake along for a few days hadn't gotten us out of the habit, so the back seat was still covered with clothes.

I grabbed fistfulls of pants and shirts and skirts, searching pockets, then tossing them onto the floor in all directions. When I made it to the bottom of my clothes pile, I went back to a favorite pair of pants I'd worn a lot and checked those pockets again. No ticket.

I pulled out my bag and jammed a hand into it, digging wildly. Admittedly, I'd re-worn a lot of the clothes I'd brought. If I were in school, I'd never dream of wearing things twice without washing, except maybe a pair of jeans. But while we were on the road, it seemed okay. We were mostly just sitting all day long, not out jogging or working in the garden. Plus, who did we have to impress? It was just me and Emmie. Most people we met, we just saw once as we were passing through a town. They'd never know I was wearing the same outfit I wore the day before and the day before that. I guess I probably grabbed something clean when Jake was with us, and I was glad I had when I rode my bike into Buffalo and met Bill. But otherwise, I'd gotten in the habit of rotating through a few favorite outfits. So my bag was half-full of clothes that hadn't been pulled out since we left California.

I sifted through them for half a minute, trying to peer into the darkness at the bottom of the bag, before I got frustrated and just dumped it all out on the floor. Clothes tumbled out along with some other things I'd stuffed in there, and then on top of the pile, a book.

I hadn't packed a book.

It had landed with the back cover facing up. It was just a blank, cream-colored cover, with a dark blue spine. I could see a title printed on the spine in embossed, gold lettering, but I turned it over instead so I could see the front cover.

Collected Works of the Beat Poets

I'd never seen the book before. It wasn't mine. I turned to Emmie, but she just shrugged. Even if it had been hers, why would she have hidden it in the bottom of my bag under all the clothes that I hadn't worn for the last month. I opened the book somewhere in the middle and let the pages flip slowly through my fingers as I watched names and poem titles flash by: Allen Ginsberg, Gary Snyder, Lawrence

Ferlinghetti, Gregory Corso... I ended up at the front of the book, the first page slipping past my thumb, leaving nothing but the front cover in my left hand. That's when I discovered something had been written inside the cover.

Bets,
Here's something for you to read on your trip.
We hope you have a great adventure.
We love you,
Mom and Dad

My world spun. They knew. Somehow they knew. They had known all along. While I was sneaking around with my secret, trying to decide if I should go or not, packing my things, and slipping out in the middle of the night, they had known.

When had they found out? Early enough that they had time to buy a book and write a note to me on the inside cover. "We hope you have a great adventure."

I read it, over and over again. My parents knowing and not saying anything, just letting me go, letting me sneak away while they slept—the thought made me embarrassed and relieved at the same time. It was like I'd gotten caught trying to hide my secret, only to discover I didn't need to hide it in the first place.

I tried to sift through all the possibilities. How they could have found out, what gave me away, why they hadn't said anything. I thought back to Cassie's speeches to me, how certain she was that my parents would never allow me to drive cross country to a music festival, and I marveled at the fact that they had known and let me go without trying to stop me. There were no answers for any of my questions, and trying to puzzle out something that had happened a month ago wasn't much use.

I turned to Emmie and said in a whisper, "I need to get to a phone."

☮ ☮ ☮

We found a phone booth in the next town we came to, and Emmie went into a nearby store to ask for change. I remembered the day I needed to call Emmie, remembered how I was too nervous to ask for change for the phone and went into the post office to buy stamps instead. Emmie came out of the store and dumped a handful of dimes into my hand. A month ago, I'd been concerned about what it would cost to call San Francisco from Forestville. I had no idea how much it would cost to call someone on the other side of the country. But judging from the weight of the dimes in my hand, Emmie understood how important the phone call was and didn't want me to run out.

She gave me a quick hug and told me she was going to take a walk, then she disappeared down the street. I stepped into the phone booth and closed the folding door behind me even though there was no one else around. With the door closed, the space inside felt close, comforting and protective, but smothering at the same time, like the air caught inside was running out.

I slid a dime into the slot and then carefully poured the rest onto the small triangular shelf below the phone. My finger shook a little as I stuck it into the shallow holes on the dial and spun it over and over again, afraid for a second that I'd forgotten my own phone number. The tinny voice came through the earpiece and told me how much to deposit, and I grabbed dimes from the shelf, counting them off as I put them into the slot. Then I waited.

I heard a couple clicks and some silence that was long enough to make we wonder if the call would go though. I imagined all the wires that it had to be routed through. I'd crossed all those miles, all those roads lined with poles and wires overhead. And now my call was tracing that same route, going back over all the miles I'd traveled.

Then the phone rang in my ear with a sound that was impossibly close. I waited, and it rang again. I realized I didn't even know what day it was. If it was a weekday, my father would be on base. If he was home, I thought I probably didn't want to talk with him, remembering the last time I'd seen him home early on a weekday. I couldn't really say for sure if my mother would be home or not, no matter what day it was.

The phone rang again. I'd lost count of how many times it had rung, and I thought about hanging up. I wondered if I would need to pay for the call even if no one answered. Then there was a click, a shuffling sound, and my father's voice.

"Hello?"

For a second, I didn't know what to say. I searched for words and had none. Then, without really thinking at all, I let the simplest thing slip from my mouth. It was really the only thing to say. "Daddy, it's me." Three little words, that I sent out across the country, having no idea what the response would be on the other end. The air that had escaped me when I spoke caught in my throat on its way back in, and I held it there waiting for his response.

But all that came back to me through the phone was a sigh, long and slow, and fading until it was hard to tell the difference between the breathy sound and the silence in the miles of phone line. I stood there with the phone to my ear wondering what the sigh meant. Was it anger at hearing my voice? Was it depression, a mood my father was stuck in when the phone happened to ring? Or was there something wrong with the phone line, letting me hear him, while my father heard only silence. I repeated, "Daddy, it's me," and then added stupidly, "It's Bets." I wanted desperately to hear something more from him than a sigh and silence.

"Yeah, Bets. I'm here." my father's voice said finally, as if he'd read my mind, "It's just... it's just so good to hear your voice." It was like the sigh, still breathy, the words stretched out and fading toward the end, but this time I could hear the relief, and suddenly it was like I was standing in front of my father, reading his expression. He wasn't angry. He wasn't depressed. He was just overwhelmingly glad to be talking to me on the phone. I felt the same relief wash over me, and when my knees buckled a little, I let myself lean back against the side of the phone booth for support.

"You've been gone a long time, kiddo. Your mother and I really miss you. We... well, we were starting to get worried. The postcards were nice, but... well... it's just so good to hear your voice and know you're okay."

My heart sank, and the phone felt cold against my ear. I'd been thinking a lot about myself since I'd left, all the things that had happened to me, and all the things I was feeling. But I hadn't thought much about what my parents were thinking or feeling back home. The postcards suddenly felt selfish, a way for me to feel like I was staying in touch with my parents, but with no way for them to respond.

I realized that I'd only been thinking of my parents' reaction to me leaving, thinking they wouldn't let me go, thinking they'd be angry at me for leaving without permission, but I never stopped to consider how they'd feel after I'd left and been gone for weeks. While I certainly had times when I was missing them, and I knew they must have missed me too, I didn't let myself think that what I'd done had hurt them and caused them to worry.

"Oh Daddy, I'm so sorry. I'm sorry I left without..."

"No need to be sorry, Bets." My father's words cut off my own. "I'm just glad you called. We've really been hoping you would. Where are you? You there yet?" Something had changed in his voice. The relief he'd felt after first hearing my voice had turned into something else. He was cheerful.

I hadn't expected cheerful—surprised maybe, upset possibly, angry probably. This was something different. It was his regular voice. The one I hadn't heard in such a long time, since he'd left for Vietnam. I expected he'd be angry. I'd done something I really, really shouldn't have. I knew that now. Sometime between finding the book and making the phone call, I'd figured that out. I guess maybe I knew it all along and just didn't want to admit it.

As good as it felt to hear it, I didn't know how to respond to the happy, cheerful voice coming at me through the telephone, so instead I let the words that I'd replayed in my mind pour out of me, not words I'd planned, just words that were stuck and waiting to get out.

"Oh, Daddy, I'm so sorry. I messed up. I never should have left. I'm sorry. I'm sorry. I just... I didn't know, I was... and you were... I'm sorry. I'm so, so sorry." Then I cried, big sobs that certainly could be heard all the way through the telephone line to California. My father's voice was coming through the earpiece, but I didn't hear it. It was only noise, background to my tears.

"Bets. Hey, Bets. No, no, no, Bets. Hey..." I finally heard the words. How long had I been crying? I wondered when the operator would cut in asking for more money. I sniffed in, and coughed, and wiped my eyes.

"Yeah," I croaked, not much more than a whisper.

"It's okay, Bets. I get it. I understand. I haven't been easy to live with lately, so I understand you wanting to get away." A month ago, that was all I wanted to hear from him, just admitting that something was wrong, admitting that he was difficult to be around. But there, on the phone with him, it was the last thing I wanted to hear, because I got it. Finally, I understood. It wasn't his fault. He didn't need to apologize.

"No Daddy, I understand." I hesitated. "I met..." How did I explain to him all I'd learned in the last month. How did I put into words the different perspectives on the war that I'd been given from Jerry, and Jake, and Bill, and Teddy. Each of their stories had added a layer to what I thought about Vietnam and the war. How did my father fit into all of that? He had a story that was all his own. It was different than all the others, but it was somehow part of them as well. Most importantly, I'd realized that I needed to pay attention to my father's story, instead of just my own. But that wasn't a conversation for the phone.

"Oh, Daddy, I love you so much. I can't wait to be home."

He laughed then, and I felt months of sadness drop out of me, because I couldn't remember the last time I'd heard that, a real laugh from my father. I leaned back against the side of the phone booth, closed my eyes, and smiled.

"Seems like you've got a lot more traveling to do before you're home again, kiddo." He was right. I wanted to be home right then and there, to be home with him, but I was a whole country away. "Just enjoy where you are, Bets. Enjoy who you're with. From what I read in the paper, it sounds like it's going to be a good show."

I laughed and agreed, and for a few seconds we talked on top of each other in a way that only seems to happen on the telephone, my father telling me what he'd heard about Woodstock on the news and me sharing what I was most excited about.

There was more to the phone call. Words that were just making conversation, sharing the day's events like we'd both just gotten home from a day at school or at work. I told him I'd just found the book they'd given me. He laughed again and told me my mother wouldn't be happy about me wearing the same dirty clothes every day. I asked about my mother. She was at tea with friends, but he promised to give her a hug for me. He thanked me for the postcards, and told me again to have fun. Then we said goodbye, and I gently placed the phone back on the hook.

Yasgur's Farm

20 E, 87 S, 212 W, 42 W, 55 W, 17 W

I told Emmie all about the phone conversation while the miles that were left between us and Woodstock ticked down from triple to double digits. She knew I was okay as soon as she saw me step out of the phone booth, but she listened carefully as I replayed everything that was said and seemed to share my relief.

"Cool," she nodded. "Yeah, cool," she repeated in a satisfied voice.

I didn't want to admit it, but as excited as I was to go on the trip with Emmie and see all the bands that would be playing at Woodstock, leaving without getting my parents' permission had bothered me for most of the trip. I was able to push it away, to focus on all the things we were seeing and doing each day, but it never really went away entirely. It was like the hiss on an old record. You could turn up the volume and try to just pay attention to the music, but the constant scratchy sound was always there, spoiling the music a little.

Discovering that I hadn't really snuck away after all and wouldn't be facing angry parents when I returned erased the worry I'd carried with me for the last month, and that cleared the way for the excitement that was building with each mile.

Emmie found my ticket on the floor after I dumped my bag. I'd totally forgotten about my frantic search as soon as I discovered the book. I held the ticket in my hands while my thoughts wandered, looking down occasionally at the words and symbols that covered it, but mostly just holding it. I let my fingertips trace its edges and turned it over again and again as I watched the scenery fly by outside the VW's windows.

As we got closer, we saw more people who looked like they were heading to the same place we were. We saw other Volkswagens, some like ours, given unique paint jobs by their owners. We saw other cars loaded down with people, looking like they'd piled a whole college dorm worth of hippies into the back seat. We even saw an old school bus that had been painted in a rainbow of colors. People beeped, and waved, and rolled down windows to raise peace signs in the wind.

We were on highway 87 heading south from Albany when we noticed the first road signs for the town of Woodstock: 50 miles, 25 miles, 10 miles. We weren't sure where the concert was exactly, but judging from the small dot on the map, Woodstock wasn't a big place. We drove down its main street and out the other side of town before we really realized we'd passed through it. Emmie made a u-turn, and we took a different route through town, looking for signs directing us to the concert and searching for people who looked like they were going there. There was nothing.

Emmie finally gave up and pulled over to the sidewalk where an older couple was walking. Before I had a chance to roll down the window they were already gesturing and pointing up the road.

"Wrong town. Wrong town!" the man shouted, not in a angry voice, only wanting to be heard.

The woman came closer to explain. "You made it to Woodstock, sweetie, but this is only the town. The concert was going to be near here, but they had to find a new spot when folks got upset about something so big fittin' into such a small town. Guess they didn't do a very good job of getting the word out. People been rollin' though all day long." I must have looked confused or worried. "Don't worry, sweetie. It's not far. Just another hour or so down the highway. You're headed in the right direction." Emmie and I looked at each other with blank expressions as the woman walked away. "Town of Bethel... if you've got a map, should be on it," she shouted over her shoulder.

I scanned the map while Emmie shuffled through a magazine that had an advertisement for the festival. We figured the festival had gotten its name from the town where it was taking place, and were still a little bit confused even after Emmie had confirmed the location from the advertisement and I'd located the town of Bethel on the map.

We drove through the town again and were back on the highway in minutes.

The whole trip through town was embarrassing and anticlimactic. We'd traveled thousands of miles only to discover we were headed to the wrong place. We were glad we didn't have much farther to go, but still, the excitement we'd felt pulling into town was gone, and it was hard to imagine we'd experience the same feeling again.

I was right. Pulling into the Woodstock festival was like absolutely nothing we'd experienced on our entire trip. It was hard to tell where the road ended and the festival began. We'd turned off the highway and were on smaller and smaller roads as we followed signs and took turns. There were some cars parked alongside the road, and there were people walking, but not many. We were two days early after all, but we'd expected parking lots, an entry gate, something or someone to tell us that we'd arrived. Instead, Emmie just kept driving slowly up the road until all at once we knew we were there.

The VW rolled to the top of a small hill in the road, and the field suddenly opened up in front of us. I was used to open spaces in Forestville, and we'd certainly seen the wide world on our cross-country trip, but the goosebumps on my arms told me this place was special.

The field in front of us curved around on either side in a ridge that made a perfect half circle, and it sloped down from all directions like the sides of a shallow bowl to gather in the middle. At the center of everything, was a stage, or at least what would be a stage. I could see tiny silhouettes moving around it like busy ants, and the sounds of construction drifted up the hill. It wasn't complete yet, but standing there watching it being built, I could already see what it would be like. Behind the stage, the evening sun sparkled on a pond while the sky filled with color.

All of that was amazing, but that wasn't what had Emmie and me staring silently at the scene before us. All across the hill, spreading out around the half circle from the curved ridge to the low area at the bottom, were people. People weren't packed together yet. The field was too big for that, so much space that people could spread out wherever they wanted. But there were so many people. As far as we could see, there were people.

Our eyes scanned across the sloping field that filled our view. Just like the small silhouettes working on the stage, there were far away figures that were just shapes on the endless green of grass. There were people close up, right next to us, and everywhere in between. They all seemed to be doing something. Some were walking, some dancing, some setting up tents. Others were meditating or doing yoga maybe. Some were playing instruments, the music drifting on the air, but barely reaching us, others were sitting in circles talking, or just looking around and taking everything in.

The music was days away, but already there were more people than I'd ever seen in one place. I thought back to the protest in San Francisco. The crowd there was nowhere near the size of the one in front of us, but at the protest there was an aggressive energy that made one person feel like ten. In the field, even though we were looking out at thousands, I could feel a sense of peace. It was calm, people were content, and happy. I had been so excited about the music and the bands I would be seeing, I hadn't really thought about what it would be like to be surrounded by so many people who were all in one place for the same reasons.

Emmie found a good spot to park the VW, and we got out to look around. We stood on top of the hill for a while just taking it all in again. No longer looking through the frames of the VW's windows, it was even more amazing. I tried to imagine what it would look like in a couple days as more and more people arrived. They were still coming all the while we were taking in the scene. There were cars behind us as we drove in, and more behind them. I was struck by the life in the people all around us, constantly moving, changing, growing.

We didn't really know where we were going, but since we'd started at the top of the hill, no matter what direction we went in, we'd gradually be going down the slope, walking into the giant bowl ahead of us and toward the stage at its center.

Like passing another wildly painted car on the highway, we walked by people who I immediately felt a connection to. Their clothes, the braids, the beads around their necks, or the flowers in their hair, I seemed to find something that made me feel that whoever we were walking by was like me, and just like passing that painted car on the highway, there were peace signs, and smiles, and waves.

Sometimes we stopped and talked. Where did you come from? When did you get here? What bands did you come to see? We shared stories. Lots of people had arrived from New York City, some from the nearby college in Ithica, others had come from farther away. We met a few people who, like us, had traveled all the way from the west coast, but not many. There were lots of raised eyebrows and surprised faces when Emmie and I told people we'd come all the way from California.

We passed a man who sat with a blanket spread out in front of him. On the blanket was an assortment of food: pieces of fruit, hunks of bread or cheese, cereal, pieces of candy, pretzels. There was no order to it. It didn't look like a meal, or if it was, it was a meal that rolled breakfast, lunch, and dinner into one. Along with the food there were other things: a toothbrush, some band-aids, a spool of thread, and a roll of tape. Then I saw his sign and understood.

On a piece of cardboard, he'd written in scrawling capital letters, "GIVE WHAT YOU HAVE, TAKE WHAT YOU NEED." Emmie reached in her bag and pulled out a pack of gum. She said hello to the man as she bent down to place it on the blanket and got a silent wave and a smile in return. I felt funny taking something, like I had to calculate the value of the gum we'd given and stay within those limits.

But I liked the idea of it, the notion that people could give and take, getting something they needed while giving something that someone else might need. I realized that value wasn't a number, wasn't something that could be added and subtracted. A thing meant less to one person and more to another. I lifted a string of beads off my neck and over my head, making sure it wasn't the necklace with the smoothed piece of glass, the key Jerry had given me, or the necklace that Cassie had given me a month ago in far away Forestville. I put it down on the blanket, grabbed an apple, and thanked the man. I'd somehow ended up with quite the collection of beads and necklaces after all the places we'd been. I could easily give one away and still have a bunch. But I was hungry. What I wanted, what I needed, was an apple. As Emmie would say, "Cool."

We moved on. There was a circle of people all playing drums, or banging on other things, or chanting. At first, it sounded like chaos, just noise. There were so many sounds and different rhythms. There was no way they could all fit together. And then, after I listened for a minute, they did. Someone was banging on a length of pipe. Where did he get a pipe? It made a high pitched ringing sound that was tuneless and annoying at first. But the more I listened, I could hear that the ringing was the beat that all the other sounds fit into. The drums, the banging, even the chanting, all somehow blending together into something that was random, and musical, and beautiful.

I thought about all the different people we'd encountered on our trip. They were all different, all moving through life at their own pace, doing their own thing, following their own rhythm, and yet, somehow, all fitting together. Back in Parachute, Jerry and Charlie were living their own lives, then I came along, changing them while they changed me, fitting together. Emmie and I were perfectly happy driving along on our own, until Jake decided to sneak into the VW one night. He fit in so well with us that we still felt the loss in the empty space he'd left behind.

We left the people making music and eventually ended up on low, flat ground with the stage ahead of us. Towers loomed on either side, their metal frames looking too delicate to support the massive boxy speakers that would send music out toward everyone gathering on the hillside. Being up close to the stage, it was easy to imagine standing in the audience and listening to some of my favorite songs.

In just a couple days Janis Joplin would be up there. Jerry Garcia would be joined by the rest of the Grateful Dead, filling the fields around us with their groovy music. Richie Havens would be singing about peace and love, the sound of his guitar and his voice touching each of us. The Who! They were playing shows all over the world, and they'd be up there. Joan Baez, Jefferson Airplane, Jimi Hendrix—back home, I had a box full of their records, and they'd all be up on that stage.

But standing there, looking up at the wooden structure that was still being built, I couldn't shake the feeling that what mattered the most wouldn't be happening up on the stage. It would be happening out on the hillside. I knew that years from now, people would talk about all the music that happened at Woodstock, but they'd also talk about all the people who were there. All the people who came from New York, and other states, and from as far away as California. All the people who helped each other out by giving what they had or taking what they needed. All the people who somehow fit together, even though they were playing in different keys to a different beat. I was excited to be one of them.

We picked our way back up the hill. It was harder going up than it was going down. It wasn't just that we were walking up the slow but constant incline. There were more people. Already, in the few hours that we'd been there, the crowd had grown, or more people had come down from the curved ridge that circled us to fill in the empty spaces on the hillside.

We also discovered that we weren't entirely sure what direction we needed to walk in. Coming down the hill, it was easy. We could see the stage from everywhere, it was at the center of everything. Going back up, we were faced with a wide hillside surrounding us on three sides. Had we come from the center, or over to the left, or to the right? Changing direction by just a little bit as we started off from the center could put us in an entirely different place once we were up on the ridge. Rather than walking a straight line, we kept shifting from left to right as one place or another looked familiar, but everyone and everything looked familiar. We were in an endless field full of beads, and bell bottoms, and hippies.

When we finally reached the top of the hill, we didn't end up exactly where we'd started, but a look back at the view of the stage at least told us which direction we needed to head. We walked along the ridge, looking for the VW in a sea of people and cars. We saw a few other campers, mistaking them for our own until we got closer, but we eventually got back to where we'd started.

We didn't recognize our VW at first. It had the right paintings on its sides, and it was parked in the right spot, but we were looking for a VW that was the way we'd left it, all our stuff inside, and the doors and camper top still closed. So when we saw one all opened up, table set, dinner cooking, I guess we just figured it wasn't ours and kept moving.

"Hey, flower child," a familiar voice called from behind us. We whirled around and ran back toward the VW we'd just passed to discover a boy who was supposed to be hundreds of miles away in another country.

Music and Mud

There were squeals and hugs and tears, most of them Emmie's. I knew enough not to get in her way. She ran the few steps between them and leapt the last few feet, wrapping her arms around Jake. I stood back and watched, laughing, and crying happy tears. It didn't make any sense. Jake had left for Canada. We had said goodbye. We'd cried about it, and he was gone. Except, he wasn't.

When Emmie finally released him, I stepped up and took my turn. I'd figured a lot of things out since I first met Jake, and I knew that there was something special between him and Emmie. Something that wasn't there between the two of us, and that was okay. I hugged him anyway, a long hug, the best kind, a hug that I gave to him and he gave back.

When we finally pulled apart, I looked him in the eye. "I am so glad you are here." The words came out slowly, like there was meaning in each one. I was glad to have him back for so many reasons: because he hadn't run away after all, because I was excited to be at Woodstock with him, and mostly because I missed him. I'd let Jake into my life, and I wanted him to stay there.

Emmie and I had been gone for longer than we'd planned. The walk back up the hill had taken a long time, and once we'd finished our hugging and gotten over the surprise of Jake's return, we realized how hungry we were. So we were glad to have dinner already set out on the table for us. We sat down and ate, not talking for a little while and just enjoying that we were together again.

Finally Emmie asked the question I'd been wondering since we'd discovered Jake sitting by the VW. "Why did you come back?" He just shrugged and smiled. That response might have been enough to explain Jake surprising us in the middle of a music festival hundreds of miles from where we'd last seen him. But there was more to Jake's story than that. There was a war, and a draft, and there were papers with his name on them, telling him to report for duty. Those were things that a shrug and a smile couldn't explain away.

Emmie's question lingered unanswered in the silence, and our faces must have told him that we expected more. He finally gave in. "What you'd said before I left stuck with me. I kept turning it over and over in my mind, and I finally decided it wasn't right to leave, wasn't right to just run away. One minute I was walking down a highway with my thumb out trying to catch a ride north, and the next I'd crossed to the other side of the road and was hitchhiking back to the border.

I asked the question I knew Emmie didn't want to ask. "What are you going to do?" Jake changing his mind about going to Canada was fine, but the draft board still had his name. His number had come up. They wanted a soldier, and they were expecting Jake to fill a uniform and pair of boots.

There was a shrug and a smile again, but he already knew it wouldn't put the question to rest. "I'm not going to fight in the war," he said with determination, looking at Emmie when he said it. That seemed to satisfy her, and she gave a quick nod. There were still unanswered questions. Jake could be arrested for avoiding the draft. If he wasn't, he'd still end up hiding out, not being able to go home, not being able to go back to school. The group Emmie and I had encountered just days ago only taunted us with words, but there were people who were angry enough to turn violent, and we'd heard stories of draft dodgers who'd ended up in the hospital before being hauled off to jail. But none of that seemed to matter for Emmie, and I understood why. She'd already given Vietnam one important person in her life. She didn't want to give the war another.

It was hard to sleep that night. It would have been a struggle even without Jake's arrival. We'd been on the road so long, the fact that we were finally at Woodstock was still sinking in, and our arrival wasn't something that could just be pushed out of mind. Woodstock was all around us, and it had a life of its own. Not everyone was ready for bed when we were. There was an energy—voices, laughter, singing—that didn't go away just because the sun had gone down. The noise alone didn't keep me awake; I wanted to be a part of it. Even though my body was tired and needed rest, my spirit wanted to join in everything that was happening around me, but at some point, exhaustion finally won, and I drifted off to sleep.

☮ ☮ ☮

The three of us spent the next day wandering around just as Emmie and I had done the day before. When we'd left the VW in the morning, we looked down the road we'd come in on and were surprised to see it completely packed with cars. If we wanted to leave at that point, we would have had to walk. It was easy to see that the hillside was filling up. There was less and less grass showing, and it was harder to walk around. We had to push past people and in some places we had to veer off to one side or the other to avoid an area where people were grouped so close together that there was just no getting through.

Our tickets were long forgotten, and my panic when I thought I'd lost mine seemed silly. There was no one checking for tickets, no one stopping the endless flow of people coming in from the road to join the crowd in the field.

Already the area down by the stage was impassable. People must have decided that comfort, food, and a place to sleep were less important than a closeup view of their favorite bands. We talked about it and decided that we'd rather be able to walk around, take in the whole scene, and return to the comfort of the VW when we were tired. So even though we could have squeezed in, pushed our way closer to the stage, and grabbed a better view of the music, we walked by the small patches of open grass that remained, leaving them for others. In an hour or two, they'd be gone, and the people closest to the stage would have thousands of people behind them pushing to get closer, all before the first notes were played.

The day passed. We talked and wandered and enjoyed each other's company. I was anxious for the actual festival to begin, to hear the music we'd come to see, but at the same time, I simply wanted to enjoy where I was and who I was with. My father's words echoed in my brain.

The music started late Friday afternoon with Richie Havens. We were confused when he came on stage first, and only found out later that the acts scheduled to play first were late because all the roads leading to the festival were clogged with cars. Everyone, it seemed, was headed to Woodstock. It started to rain a little bit around ten o'clock, and we thought about heading back to the VW, but Arlo Guthrie and Joan Baez were performing next and we wanted to see them. Joan Baez didn't finish playing until two in the morning.

Saturday's music started around noon. We didn't stand there all day listening to every band. Some we really wanted to see, and others were just background music for our wanderings. We joined in with groups that were dancing or practicing yoga, and in the afternoon we worked our way down the hill and around the side of the stage to swim in the pond. Most people hadn't brought a swimsuit, but that didn't stop them.

Walking from place to place meant weaving our way through the crowd. Sometimes there would be places where no one was moving, where everyone was packed together so tightly that there was no way to push through. Somehow, other places naturally turned into rivers of people, where crowds were always moving in an endless line toward one place or another.

We were standing on the edge of one of those streams of people when I saw him. It was just for a second, half a second. What I could see was constantly changing. An opening would form between two people and then close up, only to open again in a second and offer up a different view. Through one of those openings, just for an instant, I thought I saw Seth, standing there, motionless, staring at me.

Then he was gone, like he was never there. I was certain that I'd seen him, and at the same time convinced that he couldn't possibly have been there. I was just being silly or paranoid or something. There were so many faces, so many people with long hair, so many guys with thin beards starting to grow on their cheeks. It could have been anyone and everyone. I searched for the face again, twisting my neck from side to side, trying to see between people before the openings closed up. I realized I wasn't breathing and let air escape my lungs in a long breath.

A quick look at Emmie and Jake told me they hadn't seen anything, so I shook my head at how foolish I'd been and convinced myself that I'd just imagined it. We grabbed each other's hands so we wouldn't get separated, stepped into the flow of people, and let it take us to another part of the long sloping hill. There was music to enjoy I told myself, and it was silly to worry about someone who we'd left far behind.

The Grateful Dead started playing after ten o'clock on Saturday. They were one of the bands I wanted to see the most, but they only made it through four songs. We heard the next day while chatting with some camper neighbors that problems with their equipment and a wet stage combined to give them electric shocks whenever they touched an instrument or microphone.

Janis Joplin didn't come on stage until two in the morning. I absolutely had to stay up to see her. I'd played her songs so many times at home, I'd nearly worn out the needle on my record player. I remembered with a smile the day my mother burst into my room wondering what I was screaming about, only to find me sitting on the floor with a record spinning in front of me, Janis blaring from the speaker.

She sang at Woodstock with a voice that was both scratchy and soulful. She shouted and screamed and soothed. I didn't really know Janis's story when I stood there that night surrounded by almost half a million people. I didn't know where the pleading desperation that I heard in some of her songs came from, but I was struck by the way she mixed it together with a giggling sense of humor and what seemed to be a limitless energy.

Listening to Janis Joplin that night, I realized we were all doing that same thing in 1969. Smiling and laughing and putting our energy into all the things we did every day: going to school or a job, delivering groceries, cleaning the house and making dinner. All the while, we wanted to scream at everything that was happening around us. The war and the draft, racism and inequalities, people going off to war and people running away from it, people willing to offer a handshake to a stranger and people pulling a knife on them instead. We all wanted to scream about it, and we all wanted to forget about it and smile and laugh and think about something else. Janis was somehow able to do both those things up on stage in front of what seemed like the whole world. I stood in the crowd and let her music move me, feeling her joy and her sadness.

There were three more bands after Janis. The music ended after nine o'clock Sunday morning. By then we had dragged ourselves back to the VW and collapsed into bed. I'd gotten used to the sun filtering through the camper sides waking me up each day, but nothing could have kept me from sleeping that morning.

I felt lucky to have the VW to come back to each day. It was fun being part of the endless crowd that was spread across the hillside, but it was also nice to have a place to return to that felt like home.

We were also lucky to have cupboards full of food. While the Woodstock organizers had focused their energies on putting music on the stage, they weren't expecting the number of people that had converged on the farm and nearby town. There were people selling food, but it was not nearly enough to feed the crowd. Stores in town were sold out of everything. People in the surrounding areas gathered donations, mostly sandwiches and fruit, that were bought in by helicopter, and a group called the Hog Farm Collective set up free food lines, giving people rice and vegetables, and coming up with a plan to pass out thousands of cups of granola from the stage to help feed the people up front who didn't want to risk giving up their spots so close to the music to head to the food lines.

Joe Cocker started things off on Sunday, ending his set with a version of The Beatles' song, "With a Little Help From My Friends." It was a good song to play for the four-hundred thousand people who were settling down to their third day on a hillside, helping each other out, making sure their neighbors were comfortable, and doing their best to turn strangers into friends.

Then the rain started. It had rained here and there throughout the weekend, making things muddy and messy, but this was different. We saw the clouds gathering first, saw the far-off flashes of lightning and heard the thunder. And it was all moving toward the stage and the hill and the people. Someone on stage starting to chant, "No rain, no rain, no rain," in hopes that so many voices sending out their positive thoughts could change the weather. It reminded me of the voices shouting, "No war!" in front of City Hall in San Francisco, but neither chant could hold back the inevitable. The rain came, and for a while, the music stopped.

The man whose voice was coming through the speakers did his best to assure everyone who was stuck outside in the storm that everything would be okay. "Just sit tight. We're going to ride this out together. Check on your neighbor." But those encouraging words were mixed in with more urgent calls for people to get off the towers that held the speakers and lights, calls for people to find a safe place to ride out the storm. Along with sheets of rain came lighting, and we were glad for the safety of the VW.

We invited four others who looked particularly wet and frightened to share our space, and for several hours we huddled there, sharing stories and food. We listened to the rain pounding on the camper's roof, jumped at the sound of thunder that felt like it was just outside the rain streaked windows, and waited.

Then, the rain slowed, the thunder and lightning stopped, and we heard the sounds of guitars being tuned and voices checking microphones. We opened the big sliding door and looked out on the wet, muddy scene. Not everyone had outlasted the storm. Some people had left during the rain, and the hillside was speckled with patches of empty, muddy ground. But those who had stayed were ready for more music.

I let Emmie and Jake wander off on their own. We'd spent the entire weekend together as a trio, and they'd both been fine with that. But I also knew how happy they were to be together, and I decided they needed to spend some time as a couple. I didn't mind walking around on my own. As big as the festival was, as many people as there were, after three days, I knew my way around and felt comfortable. After all, I was surrounded by people who were all about peace and love.

I followed my feet wherever they took me, picking my way around soggy tents and people still huddled in sleeping bags. At one point, I stopped to watch a group that was sliding down a muddy hill. There was chanting and drumming as they cheered each other and took turns running to get up speed, then slipping and sliding down the hill, which got slicker and muddier with each pass. I watched and laughed, but brushed off invitations from the group to join in the fun. Maybe if I'd been stuck out in the rain, I wouldn't have cared as much about staying dry and clean.

Without thinking much about it, I made my way closer to the stage. It was easier now that so many people had left during the rain. I watched the performers, let the music flow through me, and enjoyed being a part of the crowd that surrounded me. I was so relaxed, I barely jumped when a voice behind me spoke close to my ear.

"Hey, girly girl."

I spun around.

Seth.

He stood in front of me, smiling. He looked as if the rain had washed all the color from him, leaving behind only the brown of mud. His clothes were covered. The sandals he wore blended in with his feet in the same brown. His hair hung down in his face, covering it in lank, wet strands. But it didn't cover his eyes. His eyes I could see, and they burned a hole through me.

"You having fun, girly girl?" he said in an oily voice, his smile widening, but his eyes narrowing.

Just being near Seth made me want to take a step back, made me want to turn and run. Instead, I stood my ground and spat words at him. "What do you want? Get away from me!"

He didn't seem to care and took a step toward me, forcing me back anyway. "I want my camper back, girly girl. I had to bum rides all the way here, but now I'm ready to leave this mud pit. I had to walk the last few miles to get here, but I want to drive out, and I'm going to take you with me. Then I'm going to figure out a way to pay you back for ditching me back in the middle of nowhere."

He clenched the fingers on his right hand as if they still hurt from the door that I'd slammed closed on them. Then he reached behind his back, and a sharp cry of surprise escaped my mouth when his hand came back into view holding a knife.

At first, I could only think, "How did he get his knife back?" I replayed the memory of the knife turning end over end before slicing into the water as Emmie and I watched it disappear below the surface, and my mind slowly moved from that memory like I was feeling my way through the dark, finding my way back to the muddy field in front of the stage where Seth pointed a knife at me. Stupidly, I realized it wasn't the same knife, but the knife Seth held in his hand was just as sharp and just as menacing.

"Where's it parked, girly girl? Take me there. Now!" Seth's voice barked. I was terrified, but my hands clenched into fists. Of all the horrible things Seth had done to me and to others, his nickname for me was still the thing that aggravated me the most. "Go! Walk!" he growled, jabbing the knife toward me.

I walked. Seth settled in behind me. A lot of the crowd had cleared out, but we were still surrounded by people. I thought about just screaming for help or running to someone and grabbing them to get their attention. But every few steps, I felt the point of the knife in my back. It never occured to me that the knife could just be an idle threat; I knew he was angry enough to use it. I was hoping that someone would notice the knife and wonder what was happening, but there was some pretty amazing music happening on the stage, and everyone's attention was up there.

So I just walked, retracing the route I'd taken when I left Jake and Emmie back at the VW. If I walked too slowly, I felt the knife prick the skin on my back, and a couple times when I walked faster trying to get away from its point, Seth put a muddy hand on my shoulder, squeezed until it hurt, and then pulled me back town him.

There was a constant hiss of words twisting their way into my ears. Seth retold the story of the night we left him on the side of the road, walking me through the struggle of hitchhiking across the country, and listing all the wrongs I had to repay. I heard all of it with a growing panic. Seth was creepy before, but now there was no question that he was dangerous.

My mind raced. We were just minutes from where the VW was parked. I was doing my best to take a wandering route to waste time, but we'd eventually get there, and then what? If I was lucky, Emmie and Jake would be there, but I couldn't count on it. Seth would shove me into a seat and he'd drive away. It could be hours before Emmie and Jake came back to discover the VW was gone. By then, I'd be miles away with Seth. I had to do something fast.

We arrived back at the hill where the people were sliding down in the mud, and I immediately had a plan. There were still people chanting and banging on drums, running, and sliding. I slowed my walk just a little bit to get the timing right. A woman ran past us, letting her feet slip out from under her at the edge of the hill and rocketing down on her back. I stopped for half a second to let her by and took advantage of Seth's distraction as he watched her slippery progress toward the bottom of the hill.

Then I spun around as quickly as I could on the muddy ground and let the momentum push my shoulder into Seth's chest. He made a gasping sound as the air was pushed from his lungs, and my sudden motion knocked him off balance. He teetered on the edge of the hill, his arms pinwheeling wildly for balance, the knife slipping from his hand and flying off into the mud.

Seth fell forward onto his chest. He put his hands out to break his fall, but they only slipped out from under him, and he landed with his face in the mud. The momentum I had when I pushed into him carried me forward as well, and I landed on his back.

We slid down the hill, Seth in the mud and me riding on his back. I instinctively grabbed for something to hold onto and ended up with fistfulls of his hair. Seth's face and shoulders plowed through the muck, pushing a stream of mud to either side and leaving a track that marked his slippery progress down the hill. It wasn't easy staying on top of him. He struggled as we shot toward the bottom, his arms still flailing. Maybe he was trying to find something to hold onto to stop us from sliding farther or trying to push up far enough to get his face out of the mud. Either way it was useless.

We reached the bottom of the hill and came skidding to a stop. Seth struggled beneath me, but I didn't move, and with all of my weight directly on top of his back, there was no way he could get enough traction to push me off. It occurred to me later that he may not have been able to breathe with his face buried in the mud, but at the time I didn't care. All I was thinking was that if I was on top of him, he couldn't do anything to me. Maybe I was screaming or yelling or something without realizing it, because people eventually came over to make sure I was okay, or maybe they came over to see if Seth was okay.

I told my story to whoever was close enough to listen. I kept it simple. Everything that had come before was history. All they needed to know was that the guy on the ground under me had pulled a knife, threatened me, and was planning on stealing our camper and taking me with him.

A woman, so covered with mud from her shoulders down that it was hard to even tell where her clothes ended and her skin began, bent down in front of me and reached out a hand to help me up. Somehow, amazingly, her long blond hair was still relatively mud-free and she'd managed to keep a flower safe above her left ear. She looked kind enough and managed to convince me to get off of Seth.

He sprang up immediately with a snarl on his face, only his eyes and teeth showing through the mask of mud. His hands reached for me, and he had time to take one step before two skinny hippies each grabbed an arm and held him back. They looked too thin to have any muscle on their bodies, but they both had two or three inches on Seth and their long arms held him tightly. Although Seth still struggled, yanking at his arms and kicking up mud, the pair seemed to hold him in place without much effort.

"Not cool, my friend. You need to chill."

"Yeah, just relax man. Peace."

Seth growled at them both, twisting his head from side to side toward their faces and spewing curse words along with drops of mud.

"I found this," a third hippie said in a slow, drawn-out voice that sounded too relaxed for the scene that surrounded him. He held the handle of Seth's knife loosely between two fingers, letting the blade point down toward the muddy ground. "It's a knife." Again, his words were slow and calm, only drifting out of his mouth, his tone giving only a hint of curiosity but no indication that he was holding the weapon that Seth had been threatening me with just minutes ago.

"Oh, man, not cool," the first hippie said in a disappointed voice. "Seems like things went down the way this girl says." He looked at his partner. "We gotta bring him to the fuzz I think, huh?"

The other nodded. "Yeah, there's been a cop hanging out around the first aid station. Let's take him there. Bring that knife with too." The pair turned and walked off with Seth between them, kicking and yelling. I could hear their voices as they walked away.

"Peace, friend. It's cool. Just chill."

Peace

I waited for Emmie and Jake back at the VW, and when they returned, I filled them in. Emmie was nervous about Seth being there, amazed that he'd somehow made his way across the entire country and then found one of us among hundreds of thousands of hippies, who pretty much all looked the same. I shrugged. Yeah, it was surprising that he'd made it all the way to Woodstock. He hitchhiked I guess. I felt sorry for whoever had picked him up, and it was surprising and more than a little creepy the way he'd found me, sneaking up behind me like he'd been there all the while.

But I'd also seen Seth getting dragged off to the police. He was angry and kicking and screaming, but he also looked defeated. He'd crossed the country looking for us, and just when things looked like he was going to get what he wanted, he ended up face down in the mud, pinned down by a girl half his size. Whatever the police ended up doing with Seth, I was confident he wouldn't be looking for us anymore, and if he did, there'd be three of us. Besides, there was still music left to hear.

The crowd was thinning out. The rain had chased off a lot of people, and now it was getting late. Everything was supposed to end Sunday night, but because of delays from the rain and from things just not seeming to work right up on stage, there were six or seven acts still waiting to perform while the sun was dropping below the surrounding hills. Some people had decided to see things through to the end, but for others, three days of peace and music had been enough. We'd come a long way. We were staying.

It was another night full of music. David Crosby, Stephen Stills, Graham Nash, and Neil Young were four musicians who had played in other bands or had made music on their own. That night was only the second time they played together in front of an audience. Weeks later, their friend Joni Mitchell would write a song that they would play and make popular. It was about meeting someone on the road to Woodstock. It was about going down to a farm, setting your soul free, and joining half a million people in song and celebration.

Joni Mitchell sang the song too, in a voice that was slow and sad, with the haunting notes of an organ playing in the background. The refrain of her song would stay with me long after I'd washed the mud of Woodstock from my hair.

We are stardust, we are golden
And we've got to get ourselves back to the garden

That's how I felt that last night in Woodstock, looking up at a sky that had finally cleared of rain, a sky where just a few stars glinted down at us. We were stardust, we were golden, and as muddy as the hillside was, we were surrounded by people who were full of love and wanting peace. I wasn't quite sure what Joni Mitchell meant when she sang that last line, but it seemed like she was singing about a perfect and peaceful place. We had, indeed, gotten ourselves back to the garden.

The sun rose with a band called Sha Na Na. I didn't have any of their records, but I'd seen them on TV once or twice. They had a 50's style rock and roll sound that involved a lot of dancing and jumping around on stage. It was a good way to start the morning.

Jimi Hendrix played last. I don't know how the people who organized the festival decided the order for performers. Some of it was decided for them by bands stuck in traffic and rain delays, but someone must have decided to make Jimi Hendrix responsible for wrapping up a music festival that stretched on for more than three days and nights. They made a good choice.

Maybe it was because he'd taken an instrument that everyone else played right-handed and flipped it upside down so he could play it left-handed, but somehow, Jimi Hendrix was able to make a guitar sound, not just like a different instrument but like a whole room full of different instruments. It was a shame that so many people had left by the time he took the stage, but those who stayed were witness to a show that was like no other.

Toward the end of his time on stage, a familiar song twisted and turned like the guitar had a mind of its own, and then became the first notes of "The Star Spangled Banner." The tune drifted over the remaining crowd, and people who had spent a long three days living in a field and in the mud, hushed, stood still, and listened.

The distorted sound of the guitar ground in my ears, and the whining notes pierced the morning. Goosebumps prickled my arms when I realized that the horrible, grinding sound that seemed to break the melody in two came at the point when I was silently mouthing the words about rockets' red glare and bombs bursting in air. Jimi Hendrix had somehow created the sounds and chaos of war using only the six strings of his guitar. Then just as suddenly, the guitar jumped back into the notes that caused people to stand at baseball games, take off their hats, and put their hands on their hearts.

There, standing on a hill surrounded by people who were tired and hungry and muddy but still raising two fingers in the air calling for peace, it all made sense. We were a country that felt like there was a lot of things wrong with it. I'd run away from some of those things when I left home, and I'd seen a lot more of them on the road. There were people who were full of hate, and that needed to stop. We were dropping bombs in places where we had no business being, and that had to stop. We had lots of people who were hurting and frightened and alone, and many more who weren't being given the opportunities that others took for granted. We needed to fix all of that. But, like those pure, piercing notes Jimi Hendrix played after the distorted chaos he'd created with his guitar, I was also pretty sure we were going to be able to pull ourselves out of the mess we were in, get back on track, and find the notes that made all of us want to stand up together and put our hands on our hearts.

Returning

Getting to Woodstock was not the end of the story. It was the beginning, or maybe it was the middle.

We had a country to cross again. Jake stayed with us. He was still in trouble, or he would be if he got caught. He was a draft dodger, and there was no way around that, but having him travel with us felt less like he was running and more like he was going toward something better. Avoiding the draft was just one way to protest the war, just one way to show people that it wasn't right. Even though he knew there might be consequences, he'd decided to stay in the country, to stay with Emmie, and to do whatever he could to convince people that the war we were fighting wasn't right. The long drive back to California gave Emmie and Jake lots of time to make plans and organize. They were already talking about a trip back to the east coast and a visit to Washington, DC, to join the growing anti-war demonstrations there.

We stopped in Parachute on our way back home. Emmie and I convinced each other that it made sense since we were passing through that area anyway, but I knew we would have gone hundreds of miles out of our way just to visit there again. We had lunch at the diner where we introduced Jake to Charlie, and then I stopped by Jerry's store. I sat with him and talked, running my fingers along the edges of the key he'd given me and sharing some of the lessons I'd learned and the memories I'd gathered. He smiled and nodded and seemed pleased.

About a half-day's drive from Parachute, on a dusty section of highway with nothing else in sight from one horizon to the other, I pulled off the road and into a gas station. The owner sat motionless on a rocking chair out front, but when he saw me get out of the VW, he stood slowly and ran a hand across his bald head like he was straightening hair that had disappeared long ago. He didn't say anything at first. There was a mixture of surprise and hesitation on his face, and while he mostly just stared at me, I caught his eyes flick to the VW's windows to see who else was inside, or more likely to see who wasn't.

"We owe you for some gas," I said, reaching a hand into the bag that now always hung against my hip, and pulling out a small roll of bills. Unlike our trip east, we wanted to cover the miles between us and home as quickly as we could, and we'd avoided stopping in towns to work. We were short on food and low on gas, and I was holding all the money we had left, but we all agreed this stop was important.

"Name's Bets. That right?"

I marveled at the man's memory, but then realized that we'd crossed a country full of people and places and faces while he sat in his rocking chair staring out at the same scenery all day. If the details of our first stop at the gas station had faded in my memory, it was only because so much had happened since then.

"Yes, sir. We need some gas, and we owe you for the gas we took before." I looked down stupidly at the money in my hands and my shuffling feet. "Sorry about that."

The man laughed a little. It was a dry and dusty laugh, like he was coughing up some of the dust that surrounded us. "I see you got rid of your friend."

I couldn't help but laugh in reply, a short choking laugh, like maybe I'd inhaled some of the same dust the man had been breathing, but mostly it was the absurdity of the man referring to Seth as my friend. "No, he's not with us anymore," and then I added, "He wasn't my friend."

The man filled the VW's tank, and we chatted a little, while we listened to the rhythmic sound of the pump. I told him where we'd gone and where we were going to. He asked me about the weather. When the pump shut off, he glanced up at the numbers on its face and told me the price. I doubled it and counted off bills, but the man was shaking his head before I even tried to hand them to him. He took some convincing, but I finally got him to take the payment for the gas I bought plus some money to cover the cost of what Seth had stolen. We shook hands, and the man's smile alone was worth the stop.

Then we watched the miles on road signs decrease by fives and tens as we got closer to California. I was anxious to get home, wanting desperately to see my parents, but I was trying not to think about the end of our trip and leaving Emmie. She'd become a friend over the last year through letters alone, and spending the summer with her had only brought us closer. We told each other we were going to stay in touch, going to write letters, and visit. I hoped we did, but I knew sometimes promises like that didn't work out. There was school, and jobs, and trips back east with Jake.

I made her stop a mile before my parents' house. I didn't want our goodbye to get mixed up with my parents' welcome home. We hugged and shared smiles, and told each other again that we would stay in touch.

"Thank you," I said finally. I could have explained all the reasons, all the ways that the trip we'd taken together had helped me, but I didn't have to. I knew that Emmie understood.

"It was cool, Bets." We hugged again.

"Yeah, cool," I agreed.

☮ ☮ ☮

My parents were sitting on the front porch waiting for me when we pulled into our driveway. Maybe they'd heard the VW coming. After crossing the country twice, it was sounding more and more like it needed some attention from a mechanic. Or maybe they were just sitting there because they were as anxious to see me as I was to see them.

My door was open and my feet were on the ground before the VW rolled to a stop. My parents came off the porch, and we met halfway, in a three-person hug. I was reminded of my father coming home from Vietnam, except now I felt like I was on the other side of things. I was the one being welcomed home. I'd left on the cross-country trip to get away from my house, my parents, everything, but I'd never been so happy to be home.

Maybe it was silly to say goodbye to Emmie before we got to my house. She and Jake got out of the VW. They weren't just going to drop me off and pull away, so I made introductions. My parents already knew who Emmie was, even though they'd never met her. I introduced Jake as Emmie's friend. They knew from Emmie's letter left behind on my desk that we had been traveling with a friend of Emmie's. At that moment, they didn't need to know that the person we'd left with wasn't the same one we brought home. I could fill my parents in on the details later.

Emmie and Jake were friendly and polite, and my parents seemed pleased to meet them. I watched them chat for a minute and was surprised at the contrast between my father and Jake. My father had made a life out of the military and had gone to Vietnam because it was his job, his duty. Jake was risking his freedom and maybe his life with the same conviction. He'd decided that the war was wrong and that he had to bring others around to the same thinking. I guess that was duty too.

I couldn't imagine telling my father that Jake was a draft dodger, not after everything my father had been through. I wasn't sure how I'd leave that part out of the story when I sat down to tell my parents about everything that had happened. Maybe I would tell them eventually, but I couldn't do it while they were standing there eye to eye. My father might disapprove of Jake for his stance on Vietnam, and I suppose Jake might disapprove of my father's part in the war. But seeing them together, I admired them both.

We pulled my bike down off the VW, and then there was another round of goodbyes. Jake shook my father's hand, and Emmie hugged my mother. I giggled a little seeing my mother's tidy pants and styled hair next to Emmie's flowing dress, braids, and beads. I hugged Jake, and then Emmie again, not wanting to let go. Then, I stood at the end of the driveway with my parents, watching the VW head down the road and disappear over a hill.

☮ ☮ ☮

It would have been nice if everything was better with my father; it wasn't. There were still days when he couldn't go to work or wouldn't leave the couch, and nights when he would wake up screaming. Years later people would give a name to the problems that soldiers had when they came back from a war: Post Traumatic Stress Disorder. People would take those horrible sounding words and shorten them to PTSD, which sounded less horrible but meant the same thing. But in 1969, we didn't have a name for it yet. We just knew that my father had gone to war, and when he came back, he brought some of the war home with him.

So everything wasn't better. I'd traveled all the way across the country with Emmie to get away from a bunch of problems, but they didn't go away. They were still there, waiting for me when I got home. What was different, was me. I'd figured out that running away from problems didn't make them better, and it didn't make them go away. I'd also figured out that my father wasn't a different person when he came home from the war. He was the same person I'd loved before he went away, the same person I'd missed while he was gone. The only difference was that he'd come home with a problem.

Once you figure out the reasons behind something that you don't like, it becomes a little easier. Understanding a problem doesn't make it go away, but it does help you deal with it. Once I understood the reasons for the changes in my father, I could support him instead of running away, I could focus on what he needed instead of what I wanted.

Little by little, he started to get better, but it wasn't a change I noticed right away. There were fewer nightmares, fewer angry outbursts, and when they did happen they were less, smaller, shorter. There were more days when everything seemed normal, when my father reminded me of the way he was before the war.

The war didn't get better right away either. With generals continuing to send soldiers to fight and politicians struggling to find a way to leave Vietnam that didn't look like total defeat, the war would drag on for another six years, ending with dramatic helicopter evacuations from the rooftops of Saigon.

The peace and love that we all felt at Woodstock faded long before the war ground itself to an end. There were other music festivals, but none seemed to bring people together the way Woodstock did. A little over a year after his stunning performance of "The Star Spangled Banner" at Woodstock, Jimi Hendrix was found unconscious in a London apartment and died in the hospital, his death blamed on an overdose of sleeping pills. Sixteen days later, Janis Joplin died from a heroin overdose, leaving behind an unfinished album to be completed by others and released after her death. Jimi and Janis were both only 27.

Meanwhile, protests and demonstrations spread and grew around the country. Draft cards were burned, sit-ins were held, and songs were sung. Emmie and Jake stuck to their plans and traveled the country again, taking part in demonstrations where they found them and doing what they could to change people's minds. I ventured down to San Francisco to join them once or twice and went as far as the state capitol in Sacramento, but other than that, I stayed close to home. There was lots of healing to be done in our country, and peace would eventually come. For me, the healing had to start with the people closest to me, and our peace would be found in the time we spent with each other.

Acknowledgments

Cross Country exists because of people who read *Miss E.* and wanted more. Thank you for reading and helping me to discover that Bets had another story to tell.

Thank you to *Cross Country*'s early readers. Over these many miles, you smoothed all the sharp edges. Special thanks must go to my favorite middle school book group. I shared a very early version of *Cross Country* with them, and they shared a roomful of energetic opinions with me.

Thank you to my family. They gave me the time I needed to imagine and write and create. Their support and encouragement is endless, and they are my absolute favorite people to be with. I'm looking forward to our next cross country adventure together.

At the heart of this book is music, and not simply because it's a story about a trip to Woodstock. It's a story about a time when music had a voice, a message, and the power to move people. For that reason, I also want to thank the voices that sang to me while each page of *Cross Country* was written. Janis Joplin, Jimi Hendrix, Stephen Stills, Neil Young, Richie Havens, and Grace Slick were the soundtrack to my writing. Their music helped me imagine what it would be like to hop into a VW, set off across the country, and enjoy three days of peace and music.

About the Author

Brian Herberger grew up with a driveway full of Volkswagens parked in front of the house. He was born too late for the 60's, but he's always loved the music and activism of that decade. He happily camped in the rain and the mud for the 25th anniversary of Woodstock, and has driven his family across the United States several times.

Brian is an educator and works for a large school system outside of Washington DC. *Cross Country* is his second novel. You can find out more about Brian and his books at brianherberger.com

90983689R00208

Made in the USA
San Bernardino, CA
23 October 2018